RESTORED GRACE

BAY TOWN BOOK TWO

KATHLEEN J. ROBISON

ISBN: 978-1-951839-62-8

Celebrate Lit Publishing

304 S. Jones Blvd #754

Las Vegas, NV, 89107

http://www.celebratelitpublishing.com/

To Foothill Ranch Library Writers and Critique Group.
My dear friends, Skye, Stella, Mary, Rick,
Mari-Lynn, Rain, Sam, Kayla, Robert, C.G, Hiromi, Holly,
Deb, Priya, Lilly, and my loving husband, Bruce.
And to all others in our group who have come and gone.
Thank you for embracing the brokenness of Carol Scape
and for loving all the people in Bay Town.
To God be all glory.

CHAPTER 1

C arol swept down the drug-store aisle, humming a tune when a teen girl turned. Her eyes widened, and she froze like a frightened rabbit. Before Carol could manage a smile, the girl spun back. She peered at the toothpaste shelves like she was choosing a shade of lip color.

"Too many to choose from, right? Mint or bubblegum? Gel or paste? Almost as many as the selection of shampoos." Carol chuckled.

But the girl's attention remained fixed on the rows of slim rectangular boxes and fancy canisters. The selections seemed to overwhelm her. Toothpaste just wasn't that interesting, thought Carol.

The teen touched one box but pulled back her hand. She bit the tip of her hot-pink fingernail, a contrast to the short, pleated skirt and polo shirt. Finally, she reached for a box.

"May I help you with your choices?" A young male clerk appeared out of nowhere. He wore a blue vest emblazoned with the drug store logo. Puffing out his thin chest, he adjusted his glasses.

The dark-haired teenager dropped the box and stumbled backward.

"I'm so sorry," said the clerk. "I didn't mean to scare you."

Backing away, he lifted a hand and offered a weak wave. "Let me know if you need anything. I'll be in the next aisle."

Carol picked up the box. Her long, graying red hair almost swept the ground as she bent over. She hiked up her layered gauze skirt that covered the dropped item.

"Here you go." She held out the toothpaste.

The girl's eyes brimmed with tears.

In a hushed voice, Carol asked, "Are you okay? Do you need some help?"

The teen made no attempt to take the toothpaste but instead, turned and hurried down the aisle, disappearing around the end cap.

A musky cologne floated in the air. Carol spun around, and a nicely dressed man blocked her path. She lurched forward, catching herself and her fringed shawl tangled between her hair and an oversized hobo bag.

"You 'bout scared the daylights out of me," she said.

The cologne overpowered her, and she found him attractive. *A sharp dresser, that's for sure.* Her gaze lingered, and she fought to push down rising old habits. She looked him over, searching for something wrong with him.

The sleek suit fit him perfectly. *Who wore a full suit out in public these days, anyway?* A crisp white shirt and pristine solid gray tie with a subtle sheen set the look that screamed expensive. Even his tan-colored, laced-up shoes registered pricey. Carol blinked long. She'd sworn off men this year. They'd always been her weakness, but she had resolved a new lease on life. But then he spoke.

"Well, hello, ma'am." He tipped his hand to his forehead. "I do apologize. I didn't mean to startle you." His eyes traveled up and down her form. He smiled. "Guess I just can't ignore a pretty face. Pardon me for the intrusion."

Carol blushed. His southern drawl charmed her...for a second. She wasn't buying it, but it didn't mean she didn't enjoy it. Men. She knew his type all too well. Fancy or not.

Better yet, she knew herself, and she wasn't exceptionally beautiful, thin, or young. In fact, hers was a mature face, but she applied her makeup tastefully. Her curvy figure carried a few extra pounds, and she was a woman some men found attractive.

His glazed blue eyes and slicked-back hair gave her a slight chill as she stared at him. Freeing her hair, she pushed it back and adjusted her purse. She was a sucker for compliments, and she hated that they meant so much. Still, she smiled, and creases formed around her lips.

"Oh, my goodness. That's a line if I ever heard one." She winked, then felt shameful. All these months of trying to rid herself of old habits came flooding back. Flirting. It always brought a momentary false elation. "Well, sir. I've got to run." She took a step, but he didn't budge. "Excuse me." She waved a hand, shooing him out of the way.

He continued blocking her path. "You didn't happen to see my…niece, did you?" He raised his hand, motioning with his palm down just slightly under her height. "Straight, dark hair? Plaid skirt, white polo shirt?"

Carol's eyes narrowed, and she started to point, realizing she still held the toothpaste box. "Why…no. I didn't." She wondered why she lied and replaced the tube.

"I thought I heard some conversation in this aisle a moment ago."

"Oh, that was me. The clerk. I was speaking to the clerk." She rambled on about all the toothpaste selections, hoping to keep him captive while…*while what?* Her stomach fluttered, thinking about his so-called niece. Why did she doubt him?

He looked beyond her, and he clenched his jaws. "Ashley, girl! You stop right there." He bellowed as he brushed past Carol, taking long strides to the front of the store.

The teen girl stood frozen between the exit doors.

The man in the suit grabbed her arm and led her back

into the store. She didn't struggle but went willingly with her head hanging down, holding some small item.

Carol forced herself to approach them. "Are you all right?" She ignored the man and stared at the girl, hoping she'd look up. She didn't.

The man swung around, holding the teen's arm. He smoothed back his already slick hair with his free hand. "We're all good here. Ashley, here, well, she often forgets to pay for things. Thank you for asking."

Carol shuddered at the fire in his eyes. She watched as he loosened his squeeze on the girl but didn't let go. He raised his other hand and clamped it on her shoulder. With the awkward hold, he directed the girl towards the checkout counter.

Carol glanced around, ran to the end cap, and picked up a random item. She hurried to the checkout line, where an older woman waited. Her grocery basket was piled high with tissue boxes and bags of cough drops. *Shoot.* Carol tapped her foot, then touched the woman's hunched shoulder.

"Excuse me, ma'am. May I go ahead of you?" Paying no mind to the item in her hand, Carol held it up before the woman as if it pleaded her case. "I only have one thing, and I'm late for work." Another necessary lie. "May I? I hate to ask."

The woman's white hair framed a wrinkled face. It grew more wrinkled as she frowned at the item Carol clutched. "Oh, all right," she said.

"Bless you. Thank you so much." She hurried past and bumped the woman's filled basket. "Ouch." Carol rubbed her hip.

She thought she heard the old lady mumble something about age, but Carol paid no mind.

She now stood behind the young teen. The man in the suit bent forward and cooed something into the girl's ear, and she shivered.

Carol's body had the same reflex.

The man straightened. "Now, darling. Your uncle will take good care of you. Don't you worry your pretty little head none."

The girl's gaze locked on Carol.

Carol whispered, "Honey, are you sure you're okay?"

She caught the man's piercing stare in her peripheral vision. She ignored him, hoping the girl would answer. Finally, she shook her head and looked down.

He placed a hand on Carol's shoulder and whispered, "Ma'am, you best mind your own business."

Carol pushed off his hand. "Get your hands off me."

He winked as he paid for the girl's item and ushered her out of the store.

Carol strained her neck towards the store-front window and watched them walk to a sedan. It was a strange shade, like blue ice. He shoved the girl in and lit a cigarette before taking the driver's seat.

"I hate seeing that man." The clerk shook his head.

"You've seen him before?"

"Yes, ma'am. He's been coming in about once a week for a month now. Usually just buys cigarettes, but this is the second time this week that he's had that scared girl with him."

"Do you think she's in danger?" Carol shivered at the recollection of a teen abducted in her town just last year.

"Mmm, hmm."

"I knew it. The poor thing, she looked so scared."

"Yup. I don't trust him. What did he say? She was his niece?"

Carol nodded. "That's what I heard. But I don't believe it. No niece would be with an uncle that frightened her like that."

"Heck, no. She was like that the last time they came too. Maybe he's an abusive uncle or something."

"Did you call the police?"

"Yup, but the guy was gone by the time they got here.

They just wrote down the time and took notes. The police can't do nothing if the girl don't say something."

"She's too scared." Carol swiped the back of her neck and peered out the window.

"Excuse me? I thought you were in a hurry?" The little old lady glared.

Carol threw her item on the conveyer belt.

"That'll be $18.88." The checker chuckled.

"What?" She frowned at the register, ignoring her item. "Why so much?"

He held up an Early Response Pregnancy Kit. His lips were pressed tightly, but his body jiggled from the laughter he held back.

Carol rolled her eyes, then squinted at his name tag. "Ha. Ha, Bubba. Never mind then. For goodness 'sake, keep it. I certainly don't need it."

She exited the store and searched the parking lot.

"Dang it." She yelled, and a passerby gave her a strange look. "They're gone." Glaring at the man, she asked, a little too harshly, "You see a blue car driving around?"

He stared at her and pointed out three spots—parked vehicles, all different shades of blue.

Carol let her bag drop off her shoulder and glared. "I ain't crazy. I can see those too."

He backed away and hurried off, shaking his head.

Carol's body slumped. "Sorry." She called after the man. *He thinks I'm a crazy woman. Well, maybe I am.*

She walked to her neon orange El Camino and slid in. She threw her tote on the passenger seat, and her long hair caught on a ring. One of many on both her hands. She yanked her hand, and a few strands tore loose. She screamed. Empty helplessness filled her. Helpless at the hands of a man. Not just a man, a predator.

Taking a deep breath, she then blew out and did this three times. A routine she'd put in her self-calming repertoire this past year. That and prayer. The action helped with her new resolve of trying to live a life of grace. She sighed. *Your grace, not mine. But Lord, please do something, will ya?*

Carol remained quiet and pulled onto the road, but soon rolled to a stop at a red light. She glanced at the console, and the fuel indicator light was on. She turned to the nearest gas station. The Quick Stop had only one island and two pumps. Fortunately, there was no line.

A light breeze cooled her heated face as she stepped from the car. She removed the gas cap and lifted out the pump handle, but a "Pay Inside" scrawled on white paper was taped over the card reader. She returned the handle, but gas dribbled over her fingers. *Great. Just great.* Shaking off the droplets, she grabbed her wallet and headed inside.

The sun reflected off something shiny just behind the building. It blinded her, but she paid no mind and walked into the convenience store.

Something smelled familiar. Shrugging it off, she picked up a cherry hand pie, grabbed a bottle of sweet tea from the nearby cooler, and placed them on the counter. "I'll take thirty bucks on Pump number one.

The attendant behind the counter had his attention fixed on the back of the store.

She sniffed again and chuckled, wondering why a gas station attendant would wear such a strong cologne.

Carol held up her hands. "Hey, mister, do you have a restroom here? I need to wash up."

He nodded toward the back.

The aisles were stacked high with snack items blocking her view. Seeing some movement near where he indicated, she glanced back. "There's a bathroom line? But the pumps are empty. You got no customers out there."

He said nothing.

"I can wait." Her fingers fluttered through the Post Card

rack on the counter. "Any of these got the Singing River on them?"

The bored attendant shifted his gaze to the back of the store once more and shrugged.

Carol waited. *Wow. He's a real talker.* She hummed a little tune. "I own a vintage shop, ya' know."

Still not a word, but he rang up her items.

"I'm always searching for stuff that represents the small towns in Mississippi. You know, like The Singing River here in Pascagoula?"

"Yeah, I know it. Whatever. Postcards are in the rack. That's all we got."

"You got any other cute little things?" asked Carol.

"Nope."

Carol shrugged. "Okay. Thanks"

She pulled out her wallet and paid. Before taking her items, she pulled out a thin stack of business cards and slapped them on the counter. "Mister, if anyone comes in here peddling local handmade stuff, give me a call. I'm down the road away in Bay Town."

He didn't bother taking the cards.

"Why, I got me the best little shop down on Main Street. Right across the street from the Bus terminal."

A clatter rang out from the back of the store, and the attendant called out. "Hey, what are you doing back there?"

Carol picked up her items and waltzed to the exit, pushing the glass door with her hip. She smiled. "If you ever need a change of pace, come see me in Bay Town, and send your friends too."

She strolled to the pump, opened the tea, and took a big gulp. After pumping gas, she pulled out and headed home.

～

A flashy license plate frame peeked out from behind the Quick Stop, and a man in a nice suit stood just inside the store. Pushing open the double front doors, he stared at the bright orange El Camino fading in the distance. Flipping a cigarette butt, he ground it out with his expensive tan shoes and walked back inside. Approaching the counter, he picked up all of Carol's business cards.

CHAPTER 2

The typical one-hour drive home from Pascagoula to Bay Town dragged into two. Between late afternoon traffic and a fender bender, the cars crawled along the highway, so did Carol's mind. Recalling the slick man in the drug store, she toiled between anger and sorrow as her heart ached for the teenager. *How did she get there? What about her parents?* Thoughts of her own family that she'd left behind seeped in.

Carol shook her head and flipped on the radio, singing along. The irony of drowning her sorrows while listening to heartbreak pained her as she tried to ignore the meanings behind the words. Finally, she silenced the tunes and let the beautiful drive along the Gulf Coast work its magic. She glanced out her window, happy that she'd taken the beach road home instead of the central highway further inland. The serene beaches and lapping waters calmed her spirit, reminding her of God's awesome splendor. She could almost feel the gulf waters bathing her soul, cleansing her as white as the sandy shores.

Before long, blue skies faded to gray, and the huge, billowing clouds darkened her world. How could such a magnificent landscape hold such wickedness? The fearful teen's face rose before her. Carol prayed for the girl, but still, she tapped her steering wheel, wishing she could do more.

By the time she arrived in Bay Town, it was too late to go to her shop before Bible Study. The day's paperwork would have to wait. She drove straight to her friend's house, knowing she'd be a little early for the weekly ladies' gathering.

Carol parked in front of the cottage and trotted up the walk. She reached for the front door. Locked. Ever since last year, everyone took extra precautions in locking up their houses. Though no more incidents had occurred, the girl's abductions kept the town on high alert. Especially Melanie. Her daughter, Lacey, was one of the girls. Fortunately, her kidnapping was a failed attempt. The support of their church family and a strong faith helped them to cope in the aftermath. Carol hoped that one day, her faith would be as strong.

Knock. Knock. "Hey, Mel. It's me."

"Coming." Melanie swung open the door and pushed out the screen.

Some people hated early guests, but Melanie never minded. That was Melanie, thoughtful to the core and fit. Melanie was a good fifteen years younger than Carol, and unlike her, extremely athletic. Carol had never been one to love exercise. She chuckled to herself, thankful that a long time ago, she'd decided not to stress over her weight. Content with her slightly curvy figure, she slapped her hips and took a deep breath.

"Mmm. Do I smell chocolate? What are you baking in there, girl?" Carol hugged her friend.

"Brownies. Lacey made them."

"That girl can sure bake."

Waving her through the living room, Melanie said, "Let's sit in the kitchen before everyone else gets here."

Melanie's charming cottage on the gulf oozed farmhouse chic, with an eclectic pop of color scattered about. And plants? That girl had a green thumb. Carol grinned. As she walked through the house to the kitchen, her hands slid across some pieces hand-picked from her own shop. Their friendship had blossomed over the past year, and as rough as the year had been, Carol couldn't be more thankful for Melanie and the tight bond that rose from their trials.

"So, how was your day?" Melanie walked to the counter and held up the coffee pot.

Carol shrugged. "Do you know I almost bought a pregnancy test kit today?"

Melanie spun around, and her jaw dropped. "Excuse me?"

A smile crept across Carol's lips, then she doubled over, slapping her knee as she exploded in laughter. "It was a mistake!" She screamed. Snorting and coughing, she choked. "Mel, I grabbed the pregnancy test by accident. You don't think I'm messing around, do you?"

"Well, I didn't think you would, but..." Melanie shook her head, a strand of hair falling from her loose ponytail. "I also thought you were past childbearing..." She clapped a hand over her mouth.

"Too old? You thought I was too old? I wish." Carol winced. "I haven't hit menopause yet. No matter, that'd just be wrong, and I've shut down that part of my life anyway." Brushing back her hair, she narrowed her eyes. "Well, unless the good Lord brings a good husband...never mind." She pulled back her shoulders and laughed again. "Give me a little credit here, girl."

Melanie smiled and shrugged.

Desmond Brooks walked in and raised a brow. "Sounds like a counseling session." He set a toolbox down on the kitchen counter.

Carol walked over and gave him a side-arm hug. "You'd be proud of me, Pastor. I blew it today. I got so mad, I almost started hollering, but I caught myself. The good Lord tested me twice today." She held up her fingers.

"Only two times?"

Carol hit him, but her playfulness went sour as she thought about the first infraction. It was a tiny thing, but her attraction to that creepy guy in the store still bothered her. Some might not believe it was anything, but she was working to eliminate promiscuous behavior. It was her old nature, and it often still haunted her. Her second struggle came with the outburst outside the strip mall. Carol smiled. "But I stopped myself. I even said a prayer."

"Really? Everything okay?" asked Desmond.

"Yeah, sure." But she didn't feel so sure.

"Well, give me a call if you need to talk." He walked over to Melanie. "Better yet, Melanie can help." He bent and kissed her cheek.

Melanie blushed.

"Whoo whee." Carol hooted.

Desmond grinned. "Hey, we're official now." He held up Melanie's left hand. A petite diamond ring sparkled.

"Yeah, but you better save some of that for the wedding night." Carol winked and threw a hand in the air. "So when's the wedding?"

Desmond raised an eyebrow. "It's up to the lady. I'm more than ready."

Watching the two lovebirds, Carol thought how perfect they were for one another. Both had lost a spouse. Melanie's ex-husband died just last year. Although she'd been long divorced before...before he was murdered.

Desmond squeezed Melanie's shoulder. "Okay, well, I better go. I have a sermon to work on. The leak is fixed, and the faucet works fine."

"Is there anything he doesn't do? He's the Superhero of Bay Town," Carol teased.

This time, Desmond flushed red and pushed a hand through his hair. His thick waves, piercing blue eyes, and muscular build made him quite the looker.

As he left, he called over his shoulder, "Bay Town's got lots of superheroes. You ladies included. Bye."

"So, you had a bad day?" Melanie motioned for Carol to sit, patting the chair next to her.

"I went to a sale in Pascagoula, and I picked up a couple of cool items for my shop. Then I stopped at a drug store." Carol shook her head. "That's when it all went bad." She wrapped her hands around the warm cup and sipped.

Carol conveyed the drug store incident and shared her suspicions that the girl might have been trafficked. She left out no details, and when she finished, the women sat quietly.

Light lines formed on Melanie's forehead. "I didn't think it would happen again. At least not so close to home."

"Oh, Mel, I been so busy getting over Grady's death this last year...I'm so sorry. I keep forgetting it wasn't just me that lost somebody. I don't even know why I mourn for him. At the time, he was just good company for me."

Grady was a drifter Carol had met in a bar a year ago. She didn't think he deserved it, but he died in a suspicious hit-and-run accident. He was also a person of interest in the abduction of a teen in Jackson. Carol shivered, remembering how she'd let the man crash at her house.

Melanie waved off the comment. "Because you're a caring, compassionate woman, Carol. That's why."

"Yeah, well, I hope I'm caring in a better way now. And I hope I'm compassionate and not so passionate anymore." She forced a giggle. "But never mind me. That girl today, and what happened to Lacey and Virginia last year?" She paused, "And to you too. That makes my blood boil."

Carol shivered to recall how Melanie's daughter Lacey was attacked and Virginia, Carol's shop assistant was almost trafficked. Fortunately, she was rescued along with a dozen other girls. Thanks to Desmond and Melanie, who were the real heroes, along with Melanie's ex-husband. Carol shivered again, recalling how he was found dead in his hotel room following the raid on the trafficking ring. His death was never solved.

The reality of helplessness sunk in, and the women sat in silence. Melanie fingered the Bible in front of her, and after a few moments, she opened it to the Psalms and read. As she continued, a peace settled over Carol, and a chapter later, Melanie closed the book, reached out her hands across the little kitchen table, and took Carol's hands in hers. She squeezed. The sweetness in Melanie's eyes made Carol wish she had that gentle and quiet spirit.

"We can ask God to show us if and what we can do," said Melanie.

"You always have the right answer, Mel."

"Oh, no, I don't. God did a number on me and I'm still learning and growing, just like you. He's not done with us yet."

"Ain't that the truth."

Melanie prayed, and Carol gripped her hands tightly. As Melanie's spoken words of grace flowed, Carol felt anxiety's hold loosening. Ever since Grady's death and all the terrible events that happened last year in Bay Town, Carol had finally woken up. She didn't want to go on living the life that brought her endless misery. The string of meaningless relationships and one-night stands that started so long ago was finally broken.

Carol looked at Melanie, and her heart warmed. Melanie and others at Bay Town Community Church welcomed her. They'd nourished her soul, and they hadn't judged her lifestyle but gently encouraged her as her desire to live for God replaced the lonely emptiness in her life.

As Carol sipped her coffee, Melanie's cell phone buzzed.

"Hello? Hi, Chief." She raised her eyebrows at her friend. "What?...How?..." Melanie listened. And the more she did, the deeper her brows furrowed. "That can't be…But…I see… Okay. Thank you for calling."

She clicked off and carefully placed the phone on the table. "Will Boudreaux has been released."

Carol's brows knit together. "Who is Will Boudreaux?" Suddenly her eyes flew wide. "Was that the guy who killed Grady?"

Melanie nodded. "Boudreaux won an appeal. He hired a new lawyer. Something about evidence tampering got him off the hit-and-run charge that killed Grady, but I don't know how he got off the trafficking charge." Melanie shook her head. "I can't believe it. They caught him at the crime scene in New Orleans, but the case was dismissed."

"What do you mean, evidence tampering? The video showed the car hitting Grady."

"Well, the judge ruled the video wasn't clear enough. He said the prosecution pieced together the license plate number. When they showed it in the appellate court, the judge didn't see it as conclusive." Melanie's knuckles went white.

"That's just plain crazy. Must have been an old judge." Carol shook her head. "An old blind judge."

"They had the make and model. You'd think it'd be easy to narrow down."

Carol's brow furrowed. "What kind of car?"

"What?" Melanie asked.

"What kind of car hit Grady?"

"A sedan. A Lincoln, I think. And it was a custom icy blue color."

CHAPTER 3

A s the women arrived and the Bible Study ensued, Carol's mind drifted. A blue car, the teen girl. Her fingers rustled the Bible pages, and she kept losing her place. When asked a question, she couldn't answer.

A soft, dark hand reached over and squeezed hers. Lyla, head of the Women's Ministry in Bay Town, gave Carol a warm smile. Lyla and her husband Joe were prominent citizens in Bay Town, and he was the well-loved local high school bus driver.

Chuckling, she thought how fun these women were at a Bible Study no less. The evenings spent studying, praying, and visiting left Carol with a high more real than any she ever had when she came home with a drifter after drinking and dancing at bars. That high always fell flat, leaving her lonelier than ever.

The evening sped by, and as Carol drove home, she chuckled thinking of the word *high*, but her stomach knotted when she passed the Bayou Bar on Main Street. How could people go to that place? A flood of guilt washed over her—the irony. Her past was filled with bars, drinking, and men. She had no right to judge.

Carol parked her car in front of her shop, where she lived in the apartment up above. She had an overnight parking permit that allowed her to do so, but no other vehicles were parked on the street this late. No other shop owners lived up above their stores like her, either. Most used the upstairs for storage, as she formerly had. You could enter the upstairs from inside the shop or use the stairs in the poorly lit back alley. Though she wasn't afraid of the dark, trudging up the back steps didn't appeal to Carol tonight.

She entered through the store, unlocking the front door and stepping in. An eerie silence filled the shop, except for the jingle of the doorbells. She welcomed the cheeriness of the tinkling.

Walking back to her office, she pushed aside the flimsy, sheer curtain and stepped into the workroom. She dropped her things and poked through the unfinished paperwork lying atop her desk. Nowadays, she welcomed it.

Before heading up the stairs, she peered at the front door. The streetlights outside shone in, casting a yellow glow across the wares of her shop. She walked to the front to double-check the lock. Before pulling down the door shade, she noticed a smoldering cigarette butt lying on the sidewalk and frowned. She headed for the back of the store.

Her knees creaked and ached as she labored up the dark, narrow staircase inside her shop. *I'm way too young to be feeling like this.* Carol straightened herself and let go of the railing, forcing a jauntier gait. When she reached the top, she unlocked the door, turned the glass knob, and stepped in. She closed the door behind her and ran her fingers over the smooth blue paint. Her little loft haven was her escape.

A comfortable golden ray beamed over the room from the lamp she always left on. Still, she walked over to the orange and red tiffany floor lamp and flipped it on. She dropped into her favorite overstuffed chair and sunk in. Grabbing the chenille throw, she spread it across her knees and propped her head on her fist. The dead silence in the room overpowered her. *Boy, could I use a drink*. She shook her head, shaking away her struggle.

Knock. Knock.

Who could that be, she thought? She didn't often get visitors up here. Throwing off the chenille, she walked to the window and peeked out the sheers.

She smiled and flung open the door. "What are you all doing here?" Carol hugged her guests. "Come in. Come in."

She beckoned Melanie and Desmond to the little kitchenette. After filling her kettle with water, she clicked on the stove, then lifted the lid off a ceramic antique cookie jar. A beautiful dainty cut glass platter sat on the counter, and Carol piled it high with cookies.

"Cocoa and cookies?"

Desmond nodded.

Melanie shook her head and waved off the offer. "I'm stuffed from the blueberry cobbler and ice cream at my house."

"That was hours ago, well, at least one hour. Come on, Mel. How often do you get to enjoy my baking?" Within minutes the kettle whistled, and Carol ladled heaping teaspoons of cocoa into the mugs. Pouring water, she stirred and then added a couple of mini marshmallows in each cup.

"Did you bake these?" Melanie gave in and took a bite.

"Yeah, me and Betty Crocker. We try."

"Carol, your place is so adorable. You've done a lot here," said Melanie.

"There wasn't much to do. It's such a dinky place."

"But you get the most interesting pieces." Melanie pointed around the room at the eclectic mix of colors and furnishings. "Right, Des?"

He shrugged without comment and reached for a second cookie.

"Well, I've got a lot of time right now, especially since I

don't go looking for company every evening. I mean after last year..." Carol trailed off.

Desmond and Melanie glanced at one another.

"What's up?" Carol asked.

"Well, that's kind of why we came. Are you all right? You know that call from Chief Bert tonight? I must admit. I'm a little shook up," said Melanie.

Desmond placed a hand over Melanie's.

"Well, I'm not," said Carol. In her heart, anger against the man that killed Grady was the most she struggled with. "It's been almost a year since Grady was killed, and I'm still not settled.

"Heck, he was only in his fifties." Carol tapped her fingers on the table.

"Yes, we all need to work on forgiveness, don't we?" Melanie straightened. "Anyway, you sure you're okay?"

"Don't worry about me. You know I can manage. I always do."

"Yes, I believe you can, but how about we ask for God's help too?" Desmond offered his hands, and as they bowed their heads, he prayed words that lulled her to calm and diffused her anger, but she wasn't quite ready to let go. Was it vengeance that lingered in her heart?

Melanie squeezed Carol's hand and stood. "I better get home." She smiled at Desmond. "I dragged him along, so he has to drop me off. I didn't mean to barge in on you tonight. I was just worried about my friend."

"Oh, barge in all you want. Heaven knows I get lonely here. But I'm good. I got this little place, and it suits me just fine. See you tomorrow, bright and early."

Melanie and Desmond said goodbye, and Carol watched as they headed down the stairway to the street below. Alleys sure had charm, but they had their spookiness too.

She hadn't lived in the little studio a year yet, but it was home. Having sold her house after Grady was killed, she downsized. Making sure she wouldn't have room for strange houseguests. Never again, she hoped.

Carol switched off the Tiffany lamp and pulled close the thick drapes. She cleaned up the cookies and cocoa and eyed her tablet on the small desk under the window. She was thankful for the electronic invasion that was her connection to home.

Home.

She'd thought more about her family in the last six months than she had since running away over thirty years ago.

Clicking on Facebook, she searched her sister's photos and chuckled at the funny antics of her young adult nephews. She'd never met them. But someday, maybe God would help her get that far. He'd given her the courage to reconnect, and instead of shunning her, they welcomed her contact. Well, her mom and sister had, and she hoped her dad was warming up. How could they have ever forgiven her? She shuddered and shut down the tablet.

Carol took a shower, dressed in her nightclothes, and prepped her sofa bed for sleeping. Pulling out the bed, she threw back the coverlet, adjusted her sleeping pillows, and climbed in. The cold emptiness made her shiver, but before the quiet seclusion set in, she glanced at her nightstand. As if it beckoned her, she reached for her Bible, and the pages were fresh and crisp. Flipping open to Psalms, she read:

I waited patiently for the LORD, and He inclined to me and heard my cry. He also brought me up out of a horrible pit out of the miry clay and set my feet upon a rock and established my steps.

She placed a bookmark between the pages and clutched the book to her chest. Carol talked to God like she spoke to a friend. He was her friend, but she also revered Him as her Lord. The one who saved her life and her soul.

A low rumbling sound outside drew her attention, and she tried to ignore it. The rumbling continued. Finally, she threw off the covers and walked to the window. Slipping back the drapes, she peeked out. What was a car doing idling in the alley? Beneath her window, no less. The clock on her microwave glared back at her. It was late. Glancing back out the window, she squinted. It didn't help that the streetlamp was burnt out, but as the car edged forward, she noticed a trail of gray smoke swirling up into the dark sky from the driver's window.

CHAPTER 4

The morning sun shined brightly as Carol stood outside her shop, enjoying the warmth. She began to sweep when the roar of an engine startled her, and she jumped. From the corner of her eye, she caught a streak of blue. Holding a broom, she watched as a car sped down Main Street. It was too early for tourists. Most customers didn't start shopping until after coffee time.

The early morning dew glistened on the shop windows as Carol returned to sweeping the sidewalk. A slight wind blew up some ashes, and she frowned at the cigarette butts in front of her red-brick storefront. She paused. Grady used to stand there and smoke. She forced the picture from her mind and pulled her fringed shawl tight against her chest. The shiver she felt wasn't from the cool spring breeze.

With the side of her foot, she swept the butts against the wall. Ash floated onto her shoes, and she frowned at her soiled moccasins. She finished sweeping, then began setting up. Her store's entrance was flanked by an old steamer trunk that welcomed customers to Second Chance, Carol's vintage thrift shop. She placed a pile of books atop a small round table covered with a sheer curtain made of white georgette. Two wrought-iron chairs sat on opposite sides, boasting a speckling of antique green patina over the filigree.

Carol finished placing the final pieces out front and adjusted the eucalyptus wreath hanging on the red door. Standing back, hands on her hips, she nodded—everything in place and ready for her customers.

Max, the owner of the Pink Rossette, the local florist shop a couple doors down, swept out front. He stopped and waved as his shoulder-length white hair blew in the breeze and he hiked up his faded blue jeans. Since it was still early, Carol walked down to greet him.

"Good mornin', Max." She wrapped her long hair in a bun, then bent to drink in the sweet floral aroma of fresh roses in a tall, galvanized bucket. "Hey, can I have a couple of red ones here?"

"Of course. Would you like a side of rosette with that, dearie?" Max's speech held a hint of a British accent. He grinned and slipped in his signature bud, a pink rosette.

"Would you like me to clip them short for you, as well?" The wind blew back his hair, showing off his long sideburns. Carol smiled. *Hippie.*

"You know it, Max."

"Hey, leave some roses for me," said Melanie while giving Carol a hug. "Good morning, Max. Could I get a couple of white—"

"Long-stemmed and de-thorned, all ready for you, my dear." Max pointed to a tall vase on the counter inside.

"So Mel, what brings you out so early? Got another rich client getting married?" Carol chuckled.

"I'm meeting Chief Bert at my store this morning," said Melanie.

Carol pressed her lips tightly as she thought of him. Chief Bert was a good man, and his name was synonymous with fighting human trafficking in the area. He had initiated the command to raid a run-down hotel in New Orleans where abducted girls were housed, and he'd been the one that funneled evidence to the FBI and the New Orleans PD for the rescue.

Carol looked up and nodded.

"He just wants to make sure we're all okay." Melanie's raised eyebrows questioned Carol.

An uneasiness rose within her, and it was more than the incident at the drug store. *Why would our safety have anything to do with that guy's release?*

"Carol?"

Shaking her head, Carol waved a hand across the air. "I'm fine." She shrugged, but her arms tensed as she squeezed the little red bouquet.

A blue and white squad car drove by, and Melanie hugged Carol. "I better go. There's the chief."

Blue. She shivered and more blue flashed in her mind. The girl yesterday got into a blue sedan. It was a blue sedan that hit Grady…And a blue streak this morning.

"Sure, Mel, you go on now."

Melanie pulled tight her thick tunic sweater and clipped down the sidewalk towards "Quaint Affairs," her wedding consultant business. Carol walked back to Second Chance. As she walked inside, the red light on her desk phone flashed. She had three missed calls already and when she checked the voicemails, all the calls were hang-ups. *That's weird.* She tried going about the business of the day, but instead decided that had to get some things off her chest.

Carol ran down the street and burst into Melanie's store. "I think he was here," she said breathlessly.

Chief Bert stood. "Good morning, ma'am." He tipped his hat.

"What did you say?" Melanie's words were almost a whisper.

"I saw a blue car this morning. Just barely, it streaked by, and no one else was on the street that early yet. Just him...I mean just the car. I didn't see the guy driving it."

"Miss Carol, why don't you have a seat. Sit here on this little thing." He pushed the antique chair closer to her. "I'm afraid I might break it."

He held the chair's frame with two pinkies sticking out like handling a China teacup. He giggled that familiar sound, so unbefitting his six-foot, three-inch frame.

"I'm sorry. That's a Japanese Obi slipper chair. Vintage 1957. It's a little low to the ground, isn't it?" Melanie stood and walked to a striped, brocade, wide, wing-backed chair. She removed the books stacked on the seat and motioned for the Chief to sit.

Settling in, he nodded. "Now that's more like it." His friendly tone took on a more serious note as he looked at Carol. "Tell me, who was here?"

"You said he had a blue car. I saw one." She bit her lip. "There are other things, too, and I have a powerful hunch."

"He? Who is he?" asked the Chief.

"Will Bou...Bou something...whatever," Carol grunted.

Melanie's eyes opened wide. "Will Boudreaux? You saw Boudreaux?"

"Now, Miss Carol, unless you saw his face, we got nothing to go on," said the chief.

Her brows furrowed. She hadn't allowed herself to watch the news or read the events' reports last year. She didn't even know what Will Boudreaux looked like.

"But let's just say it was him, why would he show up in Bay Town?"

"Virginia," whispered Melanie.

Chief Bert nodded. "Right. I didn't want to alarm you, but I thought of her myself. How's she doing?"

Carol's mind raced. Virginia had been one of the girls in that hotel. Carol had heard that this Boudreaux had lied about being Virginia's father when in fact, all he wanted was to use this beautiful intellectually disabled teen.

"Virginia's doing fine now," said Melanie. "She's in an independent study program and goes to church and Youth Group with Lacey."

The Chief nodded. "That's good, but Will Boudreaux's release places Virginia at risk. He's related to her somehow, and he's manipulated her before. I'm sure his prostitution ring has all but stagnated with him being in jail for the last year. I was afraid he'd be looking for her to start it up again."

Melanie shook her head. "No, it can't be."

"It was him. It had to be." Carol glanced between the Chief and Melanie. "I'm pretty sure I saw him in Pascagoula yesterday. He had another girl with him. A victim. I'm sure of it."

"Whoa there. That's a stretch."

"Yeah, I don't think so. I was driving home from a shopping trip to an antique clearance sale, and I stopped at a drug store." Carol explained the incident. "I had a terrible, terrible feeling about that little girl. I even talked to that Boudreaux." She shook, thinking how she had found him attractive for a brief moment. "I saw them getting into a blue car."

"Could you identify the man from a photograph?"

"Of course."

"Good, come on over to the station today when you get a chance."

Carol agreed, and Chief Bert shook his head. "I'm afraid this is escalating a little too quickly. If, and I do mean if, this is Will Boudreaux, we need to act. I'll call the FBI and report him, but they won't move unless I have something concrete for them."

"Concrete? Why I spoke to him." Carol's voice rose.

"Where?"

"In Pascagoula," said Carol.

Raising two hands, Chief Bert nodded. "Exactly. In Pascagoula. Not here, in Bay Town. He's a free man."

"Well, he shouldn't be," said Melanie.

"But it wasn't just Pascagoula. He is here. I can feel it. Mel, after you left last night a car in the alley sat outside my apartment. Then this morning, there were cigarette butts on the sidewalk."

"Why would he be hanging around you?" asked the Chief.

Melanie sat stoically a few moments before speaking. "Maybe it's the connection to Virginia. Somehow he must have figured out that she works for Carol at Second Chance."

"Now, wait a minute. Carol, when does she show up for work?"

"Most afternoons after school and weekends. It's part of her approved independent study program. She gets credits, and she's going to graduate this spring." A proud grin crossed Carol's face.

Melanie beamed back. "You two sure are a good fit."

"Yes, we are, and I'm thankful I have her. Hearing about her past makes me suck up my trials. God knows that poor girl has had the worst of it."

Chief Bert straightened. "I'd like to think we all saved her from the worst of it. That hotel, where Pastor Brooks found her...." He shook his head. "Miss Carol, you done a good thing taking in that poor little girl. I know there are plenty of programs for the intellectually disabled, but you've provided an opportunity for some real skills for that gal."

"Well, that group home she's in has been great, too. And that girl is talented. I love working with her. She's got a gift for style."

This time Chief Bert's laugh was deep and loud. No giggle. "Style? Why, when we found her at that bar on Main Street, that get-up she wore..." He glanced between the two women and stopped, quickly clearing his throat.

Carol stood and glared at the chief. "Why that get-up was all she knew back then, and she's come a long way. And yes, style. I like that flashy flair of hers. It suits Second Chance and me just fine." Carol crossed her arms.

Chief Bert grimaced. "I apologize. You're right. I've got no business speaking out like that."

Melanie broke the ice. "No worries, Chief. I think we're all grateful for Virginia's progress."

"Okay, well, let's finish up." He waved his hands, motioning for Carol to sit. "Let's suppose he is here. Is the girl supervised at all other times?" asked the chief.

"I think so. It seems like it. I can check with Lacey. They hang out together," said Melanie.

"Well, I think both of them need a chaperone, a protector of some sort. Everywhere they go," said Carol.

Melanie chuckled. "Wow. You have changed."

"Well, thank the Lord for that. I'm not taking in every stupid stray man who walks in off the streets anymore. I'm ain't trusting no man!"

"Whoa, TMI, too much information, there." Chief Bert wiggled uncomfortably.

"Right, sorry. But I sure as heck ain't gonna let nobody hurt our girls again."

Chief Bert cleared his throat. "Now, Miss Carol, I'll take care of this."

Carol held her head high and set her jaw. Thoughts flooded her mind—it was just wrong. No. Boudreaux was not going to hurt Virginia again.

Chief Bert gave instructions on how the women should handle things for the time being, but his words floated into thin air. She had to do something. She returned to Second Chance, and to work, but she had difficulty concentrating. Throughout the day, she thought of what she could do to help protect Virginia. But was she trusting God? She'd been learning to, and if it hadn't been for her renewed faith, she wouldn't have survived the last year. But along with this new life, old hurts surfaced, memories of her mother, and her family whom she'd left so long ago. A picture of her family floated before her face, and she toiled with decisions, old and new.

When the day finally ended, her thoughts didn't, and she toiled throughout the night.

CHAPTER 5

Carol awoke unsettled. Glancing at the Bible on her nightstand, she plopped down on her unmade sofa bed and grabbed the book. *I need wisdom, Lord.* Flipping the pages to Proverbs, she read. The wisdom part she loved. It was the fool's part that haunted her. It spoke volumes of her life, and she wanted so badly to have that wisdom. The passages soothed her soul, and she wished she had more time to study, but she had to get to work.

She'd left enough time to grab a cup of coffee at The Mockingbird Café, and as she walked down Main Street, the crisp morning air tightened the skin on her face. Patting her cheeks, she felt the dewy dampness. She breathed deep and could almost taste the salty ocean air. Birds flitted in and out of the trees, chattering about, and she pulled her ruffled knit scarf tightly around her neck.

The baristas in the Café hustled behind the counters filling orders. Carol took her place in line and glanced around. Her eyes landed on the TV monitor flashing from a corner. *Missing teen from Jackson* scrolled across the news border, running along the bottom of the screen. Leaving her place in line, she went closer to listen.

"That's terrible. Why would she run away again?" The voice came from a person seated nearby.

Carol spun around. "Excuse me?"

An older man with graying hair nodded toward the TV. A newspaper lay open in his lap.

"Yeah. That's the same girl that ran away last year in Jackson. She was rescued in that raid in New Orleans."

Suddenly, her stomach roiled. "What happened?"

"Don't know. Just that the same teen was reported missing again. That crazy mom was on the news last night. Begging for someone to find her."

"Crazy, mom?"

"Yeah. The one whose boyfriend landed up dead in an alley after her daughter went missing. She had no business bringing drifters to her house when she's got a young daughter at home."

Carol felt the blood leave her head, and she dropped into the nearest seat.

The man's paper wrinkled as he leaned forward. "Ma'am, are you all right?"

Grady spoke of a crazy girlfriend with a runaway daughter. She's what caused him to run when the police deemed him a person of interest. Wiping the sweat from her brow, Carol nodded. "How do you know all this?"

"I'm a retired journalist. I like to follow stories. And last year? That was a whopper. Anyway, they got an Amber Alert out. The teen was last seen heading southeast."

She thought of the girl yesterday—the girl in the drug store. Carol stood and headed for the exit, not bothering with coffee. Outside, she fumbled when retrieving her phone, and dropped it.

"Shoot." Gathering her scarf and her hair in a tight hold, she bent to pick it up. Frazzled, she dropped the phone again. Footsteps approached and she felt a hand on hers.

"Here you go. What are you doing here so early?" Melanie asked as they both stood. "Carol, are you, all right?"

"Did you hear? Mel, that girl from Jackson. The one Grady was involved with. She ran away again."

Melanie nodded. "I did hear about it."

"So it's the same girl. Same mom. The mom who Grady was with." Carol bit her lip. "We have to do something. This is another nightmare, and we're in the middle of it again."

Melanie frowned, "What do you mean we?"

"The girl at the drug store. Remember I told you? That must be her. And that Boudreaux guy? He called out her name. I can't remember it, but it started with an A." Carol pointed to the café. "And the news in there said her name was…oh shoot. I forgot already. Anyway, it started with an A, too."

"Carol, stop. They rescued that Jackson girl in the raid in New Orleans last year. Maybe she ran away, but why would she go back to him?" Melanie shivered.

Carol wasn't listening. "Don't you see? If it's her, then it's got to be Boudreaux. We know he drives a blue car."

"He drove a blue car a year ago. What makes you think it's the same one? You can't know for sure."

"You're right. But I'm not waiting to find out."

"Carol, stop. We can't go there. We can't panic."

Carol started walking.

"Wait, where are you going? Carol, come on…" Melanie's voice trailed behind her.

Carol walked six long blocks to the police station. The bells jingled as she pushed open the door and stepped in.

The Chief glared at Officer Blaine, the only other officer in the Bay Town Police Headquarters. "I thought you were going to take those bells down?"

The Chief sat in plain view of the front door in the old, antiquated office. No private room for him. In the back stood a solitary jail cell. The office held a nostalgic air and evoked an atmosphere much like the police station in the Andy Griffith Show, but even smaller.

Chief Bert and Officer Blaine were both on duty this morning, but then again, they always were. It was just a two-man station, and the Hancock County Sherriff's Department was their backup if they needed it. Bay Town often didn't. They'd proved so through previous events.

Carol pushed through the spring-loaded gate that separated the civilians from the police. "Chief, two things. First, I need to identify that guy. Second, I need a name."

He leaned back and scratched his head. "What about that gate, don't you understand?"

Carol looked back as she let go of the wooden panel. It hit her backside, causing her to jump. The Chief and Officer Blaine chuckled, and Carol glared.

The chief cleared his throat. "Blaine, get the mug shots of Boudreaux, will you? Now, Miss Carol, what name is it that you want?"

"The girl that went missing from Jackson last year. She was rescued in the raid in New Orleans."

The Chief scratched his short, coarse black hair. Pushing up his thick-framed glasses, he glanced at Officer Blaine, who sat typing away at his computer. Chief Bert pointed to him.

"Acadia Perrin." Blaine looked up. "That's the Jackson girl."

"Wow, that was fast," said Carol.

"Yup. That's why I hired this guy." Chief Bert hooked his thumbs into his thick belt and rocked back in his chair.

"I was assigned to this station. Came straight from Hancock Academy," said Blaine.

"Top of his class." Chief Bert grinned and puffed out his chest as if claiming credit for his more than capable assistant. Suddenly he frowned. "What do you need her name for?"

"Phone number? Can you give me her number?"

"Of course not," said the chief. "That's private and confidential."

"But you can search for it in the white pages. She might be listed," said Blaine.

Chief Bert planted his hands on his desk. "You want to tell me what this is about?"

Carol pulled back the gate, being careful to clear the way before she let it go again. "Nope. But I'll let you know if I need you."

"Wait a minute. What about the mugshot?"

"Oh, yeah." Carol stopped. "I'm pretty sure it's him. But I'll be back to check. I gotta go." She gave the door an extra rattle, jingling the bells as she whisked out.

Chief Bert scratched his head. "What in the world is that woman up to?"

With little effort, Carol found the phone number. Standing at the counter next to the antique cash register, she dialed, and pressed the speaker button.

"Hello?" A weak voice spoke.

"Hello? Mrs. Perrin?"

Silence.

"Mrs. Perrin, I'm from Bay Town? I may have some news—"

"Bay Town?" The woman's voice shook. "I have been calling you." Carol's mind raced. *Calling me?...The hang-ups!* There were two hang-ups this morning. The woman continued. "You knew my Grady."

Carol tried to draw air. Her chest tightened, and she felt as if she couldn't breathe. *Oh Lord, I gotta tell a fib. Help me.*

"You did, didn't you?" The voice escalated.

Carol still couldn't speak.

"Didn't you?" The voice screamed.

Carol hung up. Gasping for air, she laid her head upon the counter. The phone immediately rang and rang. Finally, it went to voicemail.

"I know you knew him. You took him away from me. You took him, and I needed him. And I need someone now. I have no one." An eerie chuckle escaped, "You know, Grady called me when he left Bay Town. He was coming back to me. To me. He was leaving you."

Carol looked around for her stool, and when she couldn't find it, she slumped to the floor. She'd always wondered why Grady was killed in Pascagoula. He was supposed to be going on a weekend get-away with her the night he disappeared. *Was this woman telling the truth? Had he been running back to her?*

She stroked the rough-hewn wooden planks, feeling a light film of dirt covering her palm. She felt cheap and dirty. Would this feeling never end? Stretching out her leg, she winced and pulled back. A nail protruded from the molding that she'd forgotten to fix. Raising her ankle, it was just a scratch—only a trickle of blood.

The phone call. It was a scratch. Scratching the surface of the life that she was trying to bury. Over the past year, she had learned that her former life didn't have a hold on her. But it could. She searched her mind, thinking of Pastor Desmond's recent sermons. How could she get a handle on this? Dwelling on herself didn't help, but what did? Thinking of others, loving one another, forgiving one another. Finding the strength to stand, she redialed the number.

"Mrs. Perrin?"

This time there was no pause, and the woman sputtered. "Now you're trying to get my daughter too? Aren't you?"

"What? Mrs. Perrin, I don't even know you. I...I wanted

to help. I think I have some news about where your daughter could be."

A pause. "Of course you do. You took her before, and now you want her again."

This was crazy talk. Carol wished she knew how to record a phone call. *Could she record a phone call? Think. Think.* "Mrs. Perrin, I know you're upset——"

Click. The line went dead.

Carol rubbed her temples. *Oh forget it. The woman's crazy. Walk away, Carol.* Her old self-talk survival techniques shifted into gear, but they made her feel defensive, paranoid, worthless. Anxiety rose within, and she stared at the phone again as if it were poison. Finding her purse, she grabbed her cell. *But this is my lifeline.* She dialed for help, and made two calls, and left two messages. She rearranged displays, opened shipments and took inventory. Finally, the front door bells jingled, and she moved quickly.

"Pastor Desmond, thanks for coming.

"Sure thing. What's up?"

"I called Melanie first but got no answer."

"She's out on an appointment. How can I help?" Desmond smiled.

Carol led him to the big bay window where she'd arranged a tiny sitting area in an alcove—a beautiful hideaway surrounded by huge potted Boston Ferns and various antiques. They sat, and she told him about the phone calls and Mrs. Perrin. When she finished, she blew out a whoosh of air, and continued.

"Well? What should I do? What do you think? The woman needs help, but she's crazy. I'm not worried about me, but what if she hurts someone?" Carol shook her head. "I'm at a loss, Pastor."

When she finally stopped, he leaned forward. "That woman is hurting, and she certainly doesn't sound like she's in her right mind."

Desmond spoke powerfully but always with a thread of kindness and compassion. This was his gift. Most people thought it was something all pastors were naturally endowed with, but Carol didn't believe that. In fact, he was the first clergy she'd ever trusted. But honestly, she'd never given any other man of the cloth much of a chance. And now, he was the rock that God provided to guide her.

Carol nodded. "I know. That's why I called you."

Desmond clasped his hands, resting them between his knees. Looking directly at her, he raised his brows. "I'm glad you called, Carol. Do you want to hear what I have to say?"

"I knew you was going to ask that. It seems like every time I ramble on, you ask me that." She gave him a sideways glance. "Of course, I do. Lay it on me."

"First things first. Let's pray."

Carol bowed her head, welcoming the expected peace as he prayed. His words always soothed her anxieties, and as he asked the Holy Spirit's guidance, a rush of calm swept over her.

"Amen." He reached out and patted her arm. "Now, you need to report this to Chief Bert. You need to tell him everything."

Her palms grew suddenly wet, and she gulped. "What do you mean everything? Do you mean about my relationship with Grady? I thought I was forgiven for all that?" The calming prayers previously offered faded.

"You are, Carol. Don't ever doubt God's forgiveness." Pastor Desmond gave her a mini sermon on grace and forgiveness.

She hung on every word.

"But this is also about the law and your safety. The chief needs to know enough to help you and this woman. You need to trust people too, Carol."

Trust. She was still working on that one. "Okay, I'll go see him. Then what? I think maybe that girl at the drug store may have been this woman's daughter."

"That's easy enough to find out. Chief Bert has a copy of the Amber alert, I'm sure of it."

"Why didn't I think of that? I was already in there this morning."

"You might try searching for it on your computer." His watch buzzed, and he raised his wrist. "I'm sorry, Carol. I've got a meeting in a few minutes." He stood. "I'll give you a call later."

Carol walked him outside. He said goodbye, and she gave him a side-ways hug. Her long hair tangled in his arms, and they laughed. A few towns people waved as they passed by.

"Thanks so much, Pastor. I sure appreciate your help."

"Sure, anytime. I'm praying for you."

Carol watched him stop and gaze at Quaint Affairs, Melanie's business. Her heart warmed. Her new best friend and the pastor were a perfect match, and she found the strength to grow in her new faith with the help of them both. She'd hoped to be as strong someday. She was used to relying only on herself and hoped that the day would come when it would be God and her.

As Carol walked back into the shop, her eyes riveted to the wall behind the register. Plaques inscribed with scripture hung there, and her shoulders relaxed. Pastor Desmond was just the messenger. The burden lifted somewhat, and she noted to call Chief Bert. As she laid the pen down, she saw the flashing light on her answering machine again. The number two flashed. *Two messages? Again?* She pushed the button. The first she had already heard. She didn't need to listen to the threatening voice a second time. She skipped it, and the following message began.

Mrs. Perrin's voice whispered. "I'll find you. I'll find Second Chance, and I'll find you. Grady didn't deserve what he got. But you will."

CHAPTER 6

C arol knew better. God or no God, her gut told her she shouldn't go. But as her day dragged on, she knew what she had to do. For the time being, she busied herself, and Virginia was there to help. Carol gazed after the young woman, and a vise clamped around her heart. Her eyes glazed over. It was only a year ago that Virginia…

"Oooh! These are so pretty." Virginia slipped a connected jumble of wires over her hand and jingled the bracelets on her wrist.

"Girl, come on now. I don't have all day."

"Why are you in such a hurry?" Virginia swiped off the bracelet and placed it on a small tree branch holding copper, silver, and gold jewelry. She loved arranging the displays of trinkets, herbal remedies, oils, and bling.

"Just take those empty boxes out back to the dumpster." Carol threw a nod in Virginia's direction and returned to the cash register receipts.

Her young store clerk broke down another small box.

Carol appreciated Virginia's talent with displays and how she could put things together to enhance the products' salability. Virginia was also great at selling too. People loved her, and she'd been a good fit. But slow. That girl moved at a snail's pace—not a care in the world.

Her simple mind kept her in the moment. Yet she'd blossomed since having a specialized education plan while living at The Refuge.

The Refuge. A home and a haven for battered women. Although Virginia was the first human trafficking victim, she, blossomed under the love and healing provided like most young women residing there,. Carol desired to help there. She just didn't know how. In the meantime, helping Virginia was her first priority, and perhaps others like her.

"I have someplace to be. Now go." Jackson was a long way away, and Carol needed to get on the road.

Virginia picked up a pile of cardboard, tucking it under her arm. She kicked open the back door to the alley and yelled, "It's getting dark out here. Why don't you get a light?"

Carol ignored her as she continued to count the cash. She stuffed all the checks and bills in a plain canvas bag. It had been a slow day, but enough came in to satisfy her expenditures. Her business brought a steady income that paid the bills and gave her some breathing room.

She tidied up the counter, and no lights blinked back at her from the answering machine. No new messages. *Phew.* Carol wiped her brow and hoped Mrs. Perrin was settling down.

An ache swelled behind her eyes. With her head pounding, she pulled out a migraine stick and rubbed it across her forehead. The lipstick-type tube came in a variety of scents. Peppermint, spearmint, and lavender, they were all essential oils. Not many people bought into it, but it worked for her. Beats drugs, she thought—something she'd long given up.

"Virginia?" Carol's brow furrowed. Her boots thudded as she clomped to the back door. Swinging open the screen, she peered out. *Man, it's dark out here.* "Virginia? Get back in here.

We need to go." She saw no sign of the girl, and her upper lip beaded with sweat. Stepping out into the dim alley, she called again as she moved forward. "Virginia?" A few feet away stood the smelly dumpster. Boxes lay scattered on the cracked asphalt. Carol saw a shoe peeking out from the corner of the dumpster.

"Virginia!" She screamed and stumbled over the boxes. Carol lunged and fell with a thud on top of the frightened girl who clutched a dirty ball of fur.

"Whoa there, Miz Carol, get off me!" Virginia cuddled the filthy, hissing cat. It scratched her arm and jumped away. "Come back here." Virginia squeezed out from under Carol.

Rolling to the side, Carol sat, legs sprawled out in front, brushing dirt and pebbles off her skirt. She swiped her hands together and winced at the gravel embedded in her skin. "What in the world? Are you crazy?" Carol glared at Virginia.

Virginia glared back. A light red mark rose on her chin. The cat's warning. "Me? You're the crazy lady."

Carol threw her head back and laughed. Her voice echoed in the empty alleyway that rested between the old two-story brick buildings. The two women splattered with black streaks were a mess.

Virginia stood and shook her head, blonde curls falling across her forehead. She shoved them aside and looked down. Dirt smudged her white jeans. The more she scrubbed at them, the dirtier they got. Throwing her hands in the air, she shook her head at Carol, then called into the darkness. "Here, kitty, kitty…."

"Oh no, you don't. That kitty's staying out here. Give me a hand." Carol raised a dirty palm. Hiking up her knees, she dug her heels into the ground as Virginia pulled her to standing. "I guess I owe you a pair of jeans." Shrugging, she grabbed Virginia's hand. "Come on. Let's go."

"Ouch." Virginia shook off Carol's gritty hand.

"No more working out here until I replace that bulb. And

no more chasing stray cats. You about scared the daylights out of me."

"You always say that. That poor kitty is hungry."

"Never mind, he makes do. Come on, let's get that scratch cleaned up."

Driving Virginia back to The Refuge, Carol apologized and promised to take her shopping for a new pair of jeans.

Virginia squealed and hugged Carol's neck. Always loving gifts and shopping, Virginia was easily distracted. Carol, not so much. The message from Mrs. Perrin in Jackson came back to haunt her. Being concerned for the welfare of someone other than herself was making life complicated. She worried about the girl at the drugstore. She worried about Virginia, and now…now she was worried about Mrs. Perrin.

"Thanks, Miz Carol. I'll see you tomorrow after school." Virginia flashed that beautiful innocent smile, her teeth bright behind her ruby red lips.

Would Carol always think of her as a little girl in a grown-up body? *God, help me.*

After dropping Virginia off, Carol made the long drive to Jackson. By the time she arrived, it was late, and she was beginning to doubt her irrational decision to find Mrs. Perrin. The three-hour drive took only two and a half, and it was 8:30 at night, and she still had the ride home. *What am I even doing here? That poor woman is so lost. Like I used to be.*

She checked the Map App and was surprised that it took her to a nice neighborhood with large lots in a secluded wooded area. She breathed in the pine scent from tall trees lining the streets but squinted in the dark. The absence of streetlights made it challenging to make out the house numbers. When she rounded the corner, flashing red and blue lights flooded a house up ahead. Carol slowed down. This was it—the Perrin's house. Two police cars and a plain black sedan parked haphazardly. She stopped, and a beam of light flashed on her face. Raising her hands to shade her eyes, she peered out.

"Can I help you, ma'am?" The voice muffled through her window.

Carol's old classic El Camino had no automatic switches. She rolled down the window and peeked between her fingers. She made out a man in uniform. "What's going on?"

"What's your business here?" The officer shifted the flashlight to the side, and Carol blinked.

"Nothing, sir. I'm just driving through and saw the lights." She bit her lip and scrunched her nose. *I can't even tell a white lie without feeling guilty these days.*

"Can I see your license, please?"

As she complied, another man in uniform yelled. "We're clear here. Let's go."

Handing back her license, he peered in. "You're a long way from home. Bay Town?"

Carol forced a smile and opened her mouth to speak. The police car she was blocking roared its engine, and the officer detaining her moved back. "Better get home, ma'am."

But a screeching vehicle pulled up behind her. A van parked, and a young reporter and cameraman jumped out. They started for the house.

"Oh, no, you don't." The policeman stopped them.

"Channel 2 News." The dark-haired girl flashed a press pass and ran for the porch.

The cameraman moved to follow, but the policeman held out his arm.

"You move that van, now."

"Yes, sir," said the cameraman.

Carol waited, then pulled away. Angry shouts came from the house, and the police ran for the entrance. The cameraman jumped from his vehicle with his video equipment held fast on his shoulder.

Hesitant but heeding the policeman's command, Carol drove, hoping to pick something up on the news. Leaving the neighborhood, tingles slithered up her spine as she crept through the darkness. The wooded area was lit only by the homes it hid. Passing several yards between houses, Carol finally made it to the main highway and flipped on the radio.

She drove, numbing her mind through soft rock tunes. Before reaching home, she switched stations, and 'Breaking News' blared. The missing Jackson girl was picked up at the Pascagoula bus terminal. A ticket agent refused to sell her a ticket. He said she had no identification, and he was sure she was a minor, so he had security detain her and called the police. She was reunited with her mother this evening.

Carol whooped so loud, she scared herself. Laughing, she pounded her steering wheel. *She got away. That little young thing got away. Thank you, Jesus.*

Singing and humming all the way home, Carol couldn't help but smile. That was fast. She hadn't even had time to talk to Chief Bert. And now she didn't have to. No dredging up her past. No reliving her old life. That Boudreaux. She couldn't even think of the names she wanted to call him, but he didn't get this one. Yet, her celebrating was short-lived, as she thought of Virginia. If he lost that girl, he might try to get Virginia back. Carol stepped on her accelerator and sped home.

As she arrived back in Bay Town, she drove by The Refuge. She wanted to make sure Virginia was safe. Shifting into park, she sat across the street and admired the beautiful old Victorian. All the lights were out except for the porch and perimeter lighting. She was satisfied that nothing seemed amiss and put her car in gear. She peered down the road as her truck crawled forward. One last glance caused her to brake hard. A few cigarette butts lay in the street. It wouldn't be unusual except that they were still smoldering. Red embers glowed. Through her rearview mirror, she saw nothing but shivered as she drove home.

Carol climbed up the stairs to her studio apartment above her shop and slammed the door. Her joy over the return of the missing teen was short-lived. Her tablet rested on the bistro table, and she took a seat. She opened it up and searched for the missing Jackson girl. The news was everywhere. She clicked on a website. As it opened, Carol's eyes widened at the picture of the girl. Her mouth dried, and she found it hard to swallow.

No. No. No. Young, thin with bleached blonde hair. Acadia Perrin was the name, but not the girl she saw at the drug store. He still had her. That poor scared young thing in Pascagoula was still in the clutches of that sleaze, Boudreaux. But if he still had her, maybe he wouldn't come after Virginia? Maybe all these car sightings and cigarette butts were paranoia. Her mind raced, and Carol vacillated between the relief she felt that Virginia might not be in imminent danger and the horror of the teen still in Boudreaux's clutches.

Another headache gripped her temples, and Carol headed for the shower. The hot stream pounded down the back of her neck, sliding through her hair. When the tension had released, she finished her shower and wrapped herself in her nightclothes. Carol plopped onto her sofa bed and reached for a book. The words of devotion took the weight of the world off her shoulders, and she struggled to stay her drooping eyes. Exhausted, she crawled under the covers and fell asleep.

Downstairs the phone rang.

CHAPTER 7

The aroma of freshly ground beans filled the Mockingbird Café. Bluesy tunes piping through the building ushered Carol's arrival. In her diva-like fashion, she swept in. A brass butterfly clip held back one side of her long wavy hair, and she wore a multi-flowered maxi-dress that loosely flowed about her ankles. An embroidered blue jean jacket and her teal-colored cowboy boots made quite a statement as she clipped across the gray planked floor. Heads turned, and her radiant smile greeted all. One tall, sandy-haired gentleman in a tan suit especially caught her eye. She broke the gaze.

Getting in line to place her order, she huffed at the long queue but caught herself. She determined that today she would let God handle it. After the previous evening, she didn't know what to do.

Saturdays drew in practically the whole town, getting ready for the weekend rush of visitors. She stepped in line behind the man in a suit. He was a good head taller than her, and his hair brushed the top of his white collar while his suit coat stretched taut across his broad shoulders.

He turned and nodded. The subtle scent of his cologne

matched the handsome, friendly face, and Carol felt a silly little flutter.

"Hey, Carol."

She spun around. "Hey, Mel." She then glanced back at the man, and he was still smiling at her.

Melanie hugged Carol and peeked around. "Oh, good morning, Mayor. So, do you two know each other?"

They started to speak at once, but both stopped simultaneously.

Carol threw a hand in the air. "Of course. Doesn't everyone know the Mayor?" She offered her hand. "Hey, I'm Carol."

He took her hand, and the warmth of his touch sent shivers through her. He shook gently. "Well, it's nice to meet you, Carol. I'm John."

Goosebumps arose at the sound of his smooth southern drawl, and he held her hand a little longer than customary, but Carol didn't care.

"Next customer, please," called the barista.

John nodded. "It was a pleasure meeting you, Miss Carol. I hope I'll meet you again sometime."

Carol warmed and flushed redder than her hair and blurted, "Well, come on by Second Chance, my shop on Main Street. We're open all weekend." She grinned like a high school teenager who'd just been asked to the prom.

"I'll do that," he said while proceeding to the counter, but stopped. "Hey, can I buy you a cup?"

Carol sighed loudly, grinned foolishly, but shook her head. "Oh, no, thanks. I'm with her." She pointed to Melanie and had no idea why she answered that way. "But I'll take a rain check?"

The corner of his mouth lifted, and his eyes sparkled.

Fanning her face, Carol whispered, "Hey, is it me, or is there a fire burning somewhere?" She lifted the hair off her neck. "Whoo, wee."

"Definitely you." Melanie squeezed Carol's arm. "Come join Desmond and me when you get your drink."

She pointed to a love seat and overstuffed chairs by the window. Desmond stood and joined them.

"Thanks, but I have to get to the store. Virginia will make it there before me. Today's Saturday, and Virginia helps me open." She thought for a minute and asked, "Hey, any news on Boud…." Carol's voice trailed.

She had finally identified Will Boudreaux from the booking photos down at the Police Station, and she hadn't slept well since. He was the same man she'd seen at the drug store. The man who had killed Grady and attempted to traffic Virginia was out there again, roaming the streets.

Shaking her head, Melanie blew out a breath. "Don't say it. I can't mention his name either, but I'll check things out with the Chief."

"But did you hear they found that missing girl?" Said Desmond.

"Yes. See how God works? We don't need to handle it all ourselves." Melanie beamed.

"But it wasn't the same girl. I saw the picture of her on the news. Acadia Perrin is not my drug store girl. She's still out there. In Boudreaux's clutches."

She grasped a handful of her wavy locks, twisting and turning them tightly. She had to get to the shop. Virginia would be there soon, and Carol shivered at the thought of her being there alone. Just in case.

"Carol, are you okay?"

A nod. Then a shake. Carol crossed her arms and tapped her skin, trying to remember Desmond's words when he counseled her. Let go and let God. Sometimes it was so easy, but this? This would be hard. She straightened and patted Melanie's shoulder. "I'm okay, friend."

"We'll get through this, Carol. We've done it before."

"Next in line, please." A barista waved his hand.

Carol approached the counter. "Hi there. I almost forgot why I was here," she chuckled.

"Yeah, the Mayor had a big order," said the barista.

"Well, I'll make it easy for you. Just give me a plain old black coffee."

"Bold or medium?"

"Bold."

"What size?"

"Big? Large?" Carol scrunched her face.

"Grande or Venti?"

"You guys always do this to me! Just give me a big cup of coffee."

"Would you like room for cream?"

Carol glared but answered sweetly. "Yes, please."

She heard a chuckle and turned. The mayor stood aside the counter and their eyes locked in the moment. Silently shaking herself, she couldn't but feel his smiles blowing away her troubles. *Ridiculous.* Grabbing her cup and gliding to the exit, Carol leaned against the door with her hip, giving it an exaggerated push. She swept out as beautifully as she'd swept in.

Melanie returned to her seat next to Desmond. "Did you see the mayor and Carol? There was a spark."

Desmond laughed. "Wow. That's quite a match."

Melanie hit his arm playfully. "You never know. God works in mysterious ways. Look at us."

"You're right about that." Leaning over, he kissed her cheek. "Is everything okay with Carol? She called me yesterday. It seems she has a lot going on. I prayed with her and told her to see Chief Bert."

"Yes, with Boudreaux's release, I'm a little worried. But you know Carol, she's a rock in some ways."

"More like a boulder rolling down a mountain." He motioned with his hands. "With rocks flying out all around her." Desmond put an arm around Melanie and squeezed. "I'll stop by and see her later. I'm walking the street this morning."

"Oh, that prayer walking thing?" she teased.

"Can't hurt." He raised his cup, coffee splashed out, and he grimaced. Pointing to the service counter, he walked over.

The mayor was there, perfecting his brew, and Desmond sidled up.

"You buy for the whole office there?" Desmond pointed to the two trays of coffee.

"Well, it helps with morale, especially on a Saturday. So, Pastor, who is this Carol? I don't think I've met her before." He raised his brows. "I *know* I've never met her before."

"She's great. She started coming to the church about a year ago, and six months after, she jumped right in. I think she's heading in the right direction."

"Right direction?"

"You interested?" Desmond smiled.

John stirred his coffee again. "Oh, no, not interested." He shrugged. "Maybe a little intrigued. She's quite different than…," His voice trailed off.

"Carol's her own woman. She doesn't care what others think of her, and she uses it in a good way. At least now she does." He grimaced. "Scratch that. Anyway, she adds quite a spark to our congregation."

Slow weekdays in Bay Town usually gave way to busy weekends. Billed as one of the Best Small Towns in America, tourism had finally boosted the economy. Heaven knew they needed it after the last big hurricane.

Carol rubbed vigorously, polishing the brass marker

fastened to the brick storefront. Second Chance was established in 1960. Although she hadn't owned it back then, nor even been born then, it was hers now. The last owner bailed after the hurricane, and she acquired it.

She loved the business. She loved old things, and the eclectic mixes of hard and soft materials. She especially loved fabric, textiles, and designs of all sorts. If only she'd finished design school as her parents wanted. She should have listened. Nothing excited her more than colors and fabrics. Carol breathed deep. Nothing except God, now. She glanced at her watch. Where is that girl? She thought, as she raised a hand, shielding the sun and spotted a figure coming toward her.

"Hey, Miz Carol," Virginia yelled and waved.

Carol watched the beautiful blonde swaying down the sidewalk, touching every plant, park bench, and parking meter along the way. A navy, slouchy, knit hat sat on the crown of her head as waves of platinum cascaded across her forehead. Sparkling blue eyes peeked out, and a cherub smile complimented her heart-shaped face. And those ruby red lips again.

Waving the young girl over, Carol shook a rag in the air. "Get on in here." She looked around. No car in sight. "Where'd you come from? Who dropped you off?"

Virginia giggled and skipped a little before returning to her stroll. "Nobody. I took the bus."

"Girl, you are not supposed to be alone." Carol sputtered. "I mean…never mind. Come on. We got work to do." She had a mind to lay into whoever was supposed to get Virginia to work today.

"Hey, did the kitty come back?"

Carol shook her head, and her mood lightened. In some ways, Virginia was so innocent. At least now, more so than before. For some reason, she looked at Virginia's feet, and the plain white converse were a comfortable change from those flashy, high-heeled platforms Virginia used to wear. The faded, ripped blue jeans came close to displaying too much skin, but the long tan, boxy tunic covered enough for Carol's satisfaction. "You are lucky you wore that sweater, or you'd be wearing one of my long skirts over those poor excuse for jeans."

"I paid a lot of money for these." She swept her hand across her thigh, picking at the hanging threads.

"What? Are you kidding me?" Carol raised an eyebrow. Holding up an index finger, she crooked it at Virginia. "I got an idea. Come on in."

Carol walked to a distressed tabletop scattered with short stacks of used clothing. She pulled out a pair of blue jeans and held them high. "Feel like cutting up today?" She laughed, but Virginia frowned.

"I don't get it. I don't know what you mean." Her brows furrowed.

"Cut up. Get it? Cut the jeans and let loose. Have some fun?" Carol winced.

Virginia dropped onto a nearby stool. "I don't get it. I never do."

No one was sure, but the rumor was that Virginia's disability was a slight brain impairment, because of her drug-addicted mother who died in childbirth. Although bits and pieces of the raid and rescue from last year surfaced, Carol hadn't put them together until now. If Melanie had not intervened, who knows what would have happened to the girl. Instead, the whole ordeal resulted in Virginia receiving specialized care and love from the church and the community.

Immediately dropping the jeans, Carol walked over to Virginia. "I was joking. Just fooling around, sweetie. I'm sorry." Carol took hold of her shoulders.

Virginia pushed out her lips and her brows furrowed. The pretty face scowled.

"Now, come on, you don't need to pout so fast." She squeezed Virginia and led her to the jean pile. "Honey, you're doing so well."

"Yeah, but I have one class on campus, and some kids still make fun of me. I hate going to school. Sometimes I wish Uncle Will was back."

Carol froze. Uncle Will. Will Boudreaux. The distant no-good relative. A pang hit Carol's heart. She wouldn't let Virginia return to that life. The whole town had rallied around the girl. With her mental challenges, it wasn't easy, but they helped educate her, nurture her, and, most of all, love her. She was finally finding worth in who God created her to be. Not an object for men's fancy. *Me and her both.*

"Don't say that, Virginia. You don't need him." She shook the girl gently. "He wasn't good for you. You've moved on to a better life." Carol took Virginia's chin in her hand and gave her head a little shake. "We've both moved on. We belong to God now, don't we?"

Virginia nodded. "Yeah. But I don't get Him either." Perking up, she smiled. "But He sure makes me feel good when I pray."

"For now, that's all that matters. You keep on praying and reading your Bible."

Virginia stuck out her tongue. "I can't do that. It don't make sense."

"It will one day, child. God will sort it out in your head. Why you've done so good. Before you know it, you'll be graduating."

"Then what am I gonna do?"

"How about you work for me, full time?"

Virginia squealed. "Really? I got a full-time job already?"

"Sure thing. That's how I got started. I moved here... longer ago than I want to remember. The business owner took a chance and gave me a job. I started as a clerk. Then that hurricane wiped out the store, and the owner quit. Left it to me." She waved her arms around. "It's all mine."

Carol shook her head. Everyone had taken a chance on her. The bank, the restoration grant committee. The rest of the business owners. They all helped each other rebuild. Carol nodded at Virginia.

"Yes, sirree. You'll be my full-time assistant."

Virginia hugged Carol and jumped while wiggling a little dance. Carol hesitated, but laughter broke out, and she joined in. The girls twirled, hooted, and sang without musical accompaniment.

The bells jingled at the front door, and Carol and Virginia halted like the freeze dance. They looked at each other and burst out laughing.

"I'll get it." Virginia ran to the entrance. "Hi, can I help—"

"Well, hello, darlin'."

Virginia froze, and Carol did the same. "It *was* you," she whispered under her breath.

Will Boudreaux peeked around Virginia and flashed a grin at Carol. "Yes, it is. And it's good to see you too." He gazed back at Virginia and opened his arms wide. "Ginny, sweetie, how about a hug for your daddy?"

Virginia spun around, and Carol pulled her tight. "Don't you listen to him," Carol whispered.

Virginia shook her head. "You're not my daddy."

Boudreaux raised a hand, smoothing back his slick hair. "Now darlin', that's no way to talk to—"

"You best be going, Mister. Virginia's got work to do."

He clicked his tongue and tipped his head, grinning like the Cheshire cat.

"Virginia, honey, you go back and take those jeans to the workroom," said Carol.

The girl ran. Carol watched her hide behind the workroom curtain. She knew she must stay calm for Virginia's sake. She faced Boudreaux and took a deep breath. "It's time for you to leave, or I'll call the police."

"Ha! I'm shaking in my boots, little lady. Besides, it ain't no crime to look."

Carol wished she had one of those signs that stated the right to refuse service. Instead, she said, "Then buy something and leave." Sweat trickled down her back.

He chuckled a little and raised his chin. "So, Grady been around?" An evil sneer crept across his lips.

She took a step and smacked his face with an open palm. *So much for keeping calm.* His head flung to the side, and instantly Virginia screamed.

Boudreaux shifted his head straight as he stroked his cheek. A slow chuckle arose from his throat. His shoulder shifted slightly as he reached back his arm and clenched his fist.

Virginia hurled herself forward. "Nooo! Don't you hurt her," she screamed.

Carol watched in slow motion as a body ran through the entrance behind Boudreaux. Pastor Brooks grabbed Boudreaux's arm. He didn't struggle but glared at Desmond. Virginia cried hysterically as Desmond slowly released a hold on Boudreaux.

"You better leave," said Desmond.

Cracking his neck back and forth, Boudreaux grinned. "Well, well, I guess we have a little reunion of sorts." Straightening his jacket, he then pointed to Virginia. "Ginny, I'll be back. You best be ready to join me." He turned and walked to the exit.

"Over my dead body," Carol yelled.

"You called it, babe," said Boudreaux sauntering out of her store.

CHAPTER 8

"Did he just threaten me?" Carol screamed.

Desmond ignored the outburst and pulled out his phone. "I'm calling the chief."

He nodded toward Virginia while Carol enveloped the poor sobbing girl in her arms. Hearing him speaking with the chief brought comfort to Carol, but the terror of the man's presence remained.

"Shhh. Shhh, child. Why someone was watching over us. The good Lord brought Pastor Brooks right in the nick of time." Her hand stroked Virginia's wavy hair as she held her close.

"Huh? What do you mean?" Said Virginia.

"Never you mind. We'll be just fine."

Desmond approached the huddled figures. The physical strength of his stature gave way to a spiritual intensity that soothed Carol's soul.

"Did he hurt you?" He asked.

She shook her head. "How did you know he was here?"

"I didn't. After coffee with Melanie, I went out for a morning walk, and I heard the scream." He pointed a finger upwards. "His timing is perfect."

Before Carol could speak, Chief Bert rushed through the

front door. A coat rack covered with silk shawls and scarves teetered as he brushed by. Every nook and cranny filled with treasure made it a tight squeeze for a large man like the Chief.

He righted the rack and shook his head. "He's gone. Officer Blaine is checking everywhere." He glanced between the women. "Don't worry. We're on this guy."

Carol lifted a finger to her lips and dropped a nod toward Virginia but gently pushed her away. "Listen, honey, it's kind of slow right now. Why don't you head back to the Refuge? Maybe Pastor Brooks can take you there?" Carol raised an eyebrow toward him.

"Yes. Sure, my car's outside."

Virginia shook her head, and curls flung around her face. "No. I'm scared. I don't want to go back there."

The chief and Carol exchanged looks. "Are you sure, honey?" Carol said.

Virginia's head bobbed up and down as she wiped her wet face with the sleeve of her tunic. "I want to stay with you."

Carol beamed. Someone wanted her. Not to use her, but because she was needed, and it felt good. "Sure, sweetie. Come on. You can unload that box of stuff back there."

Carol indicated for the men to wait. She walked Virginia to the workroom and turned the deadbolt on the back door. "I'll be out front," she said to Virginia.

She motioned the men toward the front door. Carol rubbed her brow and suddenly felt tired. It was still morning, and other than Boudreaux's intrusion, no customers had arrived. It was going to be a long day. "I'd like to keep Virginia with me. But I don't think it's a good idea. What if he comes back?"

"He will." Chief Bert rested a hand on his gun. "Guess I'll need to call in the Sherriff volunteers." He sighed heavily.

"Count me in. What about Big Joe?" Desmond asked.

Carol smiled at the thought of Lyla's huge husband. His presence alone could scare the daylights out of strangers.

Chief Bert removed his hat and scratched his head. "I hate to ask him. He's got young ones at home, and it is Saturday. But I know he'll say yes."

"I can take a shift somewhere myself," said Desmond.

"You got church tomorrow, Pastor."

Carol's heart warmed at his offering. Always sacrificing for others.

"Yes, and I can take my sermon and books and read on a stakeout." He pointed a finger on each hand as if shooting guns.

"What are you? A pistol packin' preacher?" The Chief giggled and said, "We're talking stakeout, not a shootout." He slapped Desmond's shoulder. "But, if you don't mind, I could use you."

"Sure thing."

"Okay, so me and the pastor here will watch your place tonight, Miss Carol. Officer Blaine and maybe Joe can take turns at the Refuge. I'll call him."

They left, and as the afternoon dragged on, Carol and Virginia ran out of things to do. For some reason, the business was slow but when the day ended, Virginia seemed to take on a heavy burden.

"Can I stay with you tonight? Please, Miz Carol?" Virginia's round blue eyes begged like a Beanie Baby doll. Her hands clasped in a praying position.

"It's not a good idea. What if he...I mean, what if..." Carol searched for words that wouldn't scare Virginia. Yet, confusion would bring on anxiety if she wasn't clear. "Honey, the best place for you right now is at The Refuge."

Virginia pushed out her ruby lips. "Why can't I just spend the night with you?"

Bells jingled. With the setting sun shining through the open door, Carol couldn't make out the silhouette of someone standing in the doorway. She squinted and raised a hand, trying to shield the glare. "May I help you?" She pushed Virginia behind her.

"No, ma'am. But I'm here to help Miss Virginia? I'm Officer Blaine. Chief Bert sent me over. At your service, ma'am."

She could hear his footsteps approaching and finally recognized the familiar police uniform. He held his hat in his hands. A gentleman raised in the south. She was sure of it by the drawl and niceties in his speech and mannerisms.

Virginia slowly stepped out, and a giggle escaped. She wore a grin that lit up the room and blurted out, "Hey, there, Officer Blaine. I'm Virginia." She walked boldly, pushing back the hair that had fallen across her forehead.

Officer Blaine's red face beamed back. "Nice to meet you, Miss." Twisting his hat in his hand, he nodded. Of average height, with strawberry blonde hair and green eyes, the freckles on his fresh face made him appear much younger than he probably was. Carol recalled meeting him just the other day at the Police Station. He was polite and helpful, but right now, he couldn't keep his eyes off Virginia.

"Son, how old are you? Why you gotta be just out of high school." Carol stood with her hands on her hips, enjoying the electricity between the two young people.

"I'm twenty-three, ma'am." As he looked up, his gaze set on Virginia again, and his brows raised.

"Oh, I'm eighteen," Virginia answered as if he was asking. "I'm still in High School, but I'm graduating this June." She twirled a curl around her finger.

He breathed out what sounded like relief, and a wide grin spread across his lips.

Carol laughed out loud. "Well, okay, Officer Blaine. What's the plan?"

He continued staring at Virginia as she pulled the sleeve of her tunic over her wrists. The toes of her shoes kicked at nothing on the floor while she stared back. Awkward silence hung in the air.

"Oh, for Pete's sake. Blaine!" Carol yelled.

Both young people jumped. Carol didn't know who flushed a brighter shade of red. "Officer Blaine. What are your orders?"

Straightening, he stood at attention without the hand salute. "Yes, ma'am. I'm to escort Miss Virginia home." He grinned broadly.

The attraction between the two young people was so thick you could cut it with a knife. Carol couldn't hide her amusement. "Oh, no need for that. I'll drive her," she teased.

"What?" Virginia's eyes opened wide. "No. He can take me. Please, Miz Carol?"

Blaine's sad face seemed to plead as well.

"I'm just kidding. Of course, you take her home. Then what? What happens after you take her home?"

"I'll stay and watch the house the next shift."

Carol nodded in agreement, but a frown formed on Virginia's face, and Blaine responded with alarm rising. "I'm sorry, miss. Did I upset you?"

Shaking her head caused her knit hat to fall, and Blaine moved swiftly to retrieve it and held it out to her.

"I don't have a home," said Virginia, taking her hat.

"Miss Virginia, I heard The Refuge is a mighty nice home."

Virginia straightened. "Well, I guess it is. It's a nice place. I have my own room, and Miz Carol…" She took Carol's hand. "She helped me decorate it. I know how to cook now. I even have some money saved."

Carol's heart filled with joy, and she breathed deep as she listened to Virginia babble with delight.

"Well, Miss, if you're ready, we best be going."

He offered his arm as if ushering Virginia to a ball. She

took his elbow, hooking her arm through his like a princess with a grand escort.

~

The Refuge was housed in an old Victorian home. Though it had not been elaborately restored, it was clean and safe. It held eight bedrooms, and with the remodel, it now housed three bathrooms, a large dining hall, a modern kitchen, and an extensive common area. The wrap-around porch made for more sitting room for outside visitors. With a paid staff consisting of two full-time house parents, the residents kept house along with the girls and women who were fortunate to have been placed there.

Virginia begged for Officer Blaine to come inside. She pulled him into the dining hall, the only place where men were allowed. The long country-planked dining table could house all eight residents and the staff. Two extra seats were always available for guests.

The housemother greeted the uniformed officer and invited him to stay for dinner. He checked in with Chief Bert by phone and got the approval. Smiling, he met and greeted each resident, quickly putting them at ease as they gathered around the table.

"Officer Blaine, we always say grace before our meals." The housemother nodded at him. "Would you like to ask the Lord's blessing?"

He smiled. "Yes, ma'am." After his short prayer, the housemother seemed pleased.

As the meal progressed, Virginia sat too close, leaning into Blaine whenever she passed food dishes. Touching his arm when speaking, she flirted with him. Discerning looks from the house parents caused Virginia to scoot away, but her giggling and demonstrative actions didn't stop. Blaine appeared not to mind in the least. As everyone ate and chatted, mealtime soon ended.

Wiping his lips with a napkin, he asked, "May I help with the dishes?"

"Oh, yes. It's my turn tonight. You can help me." Virginia stood, being so bold as to take his hand.

"Virginia, you know the rules," said the housemother. "Officer Blaine here must have duties to perform, and you have yours. Thank you, Officer, for bringing Virginia home."

"Thank you for the meal, ma'am." He smiled. "Miss Virginia, it's been a pleasure."

She pouted her lips as he turned to leave. She started to speak, but the housemother silenced her with a finger.

Officer Blaine checked his watch as he stepped down the front steps. Turning back at the house, he glanced up at the darkened windows. Lamps went on in each window. He walked down the sidewalk to a poorly lit section of the street and slipped inside his squad car. He had a clear view of the old Victorian identified by a large sign that read, "The Refuge."

Virginia stood near an open window on the second floor. The curtains were drawn back, and she leaned out with her tousled head of curls hanging about. She waved vigorously, and Officer Blaine waved back while catching sight of a blue sedan. The vehicle crept by, and Officer Blaine locked eyes with the driver as he passed. He picked up the radio transmitter and called in a report.

CHAPTER 9

Turning out the lights, then locking up, Carol took one last look around. The red light on the desk phone flashed, but she had ignored it all day. Yesterday had been a rollercoaster, and with the missing girl found, it was about all Carol could handle of Mrs. Perrin.

The stairs loomed before her as she lifted her long skirt, the hem brushing the first step. The phone rang. She stopped and took her time, hoping for the caller to hang up. She slowly edged back, but the phone stopped ringing. Click. No message. Carol moved towards the stairs but didn't take two steps before it rang again. This time she walked more quickly.

"Hello."

Incoherent babble and crying spewed out from the other end.

"Who is this, please?"

"They took her." More sobs. "They took my baby girl." A sudden change in tone as the voice quivered on the other end. "Did you hear me?"

"Yes. Who took her?" Asked Carol.

The woman speaking hadn't identified herself. She didn't need to. Controlled deep breaths came from the other end.

"It's your fault, you know. You did this to me." The voice that now spoke was assertive, stronger, almost eerie.

Carol held the phone away and hit the speaker. "Mrs. Perrin. I'd like to help." She waited for the hysterical outburst. Instead, she heard almost a whisper.

"Of course, you would. Just like you helped Grady."

"Mrs. Perrin, your daughter, who took her?"

Sobbing.

"Listen, can I meet you somewhere?" She didn't feel right saying it, but she couldn't help but feel sorry for the woman.

Abruptly, the crying stopped. "You'd do that? You'd meet me?" The voice lowered. "I can't trust you."

"Then why did you call?"

"Fine. Meet me at—"

Carol interrupted, "It will take me two hours to get there. I won't be in Jackson until 9:00 pm."

"So you don't want to help, do you? You're just like everyone else."

Carol could feel the spit of the words. "I do. I'll leave right now."

"You don't know where I live." A long pause. "Wait, you said, Jackson. Did Grady tell you where I lived?"

Carol recoiled. Eleanor couldn't know that she'd been to her house. "The news. They said your daughter was from Jackson."

"I'm not in Jackson now. I'm in Gulfport. Meet me at Johnny Reb's. I'm sure you know where it is."

The glow from the streetlight peeked through her window and Carol's eyes widened as a shadow crossed the entrance. Distracted, Carol glanced outside. A flicker of smoke blew by her door.

"I'll give you half an hour," Eleanor said.

"In Gulfport? What are you doing in...?" Click. "Wait. Wait a minute." Carol clicked off and slammed an open palm on the counter. She searched through the caller ID on the machine and wrote down the number. Grabbing her purse, she walked toward the front door and pulled out her keys. She lifted a bright orange trench coat from the coat rack. Turning the lock, she opened the door slowly and peered up and down the street. She stepped out, locked the door, and walked towards her El Camino. A pungency of tobacco smoke lingered, and Carol tensed. She turned to her car. *Shoot. Gulfport, but where?* Before opening her car door, she pulled out her phone and texted the number written on a scrap of paper.

<Mrs. Perrin. What's the name of the place again?>

<Johnny Reb's.>

"Johnny Reb's?" Carol said out loud, almost too loud. "Are you kidding me?"

Would she never get away from it? She had met Grady at Johnny Reb's. A country-western bar in Gulfport. She remembered the night all too clearly. He was a little drunk, and she was returning from a shopping excursion in Pascagoula. He approached her as she sat at a table enjoying the band, hoping someone would ask her to dance. He did. They danced and talked and drank. He made her laugh, and she had fun but instinctively quit drinking, knowing she'd be driving home soon.

Carol cringed as she remembered hoping she'd be driving him somewhere that night. That's when Grady spilled everything about a crazy ex-girlfriend whose daughter had gone missing. It should have been a red flag. Back then, Carol didn't heed red flags. Her stomach fluttered, and she wondered if she was doing it again.

As she drove along the Bay Bridge, the crescent moon shed little light on the black waters, and dark wisps flew swiftly across the night sky. Of late, she tuned into the Christian radio station, but tonight, she drove in silence. Finally, arriving at the bar, she parked but sat for a moment saying a prayer, asking for protection but not believing she deserved it. She stepped out, and a crowd of blue-jean and plaid-shirted cowboys stood smoking on the side of the building. She bristled at the tobacco smoke and marched inside. She hadn't been to a bar in six months and hadn't planned on it. But tonight, she was on a mission.

The happy country music blared, and the twang of guitars and Texas two-steppers on the dance floor tapped out a steady beat. Carol smiled. She did love dancing, and she tapped her foot and spun around on her heel as she searched the bar. Her mood changed quickly when reality set in. She didn't know who this woman was or what she looked like. She searched the room.

Mostly men sat at the counter, and couples sat at the tables with beer bottles scattered everywhere. Cheers and laughter flooded the room. Carol noticed a nicely dressed woman with chin-length hair, a little on the messy side. She sat by herself, sipping a glass of red wine. Her slim legs crossed and her slightly wrinkled skirt resting just above her knee. Carol shook her head. Not Grady's type, she thought, but then their eyes met.

Smiling, the woman raised her glass with perfectly manicured fingers swathed around the goblet—a diamond-studded silver bracelet wrapped around her wrist.

Carol's stomach fluttered, and taking a deep breath, she maneuvered through the crowd. "Mrs. Perrin?"

Glassy-eyed, the woman replied. "Yes, and you must be Carol."

The woman had black shadows under her eyes and lines creased around her lips, but her poised demeanor hinted at education and status. It didn't figure.

Carol recalled Grady's casual dress and his stringy ponytail. None of it lined up with this woman. Had she been that desperate? Carol knew the feeling well.

"Sit. Please be my guest. I'm sorry, but I don't know your name." She giggled a wicked sound, much like one of the Disney witches. "Second Chance? Is that your name,

Second?" This time her laugh was hearty and throaty—still evil.

Carol sat, and all her defense mechanisms of pride, arrogance, and self-assurance rose. "It's Carol. I'm the owner of Second Chance, Mrs. Perrin."

"Please, call me Eleanor." She set down her glass and offered a hand, an expensive watch blinging from her other wrist. She waved a hand toward a roaming waiter. "Glass of wine, Carol?"

"No, thank you. I'll take a diet Coke." Carol didn't drink anymore. She wasn't an alcoholic by any stretch, but her drinking went along with male companionship, which always got her into trouble.

Eleanor laughed again, and Carol felt the heat rise within her. Eleanor motioned to the waiter. "Another red wine for me and a Diet Coke for my dry friend here."

Carol wished she hadn't come. "Mrs. Perrin. You said your daughter was taken again? How can that be? They just found her."

Eleanor pushed her glass across the table. She uncrossed her legs and leaned forward. Carol was thankful for the space between them as the woman placed both hands on the checkered cloth. She looked down at the bowl of peanuts before them. None shelled, all whole and still in the basket. Yet peanut shells covered the floor elsewhere. She hadn't even noticed stepping on them when she arrived. What was this woman doing here?

"Hello, ma'am, would you like to dance?" a young cowboy asked Carol as he leaned over her shoulder. She could smell his breath on her neck.

The question was all too familiar. Did she still appear that easy...that desperate? Or was it just the place?

She placed an arm on the back of her chair and shifted. His face was too close, and he smiled. "No," she said. "No, thank you."

He persisted. "How about a drink? Can I buy you one?"

Carol was firmer. "No, thank you."

He shrugged as he walked away.

"You know. I hate this place. Grady brought me here only once. It's quite out of the way for Jackson…but you seem right at home here, Carol."

A wave of anger rose within, and Carol struggled to tamper it, controlling the urge to spit back a retort. Although she was more than curious why a woman of Eleanor's stature would go for Grady, she wanted nothing to do with dredging up her own past.

Carol asked again. "Your daughter?"

"Social Services took my daughter. She reported me as abusive the night they brought her home and took her away." She glared at Carol as if it were her fault.

Taking a deep breath, Carol discreetly exhaled. "Are you? Are you abusive?"

The woman glared and leaned back into her chair. She seemed to search Carol's face, her hair, and her clothes. "So maybe, you put that in her head? Did you tell my daughter?"

"Mrs. Perrin, I have no idea what you're talking about. I told you, I've never met your daughter. I never even knew she was missing last year until…" her voice trailed.

"That's because you were too busy stealing my boyfriend."

Carol stood. "Listen, I'd love to help. I know some people who help with runaways and abducted girls. I can give you the organization's name, but I don't think I can help you. This was a mistake. Call me if you want the information." Carol pushed back her chair and stood.

The woman rose too. She clutched Carol's arm. "Please," she pulled. "I don't know what to do." She suddenly sat and dropped her head into her hands. "I just want my daughter back," the woman choked.

Carol sighed. She couldn't keep up with this woman's mood changes, but she needed help. Carol sat and instinctively reached out her hands to comfort the woman. "I can help."

At the first touch, Eleanor drew back. She wiped away a few tears, patted her cheeks, and straightened. *The woman has issues*, thought Carol.

"How can you help me?" She asked.

"Well, there is this place called the Refuge...." Carol stopped. She shouldn't have said that. She shouldn't have offered the name or the services. This woman wasn't stable. If her daughter was with Social Services, they would most likely place her. "I mean, I know of people who can help your daughter and maybe also suggest help for her."

"You said this place is called The Refuge?"

"Ladies, may I buy you a drink?"

A familiar, over-powering cologne wafted by, and Carol spun around. He smiled at her with his slicked-backed hair and an impeccably fitted suit. It felt like a rock sank into the pit of her stomach. Her back tensed, and before her courage waned, she said, "Excuse me. We're in a private conversation."

Will Boudreaux's lips held a sickening grin.

Eleanor ignored Carol. "Why, of course." She waved a polite hand toward an empty chair. "Please join us." Her voice was syrupy sweet.

Was she that eager for male company? Carol couldn't believe it, but a layer of guilt settled on the rock in her stomach. *I've been there.* She peered back, hoping their eyes would connect. Hoping to give a woman-to-woman warning.

Boudreaux pulled out a chair and sat. "What'll it be, ladies?" He directed his attention to Eleanor. Her tipped head rested on her fist while she smiled back sweetly, heading right into his trap.

Carol was shocked that he was here, and panic arose. It occurred to her that he followed her. She had to get away. But she couldn't leave him with Eleanor.

"Listen, I can't stay. Eleanor, can I give you a ride home, and we can continue our conversation?"

"About The Refuge?" Boudreaux winked. "My apologies, I didn't mean to eavesdrop, but I heard you mention the place." Turning to Eleanor, he smiled. "Ma'am, it is a wonderful place. Why, my poor daughter is there now."

"Why, you low-life. You're a liar!" Carol blurted, "Eleanor, this man is bad news. He's the one who stole your daughter last year."

Eleanor finished off her wine and threw back her head and laughed. "She can't be serious."

Boudreaux looked Carol over. "Maybe she smokes too much pot." He chuckled.

"Are you crazy? Aren't you hearing me?" Carol couldn't tell if it was the alcohol or the wiles of Boudreaux that had an alluring effect on Eleanor, but the woman appeared amused, and Carol had to do something.

"He just got out of prison! He killed Grady. He abducts girls!" She called out Boudreaux's horrible deeds like a grocery list, but Eleanor ceased listening. It was late, and the crowd was getting louder and rowdier, and Eleanor and Boudreaux were caught up in the party. The band drowned Carol's anxious words. It was she that sounded like the crazy woman now.

They ignored her, and Boudreaux stood, offering a hand to Eleanor. She took it as he glided her to the middle of the floor. He drew her close to himself, and Carol watched the embraced couple. For once, the dance floor and the men held no draw.

CHAPTER 10

Sweat beaded on Carol's forehead as her neck throbbed. She gripped the steering wheel, the El Camino's tires spewed gravel when she turned. Laughing faces of drunks out in front of Johnny Reb's faded in the rearview mirror as she sped away.

Racing down Beach Road, Carol pressed harder on the accelerator, and her foot rattled from the pains of the old car. She watched the speedometer needle over. She didn't care if she got a ticket. She didn't care if she crashed. She repeatedly pounded the steering wheel until her hand hurt. Why didn't she heed the urge not to go? She'd brought him here. Boudreaux must have followed her, and now it was her fault he was with Eleanor.

Carol's insides squirmed like an opened jar of worms. Ugly, writhing bait, enticing weak prey. She shook, fearing the endangerment of the woman's daughter once more. And what of the fragile, sick woman? Her stomach tightened. It was as if a weight settled within her, and she wanted it to pull her down. To drown her so that she couldn't mess up her life or another's again.

Arriving home after midnight, Big Joe's SUV sat parked

outside her apartment. Carol checked her watch. Pastor Brooks must have just left. They cared enough for her safety to sit guard outside her home all hours of the night. And she hadn't even been there. She put her own life in jeopardy through her impulsive actions. Old nature, old self.

Just the same, Joe smiled and waved as she marched up the stairs. She waved back but didn't stop to thank him. She didn't want to explain her whereabouts. The men had both given up their time and sleep to protect her. *I'm not worth it,* she thought.

Sometime around sunrise, the sound of an engine awoke Carol. Hunched over her bistro table at home, she stretched, leaned toward the window, and pulled back her drapes. Peeking out, she watched as Joe's big black SUV drove away. Poor Joe, he'd been there all night, and she hadn't slept much herself. She'd never even made it to her bed, but sometime during the early morning hours, she'd dropped her head down and dozed.

Carol stretched and dressed for church. Her attention to detail in dressing evaded her. Grabbing her Bible and bag, she slipped on her boots and tromped down the back steps to her car but frowned. Going down the stairs hurt her knees more than going up. She looked up. Must be rain coming soon, she thought. The gray sky matched her mood. She flipped on the radio, hoping for some praise music or a sermon to lift her spirits, and it worked.

The short drive to Bay Town Community Church allowed a few songs to bathe her soul. Carol parked, and a few older men watched as she exited. Her vintage truck always drew their attention. As she stepped out onto the gravel, she heard whistles coming from the men. It amused her knowing they were not meant for her but for the vehicle. They walked over, surrounding the car, and admiring the mint condition of her classic.

Carol returned their greetings as she strode towards the church building. When she approached the front steps, she chuckled at Pastor Brooks. He stifled yawns as he greeted the arriving congregation.

"Hey, there, Pastor, late night?" Carol teased but was thankful for his help last night.

"Not too bad. Maybe a little later than I'm used to." He flashed a caring smile. "You okay?"

Carol waved him off, hiding her unrest. Any way at all to keep from disclosing her night in Gulfport. Not that he would judge. "Yeah, I'm all right." She went for lightening the mood. "A lot better with you at my house all night."

Loud gasps drew behind her. A few white-haired ladies gaped, and Pastor Brooks face flushed bright red. Carol chuckled at the shocked faces, then walked into the church, leaving Pastor Brooks stuttering explanations.

She quickly perused the crowd and found Lacey waving back at her. Melanie's daughter always welcomed her. That girl had invited her to church so often that Carol was certain Lacey made it her mission to make sure Carol felt welcome each week.

"Girl, stand up there, and let me see that outfit." Lacey stood and spun around. "I love the polka dots," said Carol. Fashion and fabrics were their bonds, but before they could converse, the worship started, and everyone stood, voices raised in sweet harmony. The atmosphere of worship, coupled with angelic sounds, filled the quaint little church, and Carol's heart swelled with joy.

Pastor Brooks began his sermon, and Carol appreciated him all the more as he struggled to stay alert and on topic. When he glanced at Big Joe, Carol peeked over and stifled a laugh. Big Joe's bald, dark head slumped forward with his chin resting on his massive chest, bobbing as he breathed. His wife, Lyla, left him undisturbed unless a snore escaped in which she jabbed him with an occasional elbow and made him jump.

They did it for me, she thought. Carol nodded at Lyla, and she smiled back.

As church ended, everyone filed out and milled around the churchyard. Carol spotted Virginia standing next to Officer Blaine and called out, "Hey there, Blaine." She didn't know his first name. "What are you doing here?"

Virginia piped in excitedly. "I invited Rodney." She looped an arm through his crooked elbow, but he shook it off, and Virginia pouted.

"Rodney? Your name is Rodney?" Carol nodded, giving him the once-over. He wore a blue and white checked long-sleeved shirt and khaki trousers. "Well, Rodney, you clean up pretty good there."

He blushed.

Melanie and Lacey joined them. "Officer Blaine, it's good to see you. I don't think I've ever seen you out of uniform."

Virginia squealed. "I know, isn't he cute?"

Red flushed up his neck once again. His face almost matched his strawberry blonde hair.

"Hey, Virginia, are you coming to Youth Group?" Lacey pointed to the Community Room.

Virginia tilted her chin and waved Lacey off. "Oh, no. That's for high schoolers. I'm 18, you know. Almost 19, and I'm graduating soon."

"Yeah, but you always go to Youth Group," said Lacey.

"When's your birthday, Virginia?" Carol asked.

"Two weeks. I can't wait." Virginia clapped but stopped abruptly. Her exuberance faded. "But I won't get many presents. Uncle Will always…"

The air around the group went frigid, and the smiles were reduced to thin tight lines.

Silence enveloped them all.

"Well, then we got two weeks to plan the best nineteenth birthday party you ever saw. So, Blaine——"

"His name is Rodney." Virginia cooed.

"Yeah, yeah. Blaine, can you make sure Virginia gets to work this afternoon?" Carol asked.

"Yes, ma'am. I'd be happy too." He beamed at Virginia, and the crowd said their goodbyes and disbursed.

Carol walked to the coffee table and searched through the empty donut boxes. She took a coffee cup, but the canister was empty. "Shoot."

A little old lady stood next to her, and Carol tried to stifle a giggle. It was one of the ones who had been behind her when she made the late-night comment to Pastor Brooks. The woman smiled at Carol and took the cup from her hand.

"I'll make a fresh pot in the kitchen." The woman winked. "Maybe you had a late night too?"

Carol drew back and stared at the older woman standing in front of her.

A broad smile broke out, and the woman patted Carol's arm. "Just kidding. I'm Bethie Cook, by the way. Come on. Come with me." She looked down and pointed to Carol's teal, paisley-scrolled cowboy boots. "I love your boots."

"Why, thank you. I like a little splashy flair, you know. And I'm Carol. Nice to meet you, ma'am." Carol smiled. "But no thanks on the coffee. I'll get coffee at the Mockingbird. I have to get to work."

"On Sunday?" The woman shook her head. "I guess it's a new world. Why I remember when every business on Main Street was closed on Sundays."

Carol breathed deep. "I bet those were better days because of it." She opened her arms and unexpectedly hugged the frail little woman. At first, Bethie Cook's body stiffened, but she hugged Carol back tightly.

"Well, thank you. Since my husband died, I don't get many of those."

A twinge grabbed Carol's heart, and she sighed. "It gets lonely, sometimes, don't it?"

She nodded. "Most all the time. But God gets me through." She patted Carol once more. "I must go now. Our Senior Bible Study is starting." She glanced at Carol's left hand. Although rings decked out almost every finger, none resembled a wedding band.

"We got some nice younger men in our group." Bethie Cooke waved as she walked off.

Carol's mouth gaped. "Senior Bible Study?" She repeated as she walked to the parking lot. A gaggle of men surrounded her bright orange vehicle. "Hey there, guys. You'll be late for the Senior Bible Study. You wouldn't want to disappoint the ladies, would you?"

They laughed as they trudged toward the church grounds, and Carol slipped into her car. The euphoric feeling from church lifted her spirits, and as she drove toward the Mockingbird Café, she wished the high would last all day.

Standing in front of the coffee counter, she perused the menu board. The thought of a donut still lingered.

"How about that rain check?" Said a voice behind her.

Carol tipped her head before turning. "Why, Mayor John Taylor, good morning." She breathed deep, and her first inclination told her not to accept, and she didn't know why. She ignored it. "You got yourself a deal."

John Taylor carried her steaming black coffee and a lemon blueberry scone to a corner table. Pulling out her chair, he motioned her to sit.

I could get used to this, she thought. "Thank you, Mayor Taylor, sir."

"John. Please." He pushed in her chair gently.

"John it is. So, no church this morning?"

Almost everyone in the small southern town went to church. Most went to the local Catholic Church, but Protestant churches were a pleasant, friendly rival.

"Not lately. How about you?"

Carol took a bite of her scone, licking the sugar off her fingers. She caught him staring with a sparkle in his eyes, and she grabbed her napkin, wiping off the sugar. She sipped her coffee and mumbled. "Bay Town Community."

"Along with half the town, eh?"

"Well, it's getting there." She laughed. "But not really. Our Lady of the Gulf has nothing to worry about."

"Yes. That Parish has been here since the town began."

"Is that where you attend?"

Shaking his head, he reached for his coffee. The short silence felt awkward, but his friendly face smiled back at her.

"I'm sorry, I didn't mean to pry. I just figured everyone but me always attended church around here." Carol shrugged.

John Taylor finally spoke. "I'm divorced. I've been hit and miss with God ever since. Going on five years now."

"That's a long time."

"It's a long story. One I try to forget." Crossing his legs, he leaned back in the little bistro chair. Too small for his large frame. "What about you?"

Carol dabbed at the crumbs on her plate. "Me too. My history is too long for a coffee clutch."

"Good, that means we'll have to do this again sometime." He lowered his chin and smiled at her hopefully.

Her mouth gaped. *What in the world could he want with me?* Carol's heart fluttered, and she blew out a little breath. Instead of saying something witty and flirty, she smiled. Glancing up at a large farmhouse clock on the wall, she nodded. "Mayor John Taylor, I would like that very much."

They chatted a bit, and Carol relaxed, wondering how being with a man could be so comfortable. No anxious feeling, wondering what would come next. Men usually wanted only one thing from women like her, and she often obliged. Anything not to be lonely, but that's exactly how she was left after every encounter with a stranger.

Swirling her coffee, she peered in at a few grinds and felt as gritty as the dark mud in the bottom of her cup. But as their light conversation continued, the ugliness floated away, and she hated to admit it, but she liked this Mayor, John Taylor. She lifted her wrist and jiggled her oversized bejeweled watch.

"Well, John, right now, I need to get to work." She stood.

He stood too and towered over the little table. "Great. Maybe I'll stop by your Second Chance later, and we can make plans?"

Carol's chest tightened, and her throat clutched. Flashbacks of pickup lines from men in bars flooded her mind. What if he wanted to be more than friends? Too many shallow relationships, if you could call them that, left her with a warped sense of judging men's actions. Thinking about her resolve to swear off men, she was torn, but this John Taylor was different than any man she'd ever welcomed or dragged into her life. Almost too good to be true. Or maybe just too fast and too soon. The ugly scene from last night entered her mind.

At a loss for words, she nodded and pointed to the front door. "Okay, well, gotta go. And thanks for the coffee and sweets."

His kind grey eyes stared back at her, and his neatly combed sandy-gray hair added to the handsome package. He sure was easy to look at. The amused look he wore confused her, and she didn't like that one bit. She pretty much knew why and what for with most men, but not this one. Carol turned and waved before stepping not so lightly towards the exit.

A little distance from John Taylor would clear her head. Too much going on. She just wasn't sure she needed a man to muddle things up right now. She drove to Second Chance and busied herself preparing for the day. Most stores on Main Street didn't open until noon on Sundays, so she took her time, dragging out the sidewalk displays and watering plants.

The street soon filled with people as they strolled up and down, musing over the eclectic mix of stores. Virginia and Officer Blaine walked up. Her arm hooked in his. Carol made a note to talk with her about moving too fast. As if Officer Blaine could read her thoughts, he pulled his arm loose from Virginia.

CHAPTER 11

The Sunday tourists kept Carol and Virginia busy all afternoon, but late in the day, a lull in the traffic finally came.

"Whoo-wee! I am plumb tuckered out." Carol plopped on a nearby stool aside a round display table in the center of the room. Virginia had done a creative job rearranging it. A square vase with a bouquet of red roses sat atop a floral, fringed cloth. Candles in assorted heights surrounded the flowers, and baskets of handmade soaps and dark bottles of essential oils were interspersed in between. Carol peered closer.

"Hey, Virginia, where'd we get these soaps?"

Virginia emerged from the back room. "Oh, my friends at The Refuge made them. Aren't they sweet?"

Carol picked up a bar sleeved in a gold mesh bag. "They certainly are. But next time, let me know so I can budget them into the product line. How much do they want?"

"Nothing! It's a hobby."

"Yeah, that's not happening. I'll come up with a fair price and send a check with an invoice. If they sell, we'll be buying more."

"Cool!" Virginia retreated to the workroom.

Reaching over, Carol fingered the silver, copper, and gold jewelry hanging from a handcrafted tree of twigs. Virginia had placed them perfectly, and the shiny metals sparkled under the overhead lights. Carol's chest puffed out a little. Yes, Virginia was a good fit, and she loved that girl.

"Miss Carol? I finished everything up. Can I leave a little early?"

"Why sure, honey. I think I'll call it a day too. Can you wait till I lock up to give you a ride?" The doorbells jingled.

"We're closing up in just a few minutes," Carol called out as she started for the door.

"Yes, ma'am. I'm just here for Virginia."

Virginia ran to the front. "It's Rodney. We're getting dinner, and then he's taking me home." Virginia giggled. "And it's okay with my housemother. I checked."

"Well, I guess that's that then." Carol pointed her finger at Officer Blaine. "Don't you dare let her out of your sight."

Virginia grabbed his arm. "Oh no, he won't. Bye."

As they exited, Carol shook her head. *Yup. I have to talk to them. Much too fast.* She thought of John Taylor. *Me too.* But was that just this morning? She'd been in a bit of euphoria all day since the Mockingbird. Usually, it was the church that left her feeling that way on Sundays. This was definitely different.

Carol walked to the front door, pushing it closed just as the phone rang. But it wouldn't close. She tried it again. A little jarred, she looked down to see what was stopping it. A slender foot wearing taupe pumps was wedged in the jamb. Carol's vision traveled up the leg, and there stood Eleanor Perrin.

She vacillated between shutting the door in her face and inviting Eleanor in. She chose the latter. "I'm closing, but you can come in."

Carol turned her back and walked to the phone. A check told her turning her back wasn't such a smart idea. This woman was crazy. The desk phone's red button flashed, and staring at Eleanor, Carol felt relieved that it couldn't be her. "What can I do for you?"

Eleanor stood coyly. Her expensive, obviously designer wrap dress hung perfectly around her slight frame. The tan and white geometric print was a modern, clean contrast to Carol's busy textiles and colorful patterns in her store. Eleanor stood poised and composed. Carol glanced down at her own boho get-up and then gazed at the chic woman standing in front of her.

Eleanor's leather handbag dropped from her elbow to her hands. She clutched it in front of her.

"I just came to apologize." Eleanor touched her chin-length hair. Expensive, ash-blond highlights streaked her perfectly styled cut. You couldn't tell that she'd had a late evening, except for the puffiness around her eyes.

Carol clasped her arms around her own curvy frame and stared at the slender woman. She breathed deep. "Please, have a seat." She directed Eleanor to the settee toward the front of the store. "Can I get you an iced tea?"

Even Eleanor's walk was poised and model-like. Carol huffed. Eleanor sat with her knees together, calves pressed tightly to the side and ankles crossed. *Who does she think she is? The First Lady or something?*

"No, thank you."" She gazed out the window, placing a long slender arm along the back of the tapestried settee. "That little Mockingbird Café is adorable. I had a drink there, and I even met the town mayor there. Imagine that?"

"Yes. Imagine that." Carol forced a chuckle. "I'll grab myself a tea. Be right back." She slipped to the workroom, opened the mini-fridge, and grabbed a bottle. Not bothering to get a glass, she opened the bottle and took a long drink. She glimpsed again at Eleanor's royal-like pose. The mention of John Taylor messed with her head. *This is so stupid.* She sucked air and marched back. Taking a seat in one of the antique chairs, she held up a locally brewed bottle of sweet tea. "You sure, I can't get you a glass? It's the best." Anything to change the subject.

Eleanor chuckled. Not a giggle, definitely a low chuckle. It was more like a really lovely 'humph.' "No, thank you. Actually, that's what I had. The mayor suggested it while I perused the menu board."

Carol's shoulders dropped. She took another big gulp. "So, Eleanor. How can I help?"

Eleanor leaned slightly forward. Her purse sat on the settee next to her, and her hands clenched too tightly now. "Why, Carol, I didn't come to ask for help. I merely came to apologize."

Uh-oh. Dragon lady was emerging. "Yes, of course. I'm sorry too. Thank you. No need to apologize." Carol didn't mean it. "You know, the alcohol and all. I kind of rambled on last night." She hoped Eleanor had been too drunk to notice that Carol was not drinking.

"Well, yes. To be honest, I don't remember too much myself. What were you trying to tell me?"

Phew. Dodged a bullet there. But where to start. "How'd you get home?"

That relaxed the woman somewhat as she eased back into the settee. She blinked and swept a hand across her brow— nothing to wipe back there. Every hair was perfectly combed.

"Oh, my." Eleanor waved a hand. "That nice gentleman that approached us. I believe his name was Cash Rutherford."

Carol choked on her last swig of tea. She sputtered, and a few drops dribbled down her chin. "Cash Rutherford? Are you sure?" Taking a chance that Eleanor remembered nothing, she tried to sound calm.

Though not a friendly one, a smile broke out across her face, and she tipped her head. "Why, Carol. Of course, I'm sure. He...well...let's just say he took good care of me last night." Eleanor smiled. "And this morning."

Carol couldn't hide her horror. She blew out a breath and

pursed her lips. "Eleanor, you just met him last night. Don't you think…" *Wrong thing to say.* Carol winced.

Eleanor stood and grabbed her purse. "You're a fine one to talk. How long did you know Grady before you went home with him? Oh, that's right, Grady didn't have a home, did he? You stole him from mine." Eleanor stormed to the front door.

"Wait. Please. I'm sorry. I do want to help. There is so much you need to know."

Eleanor turned her head slightly. "Oh, I know all right. Cash told me quite a bit about you." She walked that model-walk, and her pumps thudded on the wood plank floor.

"You can't trust him. His name is not Cash."

Eleanor stopped, and the door swung open. There stood John Taylor, a small pink pastry box in one hand.

"Well, hello, Mayor. It's so very nice to see you again. Twice in one day." Eleanor's voice cooed sweetly. Sickeningly sweetly.

Carol's heart sunk as she stood behind Eleanor. A wind blew, and Eleanor's designer wrap dress flapped gently around her knees. The breeze did the same to Carol, but a tangled, gauzy, maxi skirt didn't seem to have the same effect as Mayor John Taylor smiled at Eleanor.

He still wore the tan suit, no tie, and the white shirt that popped against his tanned skin, and he and Eleanor looked quite nice next standing next to one another. Carol groaned inside.

"Well, good to see you again, ma'am. I see you've found the best little shop in town." He smiled at Carol, and it helped strengthen her weak knees.

"Yes." Eleanor ignored Carol. "Charming. Just like the owner. But I must be going. I'm meeting someone." Barely turning her head, she called, "Thank you, Carol. Goodbye."

Carol's mind quickly switched gears. She stopped comparing, stopped envying, and thought of Eleanor's safety.

"Eleanor, please come back again. Or call me." She stepped forward.

Eleanor slipped on a pair of sunglasses and walked out. "Oh, I think we're done here.." She stopped and touched John's shoulder. "Now, you, on the other hand, Mayor, maybe we can meet at that little café' sometime." And with a throaty chuckle, she elegantly strolled out.

John stood with a puzzled expression that quickly turned to a smile. "I brought you a napoleon." He held up the pink box.

Carol's whole body warmed, and as much as she loved that luscious, creamy custard puff pastry dessert, she knew it wasn't the delectable concoction that caused her stomach to flutter.

John Taylor's hand held the doorknob while his eyes held hope. "Maybe we can do dinner first?"

Every bit of angst flooded out, and a light tingling filled Carol's body. She wanted badly to take him up on the invitation but held her breath. His suit fit him so perfectly, and his hair was combed so nicely. Even his shoes were polished and unscuffed.

A few strings hanging from the layers of her skirt curled out. As she pulled at them, the bracelets on her wrist bangled loudly. She breathed deep.

"Can I take another rain check?"

He stood for a moment too long. *Say something. Please say anything.*

Finally, he shrugged and nodded back. Clearly disappointed, but always the gentleman. "Sure." John looked as if he wanted to say more but held a kind restraint.

"It's just that I have church tonight." It was partially true. There was always a Sunday night service, but she didn't usually attend. Tonight she would. "You wouldn't want to come with me, would you?"

"No. Not yet. But maybe another time. I keep promising

Pastor Brooks that I'll stop by one Sunday, but not today." He sighed. "Well, I better let you go." He gazed, and his longing pulled at her, but he hesitated and made no move forward. The awkward pause between them seemed to last forever, and finally, his voice boomed unnaturally. "Oh, here."

He held out the pink box, and when she took it, her fingers brushed his, and she fumbled, almost dropping it. Her hand tingled, and electricity sparked, much like when she'd accidentally shocked herself with a live wire once. She glanced up. He felt it too. She knew it, but then he turned and left.

Carol slumped a little. When the door closed, she stomped her foot. Why was it when she should be impulsive and go for it, she couldn't? And when she needed to rein herself in, she went all out? *That man, he makes my head spin.* Sauntering up the stairs to her apartment, John Taylor's kind and handsome face filled her head and her heart. Stepping into the room, she closed the door behind her and peered at her nightstand. Her Bible beckoned her. *Guess I'm going to church.*

CHAPTER 12

C arol had a fitful sleep, but Monday morning finally arrived. The Sunday night church service hadn't stuck with her, and all she could think about was seeing Chief Bert.

She got dressed and walked the few blocks toward the end of town, and when arriving, she burst into police headquarters.

Carol pushed through the little gate that separated the makeshift waiting area from Chief Bert and Officer Blaine's desks. The chief shook his head.

"And a good morning to you, too. May I help you, Miss Carol?"

Carol threw her arms up. "Yes. What are you doing about him?"

"I assume you mean Boudreaux? Officer Blaine saw him on the stakeout."

"Where?" Carol leaned forward onto his desk.

Raising both hands as if in surrender, the chief said, "Hold on. First, sit down and give me an update on the weekend."

Carol took a deep breath. Though she was anxious to spill everything about Johnny Reb's in Gulfport, too much had happened. Her presence in the police station squashed any resolve she'd in cooperating with the chief.

"Well, I think he was in town again."

"What do you mean, you think? When?"

Carol paused. She hadn't seen his car, but she suspected Eleanor Perrin's visit yesterday wasn't entirely her idea. She had a hunch that Boudreaux drove her.

"About closing time. Virginia had just left with him." She pointed to Officer Blaine, who turned red.

Chief Bert glanced over and frowned.

"Do you think Boudreaux was checking up on her?" asked Carol.

"I'd bet he's keeping track of her schedule and her whereabouts. Officer Blaine and I already…." Chief Bert stopped, and his brow furrowed. "Hey, Blaine, were you assigned to take Virginia home last night?"

Officer Blaine stuttered. "I…figured since I was off yesterday…I just offered."

Carol smiled at the blushing officer.

The chief seemed oblivious. "Good job. Anyway, we talked about issuing a restraining order for Boudreaux to stay away from Virginia and The Refuge. We can do the same for you. I think it would be a good idea," said the Chief.

"No. I'm just waiting for him to come by again. Just you wait." Anger fueled bravado.

Chief Bert leaned forward. "Miss Carol, we don't need a vigilante. We'll handle it." He pointed to Officer Blaine. "Get the paperwork—"

"Already on it, sir." On his desk, folders and papers were stacked neatly in piles. Quite the opposite of the chief's desk. "Chief, I'll get these ready, but they need to be signed by The Refuge staff and Virginia."

"Is that a problem?"

"No, sir. I'll get the signatures."

Chief Bert nodded. "I knew I hired you for a good reason."

"I was assigned, sir," said Blaine quietly.

"So, you sure about that, ma'am?" Said Chief Bert.

"My name is Carol. My grandmother is a ma'am. And yes, I'm sure." For a moment, she checked herself. She was confident that she could handle Boudreaux, but could she protect Virginia?

"All right then, but if you change your mind, let me know. We can issue that restraining order. In the meantime, just let us know if he makes an appearance. It's best for everyone that you keep us notified."

Carol's mind fixed on Eleanor Perrin. Urged by the gnawing pit in her stomach, she knew she should tell the chief. Taking a deep breath, she blew it out and shook her head. Not yet. Besides, the thought of dredging up Grady flat out embarrassed her.

Carol headed for the exit. Still feeling unsettled, she turned. "Hey, I just want to be sure. So someone's watching Virginia at all times? I mean, what if there's more than just Boudreaux involved? Someone that we don't know about?" She looked at Blaine, and he stared back wide-eyed. Carol pointed a finger. "Listen, you can't be her personal bodyguard 24-7."

Chief Bert's brow furrowed. "Is there something going on here that I don't know about?"

Officer Blaine stood. "Sir, I'm done with the forms. I'll drive over and get the signatures. I need to get them filed at the courthouse right away." He grabbed his hat and hurried past Carol, nodding as he pushed open the little wooden spring gate.

"Wait a minute. Don't you file those on the computer, like online or something?"

Blaine was a tech geek and did everything on-line. It was the chief that preferred hard copies and hand delivery.

Moving quickly toward the door, Blaine waved the files in the air. "After I get these signatures." He hurried out.

Chief Bert scratched his head. "I must be missing something here."

"Oh, you'll find out soon enough. Now, what's the plan?"

Chief Bert straightened and rested his hands on the desk. "Boudreaux knows we're watching him, and he's going to make a move on Virginia. That we can count on. When he does, we'll catch him. I promise."

A heavy weight seemed to press her down, and her weary frame dropped onto a wooden bench. "Can't you pick him up or something? Isn't he out on parole?" If she could only trust God, she wouldn't be grasping at every straw.

"No parole. He won an appeal. No crime committed." He held up his hands to stay Carol's reaction.

"Don't you dare say a crime wasn't committed. You know it was him who killed Grady. Why maybe it was him that killed Melanie's husband too?"

The Chief shook his head. "Yes, I know, and I'm sorry, Carol. But they never connected him to Chris's death. So leave that one alone for now. From what I hear, Melanie's sister's been working on that case. Not our concern right now. Virginia is. Do you think you can speak with the folks at The Refuge?"

"Sure, what do you need?"

"Find out Virginia's schedule. Tell her they need to always keep a close eye on her. She can't be alone with that no-good uncle of hers around."

"Are we even sure it's her uncle?"

"Sad excuse for one. I'm pretty sure he had a hand in the death of her druggie, Aunt—another victim in that whole fiasco last year. Not sure of the connection, but he called the Aunt his sister. I didn't buy it. Anyway, I'll bet he wants Virginia and wants her bad."

"I'll head over there right now. I'm closed on Mondays."

She stood and reached out a hand. "Thanks, Chief. I sure appreciate your help and your offer of protection around my house. But I'm good. I can take care of myself."

"Miss Carol, don't go taking matters into your own hands."

I already did that. She bit her lip and looked up. He towered over her, all two hundred and fifty pounds. Cringing, she got his point.

Raising a hand to her brow, she saluted. "Yes, sir." She clicked her heels together and left.

Sweet smells of freshly baked cookies greeted Carol as she entered The Refuge. The housemother welcomed her into the large kitchen, taking baking sheets from the oven. She instructed Carol to remove the cookies to cool, handing her a porcelain-handle spatula. Carol twisted it in her hand. It was a piece she'd like to offer in her store.

The woman proceeded to fill a tray with a pitcher of iced tea glasses. Scooping up the cookies, she placed them on a floral plate and added them to the tray.

"Come, let's have some sweet tea on the porch."

The housemother placed the tray on a wicker table and sat in a matching rocker.

Carol rested in the porch swing, covered with rose chintz cushions. Taking the offered tea and cookies, she smiled. "Mmm. Thank you. I don't bake much, so when Virginia brings your cookies in on the weekend, I feel like I've died and gone to heaven."

She stuffed one whole cookie in her mouth. As crumbs fell, the housemother handed her a napkin, just like a mom. Carol winced a little and dabbed her lips.

"Well, let's hope heaven's a lot more exciting than cookies." She smiled. "Thank you for taking Virginia into your shop. She's blossomed with your help."

"Oh, my. That girl is talented. She's even handling simple transactions with customers. You're the ones that made her blossom."

"Well, let's give credit to the Lord." She nodded. "I think we can agree. She's exceeding all our expectations. Our hopes for her are already beyond our original goals. But there is one concern."

Carol bit her lip. "It's Officer Blaine, isn't it?"

The housemother perked up and wiped her hands on the bib of her white apron. "Yes. He was here this morning, having me sign some papers. And he's a nice enough young man…"

Before she finished, Carol nodded so vigorously, her butterfly clip came loose, and her hair flowed over her shoulders.

"Oh, you see it too?"

"See it? I'm not blind," Said Carol. "I'm sorry, ma'am. But yes, she's moving way too fast. Heck, they only met on Saturday." Carol reached for another cookie but pulled back and dropped her hands into her lap. "She reminds me of me."

The woman stared back, and Carol squirmed. Everyone knew Carol's reputation. She hadn't tried to hide her escapades in the past.

Reaching across the table, the housemother's warm touch comforted Carol even more. "You're a good woman, Miss Carol. None of us are righteous, not one. Every day is a new day, and it seems you're making good work of your days now."

Now? If only she could have started that a long time ago. Carol shook herself. This was about Virginia now. "Well, it seems we both have too strong an attraction for men. You've done a good job of keeping her protected from the world here."

"Yes, but an important part of her rehab is assimilating her back into normal society. I'm sure she can support herself while living in a group home, and with the right relationships, she'll make good decisions. But this chemistry between her and the Officer..." The housemother nodded, wringing a napkin between her fingers.

Carol sipped her tea. "Well, the good thing is that this officer is a good man. I'd like to believe he has honorable intentions, and over my dead body, I'll keep it that way."

Laughing, the housemother pushed back wisps of brown greying hair. "Well, self-control with the Holy Spirit might work better." She winked. "Maybe both. But I'm afraid right now of the free time she has. She'll probably be taking the bus down to the Police Station every chance she gets. If she doesn't scare the poor young man off."

"Well, that's why I'm here. She can come work for me those two hours after school as well as Saturdays. Is it possible for us to take turns getting her to and from Second Chance?"

"Yes! That would work perfectly. Busy hands keep one out of trouble."

Carol thought of her own busy life. Well, her old active lifestyle. Before she could berate herself again, they began working out a plan. Virginia would work for Carol from three o'clock until five o'clock every afternoon.

Although hesitant to ask for Officer Blaine's help, they needed him and agreed to ask him to transport Virginia two days a week, and they'd split the rest of the week. On Monday afternoons, when her business was closed, Carol would take Virginia with her. It was her buying day for the store. Pleased with their arrangements, the women hugged.

"How did you start this place?" Carol stood on the top step.

"A desire and an idea. God did the rest."

"I'd like to talk to you about it sometime." She tapped her

heart. "It's a good thing you got here, ma'am. I'd wished I'd had someplace like this when I took off."

The housemother's soft, kind face smiled. "Well, we do have some runaways, and we have connections in other states. Some of the girls need to get away from wherever their troubles are. For safety or rehab." Her brows knit. "You don't think Virginia will have to leave, do you?"

"Why, I never thought about it. I just figured when we caught him…What happens when they can't catch the guys that harass these girls?"

"That's why we're connected with other homes. Often, the girls are afraid to give up information about them, and sadly, the perpetrators are not often caught."

Biting her lip, Carol stopped before she drew blood. Heat flared within.

The housemother touched Carol's shoulder. "That's where complete trust comes in. Trust in the almighty sovereign God."

There it was again. *Trust.*

They said their goodbyes, and the housemother retreated inside while Carol walked to her car. She opened the door and glanced at a car driving by at a snail's pace. Her heart dropped. A blue Lincoln passed, and a grinning Will Boudreaux looked back, waving a hand. He pointed to the sign, "The Refuge."

Without hesitation, Carol yelled, "Hey, you hang on there." To her surprise, the car stopped. She ran down the sidewalk, her skirt and hair flowing behind her. Standing on the curb, she raised a hand, shielding the sun. She took a deep breath.

"Mister, you best keep moving. We got a protective order against you. You can't be within three hundred feet of this place or Virginia." She stood tall, with her hands on her hips.

Will Boudreaux's laugh sounded too friendly. If it had declared evil, it would have given Carol strength.

He lowered his sunglasses and smiled. "Well…Carol, is it? I haven't been served with anything yet, so unless I see something in writing…." His eyes traveled up and down her body. "I can look all I want." As he drove off, he yelled. "Have a wonderful day, Miz Carol."

CHAPTER 13

Tuesday afternoon, Officer Blaine drove up to The Refuge. Virginia sat on the front steps. A bottle of red nail polish sat next to her as she stroked a brush across each nail. Holding it up to the light, she squinted, then smiled, seemingly pleased with the color. Blowing on her nails, she lifted her head, and Blaine waved. Leaving the polish, she stood and ran to the street.

"I thought Carol was coming." She tipped her head, and her platinum waves spilled forward. She pulled open the door and climbed in.

"Yes, well, I'm here to take you. She's at the shop waiting.." He shook his head and pointed to the house. "Best you be telling your housemother you're leaving. Remember, Miss Virginia, you have to tell everyone what you're doing all the time."

"Why?" She pushed her lips out, pouting.

"I don't want nothing to happen to you." Pulling back his shoulders, he clarified, "I mean, it's for your own protection."

Just then, her housemother walked out and waved. "Thank you." She called.

"Bye!" Virginia squealed, then twisted towards Blaine. "I

like you protecting me." She grabbed her seat belt and clicked it. She rested a hand on Officer Blaine's arm.

He pulled away.

She frowned. "What's the matter?"

Looking straight ahead, he drove on down the street. "Virginia, I'm on official business. I'm working, and you can't be doing that in my squad car."

She waved him off. "Okaaay." She crossed her arms and huffed. "It's not like I kissed you or anything." She stared at him. "Don't you like me?"

"Virginia, I'd like to talk to you about that. You're still in high school, and I'm an officer of the law. Right now, we have a professional relationship."

"You're dumping me?" Tears threatened.

"Dumping you? We're not even together yet." His voice cracked.

Virginia squealed. "Yet?" She poked him repeatedly. "You said yet."

He laughed, but turning back to the road, he huffed. "Virginia, it's a little complicated, but we got to take it slow right now, okay?"

She fidgeted in her seat and nodded. "Okay. Whatever that means." She reached over and squeezed his shoulder.

Pulling off her hand, he placed it back in her lap. "It means you can't be touching me. At least not right now."

"When then?"

"I'll tell you when." As he pulled up to the curb in front of Second Chance, Virginia hit her seat belt button and grabbed the door handle.

"Wait." Officer Blaine turned sideways and rested his arm behind her headrest. "Virginia, I like you, but there's time for things. We have to wait."

As if she heard nothing else, she threw her arms around his neck and hugged him tightly. "You like me."

A knock on the window jarred them both, and Blaine

turned. Virginia squeezed his neck hard. Blaine peeled her fingers loose. "Step away from this vehicle," he shouted as he pushed open the door.

Will Boudreaux smirked as he complied.

Blaine stepped out. Hand on his belt.

"Just here to pick up my niece," said Boudreaux.

Virginia scooted back against the front passenger door, pulling her knees up.

Reaching into his front breast pocket, Blaine pulled out some papers. "Mr. Boudreaux? Will Boudreaux?"

"You know who I am. It seems everyone knows my business around these parts lately."

Blaine thrust the papers at his chest. "You are served, sir. These are protective orders. You are not to be within 300 feet of The Refuge home or Virginia's person."

Veins pulsed on Boudreaux's neck. He grabbed the papers and seethed at Virginia. "Did you sign these, girl?" He didn't bother to read them but stuffed them in his coat pocket. "Virginia, you rescind this order, you hear? You belong with me."

"No, sir. She doesn't," said Officer Blaine.

Boudreaux glanced between them and exploded with a loud, curdling laugh. "Oh, I get it." He peered down at Virginia. She still cowered in the car. "Coming up in the world, huh? Is he as good as the boys at the bars?"

Officer Blaine pulled back a fist, and before landing it on Boudreaux's face, a short squeal from a siren caused him to stop and turn. A squad car screeched up within inches of his open car door.

Chief Bert eased out of the vehicle and stepped forward. His eyes flashed at Officer Blaine first, then turned his gaze towards Boudreaux. "You been served?" Boudreaux scowled back. The Chief poked his shoulder. "I asked, have you been served?"

"Yes, sir, he has. I just took care of it." Blaine cleared his throat.

Boudreaux stepped back. Straightening his shoulders, he wiped a hand across his slicked-back hair. Pushing up his sunglasses, he nodded and turned toward the blue vehicle across the street. Everyone watched as he walked to his car.

Virginia cried while scrambling from the car and lunging at Rodney. He refrained from comforting her, while still standing at attention. Chief Bert's shoulders were pulled back, and he glared at Virginia. She stepped away.

Carol ran out, making a beeline to Virginia. "Land sakes. What the heck is going on out here?"

Shoppers stopped and gawked.

Chief Bert raised his hands high. "Everyone, return to your business, please. The show's over." He bellowed, then nodded at Blaine again. "You're good with reports. This better be a good one. I'll see you at the station."

"Yes, sir." Officer Blaine got in his car, never looking back.

Chief Bert watched the retreating squad car. "I guess this is what everyone but me seems to know something about?" He waved a finger between Officer Blaine's departing car and Virginia.

Carol said nothing, and Chief Bert commanded, "Come by the station and bring Virginia."

Carol nodded as he left. Virginia wrapped her arms around Carol, and they walked inside. She locked the front door and pointed to a stool. She opened the refrigerator door and pulled out a soda pop. Flipping off the cap of the bottle, she handed it to Virginia.

"Okay, what happened?"

"Will showed up." Virginia wiped her nose with her sleeve and took a long drink.

"What? Are you kidding me? Here? Was anyone with him?"

Virginia sniffled. "No. Who would be with him?" Virginia's lips turned down. "I'm all the family he's got. My Aunt Hilly is dead. They said a drug overdose."

Carol cringed. She had heard that Virginia's Aunt's death was indeed a drug overdose, but foul play was suspected. They could never prove it. "I'm sorry, Virginia. Was she related to Will?"

Virginia ignored the question. "When Will showed up today, he said something mean about me that made Rodney mad." Her voice began to rise. "Rodney was gonna punch him. If Chief Bert hadn't come, I don't know what would have happened."

Carol shook her head. *It's too late. He's too involved.* "Virginia, you've got to leave Officer Blaine...Rodney, alone."

"That's what he said."

"Honey, he's right. Especially now. With Boudreaux around, he could get hurt."

"But I like him. And he likes me."

"I know, sweetheart. But you're moving way too fast. Do you know what that means? It means you got to slow down. Get to know each other, and for heaven's sake, don't touch each other."

Virginia pouted, "He said that too."

"At least the man's got some sense." Grabbing Virginia by the shoulders, she drew her close. Her face inches away. "And if you care about him, you'll do as he says. Just give it time. Lord knows it's a lesson we both need to learn."

"What do you mean?"

Knock. Knock.

"We're closed!"

The knock came again, and Carol grabbed a tissue, handed it to Virginia then strode to the door. Mayor Taylor waved as he peeked in.

Carol smiled and unlocked the door. "Hello, John. Long

time no see." She was a little worried that maybe she'd shut him down one too many times.

"Well, they say absence makes the heart grow fonder," said John.

Carol laughed and waved him in. "Not too much of an absence, eh?"

He didn't step in but stared down at her. "Listen, I have a Board Meeting," he raised his wrist and looked at his watch. "Soon. But I wanted to invite you to dinner." He breathed deep, and his body tensed.

The bathroom door opened in the back. Still smiling, and without taking her gaze off the Mayor, Carol called out. "Virginia, can you open those boxes and take inventory?"

"Sure thing, Miss Carol."

John Taylor seemed to relax a little, but Carol's smile slowly faded. She thought about what she'd just told Virginia. *Take it slow.* The silence felt too long.

He nodded and shrugged. "All right then. You can't blame a guy for asking. Sorry to bother you." He backed away.

Carol wanted to reach out, but glancing back at Virginia, she had reservations. Finally, she followed him. "John, wait." He stopped and turned just halfway.

"I'd love to join you for dinner...."

"But?"

"But things are a bit hectic right now.".

"It's just dinner." His voice sounded on edge.

"I'm sorry. John, can we take a raincheck?

He turned back around and called out over his shoulder. "Raincheck. Sure thing." He waved a hand in the air, not glancing back.

Carol watched him cross the street, and her shoulders heaved. Anger rose. Why did she have to make things so complicated? "Shoot. He's a good man, you know?"

"Who are you talking to?" asked Virginia.

Carol spun around. "My goodness, girl, you scared me to death."

"Who was that man?" Virginia tried to peek around Carol.

"Nobody." Carol brushed past her. She straightened a few items and adjusted a few books, none of which needed her attention.

"He's hot." Virginia giggled. "Not as hot as Rodney."

Carol turned and glared. "Young lady, men are not objects for our pleasure. Virginia, you, and I, we are precious in God's sight, and in His timing, we just might be precious in a worthy man's as well."

Virginia clasped her hands together and pressed them to her chest. "I don't know what that means, but maybe you mean like Rodney?" She grinned.

"Yes, like Rodney. But like I said. Take it slow."

Virginia scrunched up her nose. "But what if he leaves me like that guy left you? Maybe you're taking it too slow?"

"Virginia, honey. You and I are in the same boat. I just met him too. Right guy, wrong time. Let's both give it time."

Virginia huffed as she walked back to her work.

Glancing back at the door, the force of massive weights seemed to press on Carol's chest. Her heart hurt. Take my yoke. My burden is light, the bible says. *Okay, Lord, okay.*

CHAPTER 14

The rest of the week went by uneventfully, and Carol was thankful for Friday night. It was the opening night of the Crawfish Festival. One of Bay Town's liveliest community events, where they would cook and consume upwards of forty thousand pounds of Crawfish this weekend. Carol glanced at her watch, turned off the counter lights, and moved for the stairs. The shop phone rang. Carol froze, wondering if it was Eleanor. She hadn't heard from her since she'd dropped by. She walked slowly towards the phone, letting it go to voicemail.

<Hey, Carol. You're coming tonight, right? Call me. Mel.>

She scrambled for the phone. "Wait, Mel..." CLICK.

Carol shrugged, but a rising warmth rose. Melanie was always watching out for her. This would be the first time Carol wasn't going to the festival with an ulterior motive of looking for a man. This time, she just wanted to enjoy being with friends. She blew out a heavy sigh as she picked up the receiver to dial Melanie back. The phone rang before she could punch the redial.

"Hello, Mel?"

A long silence ensued, and a slow laugh followed. "No, Carol. It's Eleanor."

This time it was Carol that paused. Pulling back her shoulders, she stood tall as if someone could see her. "Yes, hi, Eleanor. I'm glad you called." Carol winced.

"Oh, really?"

No, not really. "Yes, I was wondering how you were doing." Carol winced again. It wasn't entirely true. For a few days following their last meeting, Carol had been concerned about Eleanor and Boudreaux. She felt compelled to continue trying to warn the woman, but truth be told, Carol was relieved that the woman hadn't contacted her again. Though it was a quiet week between Blaine and Virginia, and everything not happening with John Taylor, Carol had tried to put Eleanor out of her mind.

"Listen, you really need to stay away from Will Boudreaux—"

"I don't know a Will Boudreaux. I don't know why you insist on calling him that. Now, if you mean Cash Rutherford, I have not the least intention of staying away from him."

There was another silence, and Carol thought she heard muffling as if a hand covered the speaker. A thickness swelled her throat, and she wanted to ask if Will or Cash was there. She didn't dare.

A sweet, mild humph sounded, and Eleanor's annoyed tone changed. "Listen, Carol. Yes, of course. I'll consider your advice, but I think you are seriously mistaken about the man. Anyway, could I please have your cell phone number?" The request was abrupt, but Eleanor continued. "Sometimes, I do need someone to talk to, especially in the evenings. And you've been so kind." The voice dripped like thick molasses.

Carol had changed her phone number since changing her life. Too many men had continued to call when they passed through town. Some even showed up at her doorstep before she moved. She was bold enough to turn them away, but it had exhausted her. Eleanor would be the first stranger who had her cell number.

She hesitated. But how could she refuse? If she was sincere in wanting to help this woman, shouldn't she give out her number? "Sure," Carol gave the number and breathed deep. "Call me anytime you want. I have to go." Pause. "Unless, of course, you wanted to talk now?" *Please say no. Please say no.*

"No. Not now. Later will be fine. We'll have plenty to talk about, I'm sure. Thank you and goodnight."

Slowly replacing the receiver, Carol turned and walked up the stairs to her apartment. Her feet felt like lead with every labored footfall, but thinking of the festival, she skipped up the last three steps.

Shouts and laughter echoed through the night air filling Carol with delight as she walked through the crowds. The flashing lights of the Ferris wheel made her head spin as the resounding tunes of musicians on stage throbbed through her, and she loved it. Thankful for the barrage of her senses, thoughts of Eleanor's disturbing call floated out of her head.

"Hey, Carol." Melanie grabbed her. "Wasn't sure if you were going to make it."

Carol spun around. "Of course, girl! Where's that handsome pastor of yours?"

"He's working at a food stand." Melanie pulled Carol and led her to the Crawfish booth. Desmond waved as the women stepped forward, but Carol stopped. Her heart skipped a beat as she looked past Desmond. John Taylor worked by his side, dumping a full sifter of fried crawfish on the newspaper-covered counter. Carol watched, and when he lifted his head, their eyes connected, but without so much as a wave, he turned.

Carol's shoulders drooped. Desmond filled up two baskets

of crawfish and handed them to the women. John continued cooking, his back turned.

"We can't eat all this," said Melanie.

"Save some for me. I'll join you in a minute," said Desmond.

Carol's gaze lingered on John's back. He appeared comical in khaki shorts wearing a long, white apron. The ties around his waist hung down his backside.

"We'll save you a seat," said Melanie to Desmond. She pointed to the corralled eating area. Picnic tables covered in red and white checked cloths filled the makeshift arena. "And bring the mayor with you," Melanie yelled.

Carol's protests were ignored as Melanie shoved her to the tables. "Oh, come on. You know you want him to join us. And I'm guessing he wants to as well," said Melanie.

I wish, thought Carol. She didn't feel like explaining to Melanie how things were going or not going with Mayor John Taylor.

The dance floor in front of the picnic area was packed with dancers. Young and old couples and families with small children. Everyone was Texas Two-Stepping, and Carol threw off her melancholy thoughts and instinctively moved to the beat. She spotted Officer Blaine and Virginia dancing, and slipping two fingers between her lips, she let out a shrill whistle. Virginia jumped up and down at the sight of Carol, waving wildly, while Blaine struggled to keep in step. Carol smiled. *Young love. This is the night for it.* She looked up. *Oh heaven, help them.*

Seeing other familiar faces that often frequented her business, she raised her fancy cowboy hat in the air and whooped.

"Yee, hah!" Carol yelled but paused as a couple on the floor seemed to stop and stare back. Before she could see them clearly, they faded back into the crowd. They looked familiar, but she didn't see enough of them. Still, something.... she shrugged and placed her hat back on her head. The beads and feathers hanging from the brim cording mixed into her long dark red hair. The gray was gone.

Melanie reached out and lifted a handful of Carol's thick, wavy strands. "Love the color."

Carol blushed and shrugged. "Oh, you know. It's been a rough week. I had an impulse moment. I know it's a little drastic."

Desmond walked up. "It's great." He planted a kiss on Melanie's cheek.

"Hey, Pastor. Better get your girl out there." Carol pointed to the dance floor.

The lively song wound down, and the crowd applauded when two musicians took center stage with stringed instruments. Plucking back and forth, the familiar dueling banjo and guitar rang out from the stage. The two long-haired country musicians, sitting on stools, played back and forth, slowly picking the tune and gaining momentum. Everyone clapped along, and the dance crowd slowly edged forward to the stage, stomping with the rising crescendo. Little children and old folks clogged on the dance floor. Big Joe, Lyla, and the kids joined in, and everyone loved it, cheering them on.

The excitement felt good. Carol glanced back at Melanie, leaning back in Desmond's arms. She wasn't envious, just confused as to what she wanted in life. There was a time not very long ago that going to an event like this meant going with someone or finding someone to take home. The dark thought didn't cook long before a large shadow emerged over her. Although the bright lights silhouetted the form, Carol knew without a doubt who it was.

"May I?" He mouthed as he waved an open hand at the empty seat next to her.

"You certainly may, Mayor." She yelled above the noise.

Sitting on the bench with his back to the table, he turned his head and smiled at Carol. Instead of watching the stage, his eyes lingered on her, and she, in turn, couldn't take her gaze off of him. She'd rejected him just days before, and here he was again.

The music stopped abruptly, and the applause was deafening. Another ballad followed, and the dance floor flooded with entwined couples. Carol hooted when Melanie and Desmond ran onto the dance floor. John stood and applauded.

"Hey, Mayor, you're slouching there, aren't you? There's a crowd at your booth." Carol playfully pushed him as she nodded towards the crawfish booth where the line snaked through the grounds.

He sat back down. "Trying to get rid of me already?" He reached down and detangled the feather and cording hanging in her hair. "Great color. Suits you well, lady."

Carol flinched but secretly enjoyed the tenderness of his touch. He turned to swing his legs over the bench, sliding in closer. She immediately felt her temperature rise as the warmth of his body rested so close to hers. A thought to scoot away crossed her mind but quickly passed. John raised an eyebrow and tipped his head towards the dancing, and though Carol longed to be in his arms, she felt she just wasn't quite ready yet. Luckily, her phone rang. She raised a finger and turned.

Clicking on the text. She froze. Clutching her phone to her chest, she swung her feet over the bench and stood. Her face felt flushed, and a moistness glistened on her forehead.

"Is everything all right?" John's brows wrinkled.

She stammered and blurted out, "I need to answer this text. I'm sorry."

"I have to get back to the booth anyway. See you later?" His chin dipped as he gazed down at her.

She nodded. As soon as he turned his back, Carol searched her phone. She caught her breath and then searched to see if anyone was near enough to see. Pictures. Someone had texted lots of pictures of her. Taking a deep breath didn't help much as she scrolled through—all photos of her at

Johnny Reb's. The photographs captured her walking into the bar, spinning around, smiling, her skirt swirled out, a band playing in the background. She scrolled. Another, sitting with Eleanor, a glass of wine in front of her, and finally, a man leering over her. She couldn't stop staring. Anger rose. Though nothing was incriminating, much was implied.

"Hey, Miss Carol, bad news?" Chief Bert was in full uniform, standing before her.

"What?" She swung her arm behind her back, her hand clasping the phone. "No, just admiring pictures of myself." She laughed nervously. "You know me."

The Chief scratched his head. "Not really. But hey, I guess selfies are the thing these days." He tipped his hat as he turned to leave but stopped. "I don't mean to spoil the night, but you haven't seen Boudreaux around, have you?"

Carol gulped. "No, why? Is he here?" Her voice squeaked.

He drew back his shoulders. "I sure hope not. I just got a funny feeling. You didn't see him, did you?"

The couple she'd seen for a brief moment floated into her mind. "No. I didn't," she said, a little too abruptly.

"And if you did, you'd tell me." He paused, "Wouldn't you, Miss Carol?"

Before she could answer, someone called him to another part of the festival. The chief nodded at her and waved as he left.

She waited until he was out of sight and searched her phone again, squinting as if it would help her think. It did. Eleanor had her number. These had to be from her. But the pictures showed Eleanor in them. She scrolled again. Boudreaux. It was him. Did Eleanor give him her number? Wiping her forehead, she searched the crowd. Her gaze was intent and thorough.

Ding.

She jumped at the vibration of her phone and opened it quickly. A single word, "Yup," accompanied by another picture, glared before her. It was an intimate moment between her and John Taylor. Captured just moments ago. His forearms rested on the checkered cloth. Strands of her hair touched his shoulder. Their faces close together, staring longingly. She couldn't tear away from the picture. Hating all the others, this photo captured the moment, the night, and her heart. But the beautiful moment was spoiled by the thought of who took the picture. So perhaps it was Boudreaux and Eleanor that she saw earlier on the dance floor.

Staring across the crowd, her gaze rested on John, where he was busy cooking. Her emotions went wild. Desire, concern, fear, and finally, anger again overpowered it all. She silenced the phone and stuffed it into her purse. Raising her soda, she whispered, "Game on."

CHAPTER 15

The boardwalk outside Bubba's Catch Shack down on Pier 1 was secluded and empty. Just what Carol was seeking early Monday morning. She'd made it through the weekend, but the secrets piling up inside haunted her—her trip to Jackson, Johnny Reb's, and now the photos. Boudreaux was stalking her. Shoving it to the back of her mind, she glanced towards the Shack.

"Mmm. Good coffee, Bubba." She held up the tin mug..

Bubba's long red beard waved in the slight breeze. He nodded, then held up an old, silver, percolator coffee pot. "Need a refill?"

"Yes, please."

He filled her cup, and Carol watched him as he retreated to the kitchen in the little metal and wooden structure. She watched the boats, lightly rocking in their slips. The gray clouds hovering directly overhead threatened rain, but so far, not a drop had slipped through. She crossed her legs and frowned at the old brown sandals thinking that maybe they weren't the best choice for the day. *The day? What would it bring?* The harrowing weekend had ended on a better note with church yesterday. Bay Town Community was always the highlight of her week, and Pastor Desmond's sermons prepared her to tackle the week ahead.

Squinting, she watched a small lone hermit crab walking sideways down one of the docks. Its shell appeared too big, and it labored dragging toward who knows where. *How in the world did it get up there?* Carol thought of her family back in New Mexico. *How did I get here? And Lord, where am I going?*

A streak flashed above her, and she smiled at the elegant white egret soaring beautifully across the sky. The bright white of its elongated expression of grace glided against the darkening landscape. She watched it fly inland when a shadow spawned over her head. She ducked as a seagull swooped down and snatched the hermit crab on the dock. It flew away with the creature wiggling in its beak. Carol's jaw dropped. "Let him go!" She screamed.

As if hearing her, the seagull dropped the poor creature, and she watched in horror as it splattered on the rocks. Carol threw her hands to her mouth and watched as the preying bird landed, picking on the dead crab.

"Hey," a voice called from a distance. "Carol, are you all right?" Melanie jogged up the boardwalk.

Shocked, she turned to stare. "Mel. Did you see that?"

"See what?"

"Why, that monster over there." Carol pointed to the feasting seagull.

The bird turned his head towards her just as it flipped its head back and swallowed its prize.

"Ewww. That's so gross." Melanie scrunched her nose. She glanced at Carol's cup of coffee and looked at the wooden shed. Bubba stood flipping a fry pan behind the pass-through window. She pointed to the cup. "And that's kinda gross too," Melanie said in a hushed tone.

Carol picked up her cup. "Are you kidding me? I love this stuff. Bubba's the only one who percolates coffee anymore." She gave Melanie the once-over. Her friend, dressed in trendy running clothes, jogged down Beach Road most every morning. This was her turnaround point. "I'd join you, but I don't have my running shoes on." She pulled up her long skirt, raising her sandaled feet.

"Sure. Next time." Melanie held out a hand as if waiting for a downpour. "So, what are you doing down here? Is Mockingbird closed?"

Carol shook her head. "Just needed a break from there."

"Because Mayor Taylor always goes there," said Melanie.

"Yeah, well, that could have been a beautiful thing. But if I touch it, he might end up like that poor little critter." She pointed to the empty spot where the seagull had previously devoured its prey.

"Carol, what are you talking about?" Melanie pulled out the red metal chair and sat. She stood quickly, wiping her backside from the dampness of the seat.

A breeze blew up, and Carol's hair swirled around her face. Her skirt flew up, and she pulled it down, covering her exposed legs.

"Melanie, I don't have the energy to control how I feel about a man. And John's not just any man. Nobody like that has ever been interested..." Carol paused. "I'm just dreaming."

Melanie's face softened, and Carol felt her warmth as she gently covered Carol's hand with hers. "Maybe you're not giving him a chance. Maybe you're afraid?"

Water brimmed behind her pale lashes, and Carol nodded. "Yeah. I'm good at that." She sucked in a breath. "You know, once, my parents fixed me up with a nice young guy. He was going somewhere. Already in Pre-Law at college." Carol focused on Melanie and smiled. "And he liked me. Yup, he was definitely interested." Drawing her hand away, she sat up straight. "Can you imagine that? A straight shooter liking the wild party girl."

"Yes, I can. We all like you, Carol. We love you."

In a barely audible whisper, she said, "He loved me too." As the words escaped, she wiped a hand across her eyes. "That was a long time ago." She fluttered her fingers at Melanie. "Go on, girl, finish your run and leave me be. I'm good. The Lord's doing some kind of work in me."

Melanie stood and stretched. "I know, Carol. And it's good work." She hugged her friend. "See you at Bible Study tonight?"

"Of course, girl."

Carol watched Melanie's slim body move rhythmically down the gulf. The screeching overhead caused Melanie to duck. "Those darn seagulls," Carol yelled.

The wind picked up, and a strong fishy smell rose from the choppy waters. Bubba walked out just as huge drops fell intermittently around the shack. "Think I'm gonna bring in the chairs and tables for a bit." The white bib apron stained with the standard breakfast fare stretched tight across his protruding belly. His red plaid shirt sleeves rolled up, exposing colorful tattoos covering his forearms. He stroked his red beard.

Carol stood and tried to tame her swirling hair, skirt, and shawl. "My goodness, maybe you should put me in there too."

He chuckled and waved as she walked to her truck. She heard Bubba yell, "Love the truck, ma'am."

Carol chuckled. He always said that. Nothing changed much down here. And she was finally starting to appreciate it, just like home. Nothing much changed there either. All her family had stayed in Santa Fe...New Mexico. Everyone but her. She climbed in just as the deluge began, escaping a soaking. Sitting behind the wheel, she reached into her purse to retrieve her keys but instead pulled out her phone. Hitting her contacts, she waited as she put her phone on speaker. She stared at the pounding rain on her windshield.

"Hello?"

"Hello, Mother...It's me, Carol."

There was a long pause. Her mother's breathing turned to a slight pant, then a door closed. "Hello, Caroline. I'm glad you called. Are you all right?"

How long had it been since she'd called? "Mother, I'm fine." This time it was she that paused. "Just missed you, is all. How's Daddy?"

Another pause. "He asks about you. Really, he does. He tries not to show it. You know a man's pride and all. But he's glad his little girl is back in touch."

"I know, Mother. But I'm trying."

"And you're doing a good job, sweetheart. Tell me more about your business, and is there anybody special in your life?"

Carol cringed. How could her mother even ask that? That was her father's biggest nightmare. Men in her life. Too many men. "Business is good. And I'm swearing off men." Carol shrugged and suddenly grew quiet. Another eerie silence ensued.

"You sure about that? They're not all bad, you know?" She paused. "Alexander…"

"Stop, please. That was a long time ago."

"I know, but—"

"You know, Mother, there is somebody." Carol hoped to stop her mother's reminiscence down her painful past. "The mayor, in fact." Carol laughed, hearing a loud gasp from her mother.

"Is he a good mayor? A good man?"

"I think so. Everyone in town likes him. And he's a real gentleman. Handsome too. He's quite the looker, mother." She chuckled.

"Oh, Caroline. That's not important." Aurora smiled. "But your father might like to hear of this."

"No. No. No. Nothing's really happening."

"Well, honey, don't let this one get away. Not like…Oh, I'm sorry."

Carol swallowed hard, her throat suddenly parched. "I know. I blew that one."

"Honey, if you're trusting God, things can be different. Much different."

Carol warmed inside. She'd kept her faith back, not wanting to disappoint her family again. Their sincere beliefs were the only thing that allowed them to forgive Carol. She only hoped her walk with God would one day be as genuine.

"Well, Mother, I'm trying."

Through the phone, she heard a door open, and a familiar man's voice spoke in the background. She peered at the windshield again and couldn't differentiate if the watery view was caused by the rain or the wetness in her eyes.

A shaky voice said, "We love you, Carol. We're praying for you." And as if she could see her mother holding the phone away, she heard an accompanying whisper, "Do you want to speak to her?"

Carol waited. The wait was too long. "Mother, I really must run. Sorry, I'm late. I'll call again soon. Bye, I love you." She reached to click off and instead spoke softly, "Mother? Tell Daddy I'm sorry." She clicked off before another word was spoken and rested her head on the steering wheel.

Her moment of silence shattered at the sound of a blaring siren. Bay Town had a Fire Department downtown, and the secondary station with a lone truck sat housed near Pier 1. The engine roared down Beach Road with lights flashing, and Carol followed. The Engine truck drove too fast for her to pursue, but the town was small enough she could assess the location of the emergency by the lights and sirens.

Carol dropped her mouth in horror at the sight in front of her. *The Refuge.* The rain at the pier was a deluge, but here, in town, the rain came in steady sheets. She paid no mind and jumped out. Chief Bert stopped her at the front steps. She struggled to get around him, knowing her efforts were fruitless.

"Miss Carol. We got this. The Fire Department got here in plenty of time. If you want to help, go on over there."

Carol peeked around Chief Bert's large wet frame to where he pointed. She spotted The Refuge's housemother huddled in the back of an ambulance, a blanket over her shoulders. Firefighters battled a small blaze behind the Victorian home. The woman didn't appear hurt but frazzled, wet, and cold. Carol ran over.

"Are you all right? What happened?"

The woman nodded. "I'm fine." With a look of confusion, she shook her head. "But I'm not sure. Everyone was gone for the day. I did some grocery shopping, and just as I walked up, I smelled smoke. I opened the front door and almost choked. I dropped my groceries and called 911."

"Do they know where the fire started?" Carol asked.

She shook her head, and they sat waiting.

Finally, a fireman walked up. "It appears that a fire may have started in a downstairs bathroom."

"Do you know if any appliances were left on in the bathroom?"

"No. The girls use the upstairs bathrooms. That would be where their blow-dryers, and irons are plugged in."

"Perhaps a candle?" he removed his helmet.

"No. We don't allow real candles. Just the LED ones."

"Good. Well, the back wall of the bathroom was connected to the kitchen. So the stove and oven suffered the most damage. It's a good thing you called so quickly. Other than water damage and perhaps the one connecting wall, we saved the rest of the house."

The rain intensified, and the fireman moved the housemother further into the ambulance for cover. Carol ran to her truck, retrieving her umbrella. She glanced down the street and froze. Anger rose within her, and she marched down the sidewalk—the wind blew hard against her body. Her thin skirt was no protection against the pelting rain. She paid no mind to her feet, squishing in her sandals, plodding through the puddles. Carol walked a half-block away from the Refuge. She approached the blue Lincoln.

"What are you doing here?" She screamed.

The window slowly slid down. Will Boudreaux blew out a thread of smoke that quickly disappeared in the rain. "Just watching an unfortunate event." He grinned.

"You have a restraining order." She yelled above the pounding storm, furious that he had the gall to show up. "Get outta here, now!"

"Why, Miz Carol. I am within my rights, you know."

"You have no rights here. Now git."

He glared back at her but remained calm. "Oh, but I do. I'm just outside of my 300 feet. And Virginia is nowhere around, right? I mean, we wouldn't want her harmed in that tragic accident over there, now would we?" He took a long slow drag on his cigarette.

"You!" Carol yelled. "You set the fire."

The car window slid up, and Carol heard guttural laughter escaping as it closed. The idling engine roared, and she watched as the car pulled slowly away from the curb, making a U-turn away from the fire.

Carol ran back to the house, slipping and sloshing. Soaked, she dropped her useless umbrellas and found the Chief. "He did it. It was him." Carol pointed in the direction of a street void of moving cars.

Chief Bert followed her finger and shook his head. The hooded rain poncho sat stiffly over his hat, but water dripped from the brim. "What are you going on about?"

"Boudreaux. He set the fire," Carol yelled.

The Chief froze, then searched the street. He stared at The Refuge sign and shook his head. "Nope. He wouldn't do that. We'd catch him for sure."

"Maybe he wouldn't, but he could hire someone! That man is evil."

Chief Bert grabbed the next fireman that walked past. "How soon before we can find out how the fire was started?"

"I'll check with the captain. He'll let you know. This rain helped the fire but will slow down the investigation."

Carol heard the words but became preoccupied as she watched the housemother sitting in the ambulance. Her hunched figure appeared to be crying. Running over, Carol asked, "Are you hurt? Can I help?"

She looked up and dried her tears. "No, I'm not hurt—just overwhelmed. I know God will take care of us. But I'm just not sure how we will rebuild that kitchen. Our mealtime together is so important."

Carol's mind raced, and like a light switched on, she said, "Don't you worry. We'll have this kitchen up and running in no time." She pulled out her phone from her jacket pocket, hitting a contact. She then touched the speakerphone.

"Pastor Brooks? Can I meet with you?"

"Hello, Carol. Where are you?"

"I'm at The Refuge. It caught fire."

"I'm on my way over. I just heard. Is anyone hurt?" His voice rose.

"No. But that's what I wanted to speak with you about. I think we have a project for the church."

"Sure. I'll be right there."

Tapping her foot, she looked around and glanced at her watch. She gave it a few hits before realizing it wasn't working. "Are you kidding me?"

A fireman turned. "Are you all right, ma'am?"

Carol laughed sheepishly. "Yeah," she said as she lifted her wrist. "It's my favorite."

He glanced at the gaudy, bejeweled, wide wrist band with the big white and gold watch face. "Yup. That's a beauty, ma'am."

Carol threw a hand in his direction. "Come by my shop. I got another just like it. Your wife will love it."

He held up his left hand and pointed to a bare ring finger. Smiling, he winked at her and walked off.

"Oh, for goodness, sakes," she said. The innocent flirtation checked her spirit, and as the cold rain poured down, Carol's heated cheeks flushed. *Lord, will you never stop testing me?* She turned her head away from the well-built fireman rolling up the hoses.

CHAPTER 16

Flinging open the door to her apartment, Carol clomped in, and rain swooshed through the entry, adding to the puddle beneath her dripping body. She slammed the door, stripped down, and picked up the heap of wet clothing. She ran practically naked to the laundry nook off the kitchenette and dumped the clothes into the washer, then ran for the bathroom.

Carol showered, and the hot spray soothed her tight muscles. As she turned off the water, she heard a light knocking. Her pulse quickened when she realized she'd forgotten to lock the door. Grabbing a large bath towel, she wrapped it around herself, not bothering to dry off. Her tangled hair stuck to her back as she pulled it free. She peeked out of the bathroom and noticed that her front door was ajar. Instinctively, she dashed, intending to shut it tight, but before she reached it, a head poked in.

"Carol? It's me, Desmond Brooks?"

She reached the door and flung it wide. "What in the heck are you doing here?"

Desmond stood in front of her, but he had already averted his eyes. "I'm so sorry. The door was unlocked, and you didn't answer. I was concerned." Desmond stuttered out further apologies and reached for the knob, pulling the door closed. "I'll just wait out here until you're dressed," he called.

Carol glanced down. Since becoming a Christian, she had vowed to never take her clothes off in front of another man again unless it was her husband. She laughed as she tightened the oversized bath towel around herself.

"Oh, for Pete's sake. Come in out of the rain. I'll be out in a minute."

The front door remained closed until she shut the bathroom door. She heard the front door slowly creak back open. A silky kimono hung on a hook in the bathroom, and she grabbed it, wrapping the flimsy fabric around her body. Looking down at her ample silhouette, she quickly dropped the kimono to the floor and donned a thick terry robe. Catching sight of herself in the mirror, she thought, *I look like a soaking wet retriever.*

Carol walked out, and Desmond stood inside the apartment, his wet, wavy hair falling across his forehead. His light raincoat was apparently water-resistant and was dotted with droplets. He hung back.

"I won't bite. Now, come in, and tell me what in the world you're doing in my apartment?"

"I'm really sorry. I shouldn't have barged in,"

The poor man looked so uncomfortable. "Oh, never mind," said Carol. "How about you go downstairs, and I'll meet you in more suitable attire. We can talk there."

Desmond nodded and headed for the front door.

"Not that door." She pointed to the door leading to the stairway that joined her shop below.

Nodding once again, Desmond left.

Carol dressed quickly and ran barefoot down the steps. She heard voices and listened before she approached.

"Good morning, Pastor." It was John Taylor's voice.

Desmond paused and stuttered before he spoke. "Oh, uh, good morning, Mayor."

Carol heard the mayor chuckle and ask, "So, are you opening up Second Chance today?"

She walked up behind Pastor Desmond, squeezing a hank of her wet hair.

Mayor Taylor breathed deep, and a smile started but quickly faded. He glanced back and forth between Desmond and Carol. "Been out in the rain, have you?"

"Yes, and no. I just got out of the shower." She smiled.

Mayor Taylor glanced again between the two. He nodded and peered at Carol. His voice held no emotion as he said, "I just came from the fire. The chief mentioned you were there, and I was concerned." He glanced at Desmond again. "No need. Looks like you're in good hands." He stepped back. "I best be going. Maybe someone else might need my help."

Carol gaped. Wait a minute, *did he think she and the Pastor?* Maybe in the past, she probably would have been guilty of whatever he thought. But not now. She glanced at Pastor Desmond, but he said nothing. "Wait, John. Come on. You can't possibly think anything—"

John raised a hand and stepped out.

"Mayor, it's definitely not what you think," said Desmond.

John froze. "How do you know what I'm thinking? But you know, folks, it's a good thing. This is a new era. The old south would have a lot to talk about here. Good day."

Desmond's brows furrowed, and he glanced between Carol and John's retreating form. "Aren't you going to say something? You should go after him."

Carol shook her head. *He's just like everyone else I used to know.* "Why? My reputation precedes me, Pastor."

"Well, mine doesn't. And yours shouldn't either. I'm sorry, Carol. This is my fault. I should have waited for you. Chief told me you thought you saw Boudreaux at the fire, and I was concerned."

Swinging around, she glared, and her breathing intensified. "I did see him. And if John, like everyone else, wants to label me as the loose crazy woman in the neighborhood, so be it." She moved toward the door. "Pastor, you better go now. Sorry for the mess-up."

He took a few steps, turned, and patted her shoulder. "Carol, just like everything else, God will take care of this."

"Yeah, yeah. I know He will. But probably not as fast as I want him to. Go on. I'll be fine."

But she wasn't fine. She locked the door after him and glanced around the quiet shop. She was tempted to throw in the towel. This living rightly was hard work. Staring at the flimsy sheer curtain in the back, she recalled how Grady tended to lurk back there. And the time he scared Melanie and Lacey half-to-death when he emerged. It happened just the day before he was killed, which was a life-changer for her.

No. I can't give up. I can't go back. She trudged up the stairs to her apartment and curled up on the sofa. She lay in silence until her eyelids drooped. Exhausted, she slept.

When her cell rang, startling her awake, Carol sat up straight. The events of the morning jumbled in her mind, and she reached for the phone. It was Virginia's Independent Study teacher, and Carol was late picking up.

"Yes, I'm sorry. I'll be there in a minute."

The teacher had been instructed not to allow Virginia to leave school alone, and it was Carol's day to pick up. Retrieving her purse, she ran down the staircase and headed for her car.

Pulling up in front of the school, Carol waved. "Hey, Virginia. Sorry, girl. I had a busy morning. Can you believe it? I fell asleep."

Virginia smiled. "That's okay. I wanted to call Officer Blaine to pick me up, but they wouldn't let me." She picked at her light blue fingernails.

Carol glanced over. "Well, that's good. You can't keep bothering that guy. You'll see him soon enough."

Virginia pouted and stuck a fingernail between her teeth.

Carol reached over and gently slapped her hand down. "Don't do that. And change your polish, will you?"

Virginia drew back as she set her hands under the sides of her thin thighs. "Why? Don't you like blue?"

"Not anymore. Listen, Virginia. I have to tell you something." Carol pulled over to the side of the road and parked. The inside of the car felt steamy and stifling. Carol rolled down the windows welcoming the fresh rain scent, and the cool air revived her. "There was a fire at the Refuge."

Virginia's doe-like eyes flew wide. Questions poured out, and surprisingly, none of them included Blaine. She was genuinely concerned about the housemother and the other girls. Wrapping an arm around Virginia's shoulders, Carol squeezed.

"Everyone is fine. Perfectly fine. No one was hurt. The kitchen is messed up, but I got a plan for that." A frown crossed her face as she thought of Pastor Brooks. They'd never had a chance to discuss the church's help in restoring the kitchen. Instead, their meeting had become a potential scandal.

"God's got our backs." She took a deep breath. "He'll make it right. I promise."

How quickly her doubt diminished, and Carol warmed a little inside, believing again. Right now, the important thing was that Virginia felt safe. Arriving at The Refuge, most of the trucks were gone, but yellow caution tape remained around certain parts of the large home. Between the torrential morning downpour and the firefighter's efforts, the water damage was indistinguishable. They had put the fire out from the rear kitchen entrance, but the assessment team tracked mud and water throughout the house.

Carol parked under the large sycamore tree in front of The Refuge, and Virginia jumped out. The housemother stepped on the front porch and hugged Virginia. The five other girls were already home from school, and they filed out of the house with supplies in their hands. The huddle brought a smile to Carol's face. As she glanced over each girl, the rags and buckets they held assured her that they would be okay. The town seemed to be able to recover from a tragedy without her. Why did she think she was suddenly the solution to everyone's problems? She stepped out of the car and jogged up the steps.

"If you got an extra pair of sweats, I'll help with the cleanup." She stood, hands on her hips.

"What are sweats?" The girls exchanged puzzled expressions.

Carol glared at the housemother. "Oh, for Pete's sake, am I that old?"

"We both are. Come on, I've got an extra pair. Come with me."

After a long afternoon of cleanup at The Refuge, Carol went home and readied herself for the second shower of her day. Happily exhausted, the manual labor had kept her mind off more troubling things.

Convincing herself she was too tired for Bible Study, she sat and picked up a magazine. She tossed it aside. The Bible Study was at Melanie's house. *Did Desmond tell her what happened this morning?* Nothing transpired between them, so of course, Melanie would understand. *Wouldn't she?*

Retreating to the bathroom, Carol went through the motions of getting ready. Primping herself, she leaned in close to the over-the-sink mirror. She smoothed on her foundation and applied a heavy hand of blush. The lipstick she chose was darker than she normally wore, and she applied it liberally. After multiple strokes of mascara, she blinked and nodded to herself. Putting her best face forward had always helped when facing her accusers. And she had faced many. She fluffed her wild, red mane and peered at her reflection in the mirror. Her dolled-up face gazed back.

Will Melanie really believe that nothing happened? She gripped the sides of the sink, then reached over and pushed the lid of the toilet down and sat. Carol struggled to push out thoughts of John Taylor and others who might accuse her of promiscuity again. She closed her eyes and prayed. A wave of peace finally swept over her, and at least for the time being, the internal turmoil passed. She stood and plucked some tissue from a box and wiped the excess color from her lips and cheeks.

Carol stood at Melanie's front door, trying not to fidget. She knocked, then smoothed down her dark gray A-line dress. She adjusted the wide belt hanging low around her hips. Plain and simple. Even her shoes—black ballet flats.

The door flung open, and Tina, Melanie's next-door neighbor, cheerfully gushed, "Welcome, welcome. Come in." She pushed out the screen door, but her smile quickly turned to a frown. "Did you just come from a funeral or something?"

Carol looked down at her dull, drab dress. "Ha. Ha. Ha."

Tina grabbed her hand and pulled her inside. "I'm just kidding...sort of. This is a new style for you, isn't it?" She pointed, then laughed. "You know we're two peas in a pod. We both love color and attention." Tina yelled toward the kitchen. "Melanie! Carol's here, and I forgot my notebook. I'll be right back."

Tina left, and Melanie joined Carol, hugging her. "Have a seat. I'm just putting out the coffee service." Melanie moved toward the kitchen.

"Wait. We need to talk."

"Oh, honey, you've had quite a day. Desmond told me all about it." She smiled.

Carol saw nothing but kindness there. "I'm so sorry. His reputation—"

"Reputation? It'll be fine. We got bigger things to tackle. Remember, we're Superheroes." Melanie raised her arm, flexing her muscle in a strong-man pose.

Before Carol could respond, the doorbell rang and continued ringing until all the women attending had arrived. She smiled, relishing the joyful mood all around her.

CHAPTER 17

When the Bible Study came to a close, Melanie asked Carol to share the kitchen restoration idea for The Refuge. She hesitated. After the fire, the kitchen needed serious work, and it seemed like such a good idea. But now it seemed daunting, and these women were busy with their own lives and families, and she wasn't so sure that she was the one to lead it. Who would follow her?

"Well, The Refuge needs help, and I thought...I'd like for us to take on restoring the kitchen." Carol began slowly and had difficulty looking each woman in the eye. Melanie's reassuring nod gave her courage, and the faces smiling back at her melted her insecurities. She couldn't contain her passion for helping the poor girls, and coupled with her anger over the destruction, she rushed ahead, her ideas spilling out. By the time she'd finished, their warm reception had floored her. They jumped in, and their suggestions tumbled over one another, and Carol took note of every proposal.

Lyla, the president of the Women's Ministry and Big Joe's wife was especially excited. "I'll talk to Pastor Desmond.. I'm sure he'll agree. Hey, whoever can make it, let's present the idea at the Town Council Meeting tomorrow. We'll get lots of volunteers." She eased forward, raising her large frame to full height. "Well, I gots to go. Big Joe is prob'ly about to go crazy, trying to put our little ones to bed," She reached her arms out to Carol. "Get on up here, Carol. You don't expect me to bend over you. Why we'd both land up on the floor."

Laughter broke out as the rest of the crowd stood to leave. Carol thanked each for their support. "Getting the approval from the church means everything," said Carol.

"Pssshhh!" Lyla waved her off. "That's what we're here for. All about doing God's work. See you at Town Meeting tomorrow. We'll present your plan there. Bye, ladies."

Carol frowned. "Town Meeting? Do I really need to be there?"

Melanie nodded. "Yup. It's the next step to get the ball rolling."

One by one, the ladies filed out, saying their goodbyes and sharing their excitement about their roles in this new project. Or, as they called it, a ministry. Carol stood in awe. A little melancholy and a little troubled, but in good company.

Tina was the last to go. Tapping a finger against her bottom coral lip, she nodded, her bouncing ombré curls moving rhythmically. "You know, I like the look. A little conservative, for you…" she waved a hand down her bejeweled jeans and giggled. "…and maybe for me too. But hey, you got a good idea."

Carol stood and hugged her. "Thanks. I'm pretty excited about this project."

"Yes. Me too. I'm hoping I can be in on the decorating and painting team." She scrunched her nose and held up her hands. "My nails don't work well with a hammer."

"I think that can be arranged. Goodnight." Carol waved as Tina pranced across the lawn.

Carol helped pick up plates and cups. She blew out the large three-wick candles scattered about the room. Melanie always set such a sweet ambiance. She started toward the kitchen and somewhat dreaded being alone with Melanie. It was still hard for Carol to accept forgiveness.

"Melanie?"

"Yes?"

Carol blinked. "Great study tonight."

"It was, wasn't it? Every Monday, I struggle with wanting to cancel this study after a long day of work. But then, after everyone gets here, I'm so thankful we do it. I sleep a little better on Monday nights."

Carol bit her lip. "Melanie, about today."

Melanie dried her hands and raised a palm. "Stop. Today is over. For goodness' sake, if someone had a problem with it, they'll need to deal with it."

"But the Pastor. His reputation."

With her hands on her hips, Melanie leaned forward, "Carol, he's not a Boy Scout, you know." She paused. "Well, maybe he is. But I'm not. And look, we're together."

"But Mel, you're just kind of naturally good. I'm not like that."

"Hush now. You know I have skeletons in my closet. We all do, and none of us are naturally good. If we've confessed and repented, and received God's forgiveness, then all of us should have an extra measure of grace for each other, as well as ourselves."

All of us? Carol thought of John Taylor. "Yes, I guess they should, but maybe they can't." She pictured his broad, proud shoulders walking away.

Taking Carol's hand, Melanie led her to the kitchen table. They sat, and Carol remained silent. A thin line drew across her lips.

"Is it John?" Asked Melanie.

Carol nodded. "It's just not meant to be. You know, we connected that one time. It was so easy. But it was pretty surface stuff, you know."

"Of course, it was your first encounter. He's a good man, Carol. Give it time."

"You don't understand. He thinks I was *with* Pastor Brooks." She didn't know what she expected to see in Melanie, but a smile arose.

Melanie shrugged, "Well, you were, weren't you?"

"What?" Carol stood. "Do you really think—"

"Carol, sit down. My goodness, you were *with* him. Just like I'm *with* you right now. Come on. Of course, I know nothing went on. It's called trust, and I trust you both." Melanie's face grew serious. "Carol, how much do you know about Mayor Taylor?"

"I don't know anything. I know he was married once. That's it. Heck, until you introduced him to me, I didn't even know who the mayor was. I never paid any mind to politics."

Melanie nodded. "He married late in life, and she was years younger. First time for both. It didn't last too long, and because he'd always been involved in the town council, everyone knew his business. About five years into the marriage, she left him. Ran off with some rich casino developer."

Carol gaped and pressed a hand to her chest. "That's terrible. How long ago was that?"

"I'm not sure."

"I had no idea, but I've been so busy with my own affairs, I never paid much attention to anyone else's."

"Well, it's been a while, and believe it or not, when you two ate breakfast at the Mockingbird last week, the talk was all over Main Street."

"Oh, the poor man," said Carol.

"No. Not the poor man. Everyone was excited that he might be seeing someone. He's the most eligible bachelor in Bay Town." Melanie touched Carol's hand. "There's no denying the attraction. Just like between Desmond and me. Doesn't make sense in our world. But you can't let that dark voice tell you that you're not good enough. Don't go there. I did, and it took me a long time to climb out."

"But he thinks something happened."

"Then tell him otherwise. You're a strong woman, Carol. Set him straight. He doesn't trust women. That's for sure. But show him he can trust you."

Carol thought about the things she still struggled with. She'd had her chance once. Someone much like the mayor. That was a long time ago, but the longing in her heart and body for companionship never diminished. Yet, the instant gratification of fleeting encounters always left her feeling empty. At this point in her life, she was learning about God's true love. Could she trust herself with an earthly love that was pure and not tarnished?

On Tuesday morning, Carol went about her routine, opening up for the day. The afterglow of bible study and the friendly women faded, and she dreaded facing her friends and neighbors. A dialogue of defense played in her head, and her arguments took center stage. She'd been here before. After a wild night, she always imagined the whispers of gossipers around her. Yet she never minded before. But this last year had been different. Her neighbors were important to her now. As she swept outside, she readied herself for judgment or something like it. The community seemed to be out in full force, but with every encounter, kindness followed.

"Hey, Miss Carol." Max, the florist, waved at her from three doors down.

Chief Bert drove by with a broad smile, and any passerby responded with a friendly 'Hey.' That endearing southern charm. It all blessed Carol. Even the Senior Walkers smiled and nodded in their matching athletic suits and one-pound weights in hand.

Carol finished sweeping and stepped inside. Her eyes rested on the wall covered with wooden plaques. Scrolled words of inspiration and encouragement stared back at her, and strength rose as she glanced over from one to the next. Her gaze stopped.

Without wood, a fire goes out. Without gossip, a quarrel dies down.

They didn't know! How would they? Carol's heart melted as she thought of each person she had encountered that morning. John never told anyone. She just assumed he had. *I have to talk to him.* Turning abruptly, she bumped a three-legged end table. A lamp teetered, and she rushed to grasp it before it tumbled to the ground. *Slow down, girl.* She smoothed down her hair, straightened her skirt, and took two slow steps but quickly grabbed her keys from the counter. *He might still be at the Mockingbird.* Carol ran.

She barged into the bustling café and looked around. The crowd had changed already. Too late for early opening business owners and people heading to work. Too late for…her gaze stopped on a tall man at the counter. His sandy hair graced the top of his white collar. A smile broke across Carol's face, and she stepped forward. As he turned, a mustache bushed out beneath a sizeable protruding nose. He nodded and scooted past her.

Yes, too late. She walked back to Second Chance. Her shoulders drooped, and she brushed her hand across the night-blooming jasmine bushes planted beneath the magnolia trees. Chief Bert waited up ahead, and she picked up her pace.

"Hey, Chief. Everything, okay?" She unlocked the shop, propped open the door, and waved him in.

"I was going to ask you the same thing." He tipped his head, removing his hat.

"Yeah, good. Why?"

"Well, you were pretty upset yesterday about Boudreaux."

"Go on."

"It was arson. The fire was set."

"I knew it." Carol threw up her hands. "Let's get him."

"Hold on there, Miss Carol. We can't go arresting somebody on a hunch."

"Watch me," said Carol. "I think I know where to find him."

Drawing back, he frowned. "What?" He gave her a sideways glance. "You been doing some investigating of your own?"

"I was in Pascagoula. That's where I first saw him, and I think he followed me." As if the dots connected, Carol followed the signs she hadn't thought of before. *The gas station. My business card.* Carol twirled on her heels and clapped her hands. "That's how he showed up here." She went on to explain the incident at the drug store and the gas station. She spoke so rapidly, that the chief had to slow her down as she rambled on.

"And you're just now telling me this?"

"Everything's been happening so fast. You know he's behind the fire. He was there, Chief."

"I think you might be right. But we better take it slow."

Carol chuckled. Why did everything in this new life have to go slow? Blaine and Virginia flashed in her brain. *Virginia.* "Not this time. We got him."

"Not yet. We don't. If it's him, Boudreaux will slip up, and we'll catch him. We just have to get him before he gets Virginia."

The mention of her name tempered Carol's excitement. "He won't get her. I won't let him."

"Miss Carol, trust me, okay? We're stepping up the watch. You just report anything you see."

She nodded.

"Good. Have a good day." He pulled on his hat and walked to the door, stepping aside as a customer walked in. He nodded. "Oh, Miss Carol, are you coming to the Town Council meeting tonight? It might be good to have you there. I'm sure the fire will come up."

Carol nodded, and a knot grew in her throat. John would be there.

CHAPTER 18

The garish parking lot lights clashed with the quaint old City Hall building. Substantial and square, the red brick historic structure emitted a nostalgic warmth. The scene inside was anything but. Carol squeezed through the crowds and saw Melanie across the foyer. She called out, but the deafening chatter drowned out her voice. With hands raised, holding onto her purse, she pushed through.

"Whoa! That's like trudging through a swamp. Where'd all these people come from?" Carol hugged her friends.

The Women's Ministry of Bay Town surrounded Carol as they chattered in excitement.

"Ain't this great." Lyla gripped her large purse tightly across her chest.

Tina stood on her tip-toes, wearing the highest heels in the group, searching for someone. Suddenly, she raised her hand and waved. The bangles on her wrist tingled loudly.

"Rudy! Rudy! Over here." Heads turned. Now nobody could miss where Carol and all the Women's Ministry stood. Rudy, Tina's husband, squeezed through the crowd, and she cooed. "Hey, Sweetie." She kissed him and said, "So glad you made it."

He shook his head and grimaced. "Did I have a choice?"

Carol loved the sweet exchange.

Big Joe side-stepped towards the group, and he gripped Rudy's shoulder. "They need us tonight, brother."

Rudy extended a hand. "You got it."

"The young 'uns all taken care of?" Lyla asked.

"Yes, ma'am. In the good hands of the Almighty with the babysitter."

As the huddle conversed, Carol remained quiet.

Melanie placed a hand on her elbow. "You okay?"

Carol nodded as she glanced down, barely able to see her feet in the tightly bunched crowd. Feeling a little claustrophobic, she wiggled her toes. It somehow made her feel somewhat in control of what could be a potentially explosive evening.

The residents of Bay Town were a quiet bunch. Still, ever since the trafficking crimes committed last year, it didn't take much for the residents to jump on any looming threat to their community. Word got out about the fire possibly being arson, and it was most likely the cause for the whole city converging on the Town Hall meeting.

Chief Bert nodded and waved everyone in. The crowd was so large, by the time the Women's Ministry entered, the seating was full.

"The meeting is about to begin. The seats are all taken, so please fill in quietly along the side walls and in the back. Silence your cell phones and your voices, folks." He bellowed loud enough that everyone immediately obeyed.

Carol looked down at her dark, drab dress.

Tina touched her shoulder and raised a brow.

"I thought I might need to look a little more serious." Carol shrugged.

"Serious? Okay, but don't let it mess with the heart."

Carol nodded and followed the ladies in. *The heart.* That was already getting messed with. As she eased through the double doors, she peeked towards the platform. The mayor conversed quietly with the council members sitting front and center with the overhead lights shining directly atop his sandy-gray hair. Her heart lurched.

"Call to order." He appeared so official hitting the gavel, but as he looked up, his friendly face brightened and eased the tension in the room.

"Thank you all for coming. I'm always thankful for our good citizens of Bay Town who rise to the call to help one another. Now, I must ask that we keep to an orderly pace here. We'll attend to all the normal city business first and leave the rest of the evening for why I assume you are all here."

A low rumble of voices rolled, and Chief Bert, standing aside the extended platform of seated council members, raised his hands. A hush landed, and business proceeded. Carol eased so far back into the crowd that she felt the railing along the wall press into her spine. She pulled one shoulder behind Lyla to hide from the view of the Council seats.

Mayor Taylor did an excellent job of running through the docket of old business. Before long, he asked for a motion for new business. A sea of hands waved all over the room. The mayor perused the crowd and pointed to Pastor Desmond standing in the back of the room.

"Pastor Brooks?" said the Mayor.

Carol froze. No other name could have emitted a stronger emotion. Out of all the raised hands in the packed room, Desmond was chosen. After the brief uncomfortable encounter on the day of the fire, Carol's defenses were up, and she wasn't sure where she stood, but she hadn't expected this. Something in her spirit rose. It felt like hope. If John and Desmond had straightened out the misunderstanding, and that's indeed what it was, maybe she still had a chance. Carol shook herself. *A chance for what?* She leaned out from the wall to listen.

Desmond took a step forward, his hands resting casually in his front pockets. "Mayor, the Women's Ministry of Bay Town would like to propose a Committee to help restore the kitchen at The Refuge."

Questions shot out faster than anyone could stop them.

"What about that fire?"

"Was it arson?"

"Did you get the person who set it?

"How did it start?"

The mayor pounded his gavel.

Chief Bert stepped up on the platform, next to the giant American flag mounted on the wall behind the council members. His uniform, coupled with the symbol of freedom, imposed a quiet reverence, and as he raised his hands once more, the room hushed.

Nodding, Mayor Taylor then pointed to the front row. A firefighter in uniform stood, but the mayor glanced to the back of the room once more.

"Pastor, if you don't mind. We'll return to you shortly. I think now would be a good time for the fire captain to give us a report before we proceed."

Desmond nodded.

"Thanks, Pastor. We'll address the committee next." The Mayor gave the fire captain a nod.

The detailed report read like a police blotter, and the crowd was quiet until the suspicion of arson was mentioned. Instantly, as if in unison, the crowd's breath drew in all at once, followed by rising whispers. Mayor Taylor raised his gavel, and the crowd hushed once again. He set it gently down.

Carol marveled at the mayor's authority. She never cared too much for order and discipline, but something inside her found new respect.

Lowering his papers, the captain addressed the crowd. "It's conclusive that the fire was set. A number of appliances, small and large, were plugged into the same outlet via a daisy chain of power strips. None were surge protectors, and all appeared to be nicked and faulty. The folks at The Refuge assured us they never used power strips, as the home is old and in need of electrical renovation."

"Is there an assessment of damage?" The mayor asked.

His hand rested on the gavel as he gazed over the crowd. He stopped. An overhead lamp shined on Carol, and a soft haze hovered in the air. She pushed back her hair and felt a glow in her cheeks. Her gaze locked with the handsome Mayor John Taylor. Whatever his eyes held, she couldn't make it out. She broke the brewing fixation by looking elsewhere.

The fire captain interrupted the short silence. "I'll leave that for the insurance adjuster."

Still, an awkward silence rested over the room as the mayor continued to gaze towards the wall where Carol hid. A Council member touched the mayor's arm, and as if in a trance, he couldn't seem to respond but kept on staring.

A giggle rose from the group of women standing around Carol. Melanie poked her in the ribs, and Carol paid no mind, wanting to melt into the ground like the wicked witch in the Wizard of Oz.

"Mayor?" The police chief's powerful voice boomed.

It seemed to do the trick as the mayor shook his head. "Uh...Yes...the damage, captain?"

Another wave of laughter went around the room. Under the bright hanging lamps, a visible red flush rose from the mayor's neck, covering his face. With a finger, he pulled at his tight collar and loosened his tie. A sheepish smile covered his face. "Sorry for the distraction, folks."

"Mayor?" Pastor Brooks spoke out.

The mayor immediately nodded and pointed to the back. "Yes, Pastor Brooks? You have the floor. By all means, take it." He chuckled as the crowd joined in.

"We're waiting for the claims adjuster to be scheduled. But the church would like to begin raising support for the restoration. And we're ready to begin cleaning up as well." He paused. "Mayor, I think the Women's Ministry of Bay Town could better address the situation. Could we turn this over to them?"

Carol peeked out behind Lyla.

Mayor Taylor smiled broadly. "Yes, of course. Ladies?"

Carol knew he was smiling. She could tell by the sound of his kind voice. She couldn't help but be warmed by what she heard and finally peeked out so she could see him.

Lyla spoke. "Mayor, we want to begin clean up this week. We all ready to start, and I have a Volunteer Schedule here." Lyla held up a bright pink clipboard.

"Thank you. Your name, please?" He raised a friendly hand. "For the record, here."

"Lyla. Lyla Johnson." She gave him a sideways glance. "Why, Mayor, I saw you last week at the Mockingbird Café. You was having breakfast with the beautiful Miz Carol here." Lyla stepped aside and ushered a hand towards Carol.

Once again, she was on center stage for the whole Town Council. Friendly laughter fluttered throughout the room.

Mayor Taylor banged the gavel lightly and raised his hands. "Thank you, Mrs. Johnson." He glanced at the council members. "All in favor of letting these kind ladies commence work?"

"Aye's," and nodding affirmations rang out.

The mayor nodded at Lyla. "Please feel free to take sign-ups." He looked at his watch. "Due to the time, I adjourn this meeting, and we'll pick up in two weeks. Thanks, folks." The gavel banged, and the mayor wiped a hand across his forehead.

"Whoo-hoo, girl." Tina clapped and hugged Carol. "He's got it bad. Get those mourning clothes off."

"Tina!" The crowd of women collectively yelled.

"What? I meant the style. She needs her groove back." Tina waved a hand in the air while the other planted firmly on her hip.

The crowd seemed to empty quickly. Pastor Brooks walked over and hugged Melanie, who stood right next to Carol. The women continued to tease in a friendly manner as Carol shook her head. Desmond raised his brows, and the group quieted. Smiling, he nodded at Carol. "You okay?"

Carol shook her head. That's why he was the pastor. Sensitive enough to care but strong enough to command when needed.

"I'm closing up, people." Chief Bert flickered the lights, and the crowd filed outside

"Carol, you didn't even get to give your proposal," said Melanie.

"Ain't that a relief." Carol blew out a breath. "I think everyone got the gist." She pointed to Lyla in the parking lot, getting signatures for volunteering all around. "Besides, I got more than my share of the floor tonight."

"Good evening, Miss Melanie." The mayor nodded. "Pastor, thanks for your help. It seems I was under a spell in there." He smiled at Carol.

She turned and gazed up. Every time he stood next to her, she was startled all over again by his height.

"Anytime, John." Desmond extended a hand, but John didn't seem to notice. "Okay, I guess we better go."

Melanie mouthed to Carol, "Call me." And she and Desmond left.

Carol and John stood gazing at one another. "I'm sorry…." They spoke simultaneously. "No, you go…."

Carol raised a hand. "Okay, me first. You're not still angry? I mean, you left the other day pretty hot after the fire." She giggled. "No pun intended."

"Yes. And I apologize. I jumped to conclusions, but thanks to Pastor Brooks, he came after me and straightened me out. I'm so sorry."

Carol smiled. "So all that staring in there was you apologizing?"

He chuckled. "Maybe." A deep sigh escaped. "But really, I just couldn't keep my eyes off you."

She shook her head. Her long waves flowed around her shoulders. "Come on, Mayor. That was embarrassing. I get enough attention in this town…well, I used to, anyway."

He stared back at her, not saying a word, but his yearning was killing her, and she wanted to kiss him. Her pulse raced, and she bit her lip hard. She took a deep breath and tried counting to ten, but it didn't work. Nothing worked, and she couldn't stop herself. Standing on her toes, she quickly kissed his cheek. Before she could lower herself, he wrapped his arms around her, lifted her a little, and pressed his lips over hers. The softness both hypnotized and frightened her, and she knew she should pull away. Instead, he did. Stepping back, he took her hand and led her to a darkened corner of the lot, away from the garish overhead lights. Wrapping her in his arms, he kissed her again and again.

The scent of the night-blooming jasmine floated through the air enveloping the couple. Spring crickets chirped quietly, and as the twinkling stars dotted the bright skies, Carol felt like she was in a dream. Staring back at her, John brushed a hand across her cheek and lowered his head. Her heels lifted off the ground again, and he lifted her chin, placing another soft kiss. She felt a wave of joy flood through her. The stubble of a light shadow on his face brushed her soft skin, but she welcomed the sandpaper reality of the deep, lingering moment.

Carol eased back down and pulled in a long breath. "Whoa there, Mayor…." He put a finger to her lips.

"My turn. It's John, not Mayor, and I don't know what's going on here or where this is taking us." His fingers brushed through her hair. "But we're not teenagers, so I don't know about you, but I'm ready for something more than dating."

Carol drew back. "Wait a minute. We haven't even been on a date." She gulped. *Don't say anything stupid. Lord help me.*

"That's my point. I want to get to know you, and that

doesn't mean casual dating. God knows that's all I've done for a while, but this time, I don't plan on dating anyone else. Carol, right now, I only want you."

Too quickly, a fire rose within. "Oh no, you don't. You can't have me. I'm not giving myself to no man!"

His mouth gaped. "I'm so sorry. I didn't mean what that sounded like. I would never take advantage of you. I apologize."

Carol winced realizing, maybe she'd insulted his southern gentleman sensibilities, but he took one of her hands in his and clasped it tightly. His strong hands felt so good in hers. He stared intently and pulled her in close, holding her to his chest. His scent intoxicated her, and she rested her head, relishing the comfort of his steady heartbeat.

CHAPTER 19

With everyone at the Town Council Meeting, Officer Blaine sat quietly in his squad car. He checked his watch. *It should be over*, he thought. The night was shrouded in clouds that threatened more rain. He grabbed the long, black flashlight resting on the passenger seat and stepped into the damp street, the smell of wet asphalt and mud hanging in the air. Branches of the sycamore trees hung over his head like monstrous arms. He closed and locked his door.

A curtain in the upstairs window of the old Victorian spread aside, and Virginia peeked out. Blaine looked up and couldn't help but smile, but he didn't wave. The night was too dark. He walked across the yard and flipped on his flashlight. Waving it back and forth, he disappeared behind the house.

Virginia stared down, pressing her forehead against the window. She saw Rodney's squad car and smiled. Something pecked at the glass. She jumped back but just as quickly peered out again and listened as another sound tinked. This time she saw a few pebbles roll off the roof below the gable. She let go of the curtain, and within minutes Virginia was downstairs. Creeping quietly out onto the front porch, she closed the door and tiptoed down the front steps in her bare feet. She wore light pajama shorts and a cami, barely covered by a thin robe. Pulling it around her, she whispered, "Rodney? Is that you?"

A rustling sound came from the bushes, and she turned just as a hand clamped over her mouth, muffling her scream. The air smelled of stale cigarettes and sweat. Raising a leg, she threw her heel back and kicked. The person holding her seethed in a hushed word, and the hand gripped her tighter. Tears ran down her face as she clawed the fingers binding her. Her eyes widened as a bright ray flashed from around the bushes. The light blinded both Virginia and her assailant.

"Let her go! Police!" Rodney's familiar voice rang out in the dark.

For a quick second, relief flooded Virginia's mind, but the man squeezed her more tightly. She jabbed her elbow in her tormentor's side, and at the same time, she sunk her teeth into a rough, bony finger. He screamed, and Virginia wriggled free, falling to the ground.

"Rodney!" She screamed.

"Virginia, run! You there, step a—" Rodney's voice shut off, and his body fell with a sickening thud.

Virginia screamed again and crawled to his still body. She looked up, and another man with a wooden bat stood over Officer Blaine. With one beefy arm, the man with the bat snatched her away.

She kicked and clawed at him, screaming all the while, and he struggled to contain her.

A door slammed, and pounding footsteps came from the house. The housefather, a short but sizeable imposing figure, ran down the walkway. Without hesitation, he drew back his hand, and his fist crunched the man's face. The bat fell out of one hand, and he let go of his hold of Virginia with the other.

The housefather faced a taller, thinner man who was cursing and shaking his bleeding hand.

"Go on, Virginia. Get in the house and call 911."

She hovered over Officer Blaine. "But, what about Rodney?" Virginia sobbed, her face streaked with dirt and falling tears.

"Virginia, do as you're told, now."

The man with the bat rose and Virginia screamed as he held it over the housefather. He dove for the man's feet, tackling him down. Grabbing the bat, the housefather threw it aside and punched the man again. The man lay stunned, moaning. Virginia screamed again.

The housefather, still on his knees, turned just as the man with the hurt finger kicked him hard. He tumbled back and flipped to standing. The man cradled the hurt appendage, and the housefather lunged for it. Grabbing the finger, he twisted. The man cried out in pain and stumbled backward, falling over the other man on the ground. "Come on, let's get outta here." They staggered and ran behind the house.

The housefather stood, panting. He nodded to his wife, standing on the front porch.

She held a cell phone to her ear and trotted to her husband. "Police are on their way."

She knelt by Officer Blaine's crumpled body and lay a hand on Virginia's shoulder. A trickle of dark liquid seeped from beneath his head. "Oh dear God, no," she whispered.

Virginia bent over him, cradling his head in her arms. "He's bleeding! Help! We need help." His eyes shifted, and he seemed to focus on her. "I'm here, Rodney," she whispered but his eyes rolled back into his head, and he went limp.

Sirens screeched in the distance, growing closer as the fire trucks drew nearer and nearer. The Refuge housefather waved the paramedics over. He pulled Virginia up and moved her aside. She struggled as he held her tight. The first responder worked quickly as two others retrieved a gurney. Lifting Blaine onto the bed, they raised it, then wheeled him to the waiting emergency vehicle. Virginia stood shaking.

Patting her shoulder, the housefather said. "Let me report this to the chief. Then I'll see if someone can drive you to the hospital."

She nodded and ran to the ambulance. "Rodney!" she cried out.

He was strapped in with an oxygen mask covering his mouth and nose. His head rolled to the side, and Virginia waved from the rear of the vehicle. He didn't respond, and lowering her hand, she clenched her robe and sobbed.

The automatic doors of the hospital slid open as Desmond and Melanie rushed in. Chief Bert had called the pastor who was with Melanie. They left their dinner and drove straight to the hospital. The receptionist was on the phone, and the two waited.

Melanie stopped. "Whoa. I haven't been here since last year." She clutched Desmond's arm. They had been treated here after the human trafficking raid, and Desmond had taken the worst of it physically. But it was the emotional trauma that made Melanie stop short.

"Are you okay?" Desmond pulled Melanie in close and kissed the top of her head.

"I'm fine, but that's a night I want to forget." Melanie forced a smile.

"We will," Desmond assured her. "Has Carol called back yet?"

"No, I've left messages, but she's not answering. She's probably the best person for Virginia right now."

The receptionist replaced the phone and asked, "Can I help you?"

"We're here to see Officer Blaine?" Desmond asked.

"Are you family?"

"No. Friends," said Melanie.

"I'm sorry, only the family can go back right now."

Before Melanie could answer, Virginia's pathetic wails came from the hallway, and Melanie ran to join her. The Refuge housefather and Virginia walked side-by-side. His arms wrapped around her shoulders.

"They won't let me see Rodney. I just want to see him." Virginia's streaked face matched her disheveled clothing. She clasped and unclasped her hands while continually swiping at her face and hair.

The housefather shook his head. "They're running tests, but they might have to do some surgery. He got hit pretty bad."

Melanie moved Virginia toward the lobby seating area, and the men followed.

The housefather explained Officer Blaine's condition as best he could. He glanced at Virginia, then spoke quietly. "It's not good. He may have a depressed skull fracture. They're going to observe him for a few days at least." He winced. "A baseball bat. Can you imagine? I didn't get there soon enough."

"Sure you did. We've got Officer Blaine on the prayer chain. He's in God's hands. You did well." Desmond nodded in assurance.

"He has a concussion, and he'll need stitches too. They think he might have also broken his shoulder or an arm. He's out and hasn't responded yet."

Desmond's cell rang. "I'm sorry, I have to get this. It's the Chief." He pointed to his phone. "Yes, Chief?...No can't get in. Only family is allowed....Oh. All right then." A grin broke across his face, and he nodded at Melanie. He clicked off, slid the phone into his pocket, and stepped over to the reception desk.

"Excuse me, ma'am. May I go in to see Officer Blaine as clergy?"

"Are you registered as a chaplain here?" He started to shake his head, and she raised a finger. "Sure. Give me your Driver's License, please."

"Thank you, but if anyone else asks, Officer Blaine has no family in town, and the Chief of Police is tied up and will be here shortly. He asked that I update him on the officer's condition."

The receptionist nodded and handed back the license and a temporary badge. "Go on down that corridor and turn left at the end. Keep following the signs to the ER. Just tell them you're clergy."

CHAPTER 20

Early the next morning, Carol stood in front of the antique armoire. She'd tried on many outfits and finally settled on one. She jumped over the pile with a light step, humming as she spun around. Breakfast with the mayor. Now that was a step up.

Applying her make-up, she used a light touch. She glossed her lips and relived John's soft touch from the night before. *Was that a dream or what?* Picking up the dress she wore the night before, she held it to her nose. His light, clean scent. *Nope, not dreaming.* Carol smiled.

She unplugged her phone from the charger, and the small box above her door clanged. The doorbell she had installed on the front of the shop rang upstairs also. Barefoot, she dashed down the stairs, checking her phone along the way.

"Shoot." Four missed calls from Melanie. Carol's cell phone had run out of charge last night. The doorbell rang again. "Coming. Hold on."

Flinging open the door, she squinted as the sun hit her, and she lifted a hand to shade the light.

"Chief? What are you doing here?"

"May I come in?" He glanced down at her feet. "Are you going all hippie on us again?"

She wiggled her purple polished toes. "Hold on. I'll get my shoes."

"That's okay. This won't take long."

"What? What's happened, Chief?"

He hit his hat on his thigh. "There was another incident at The Refuge last night."

"Again?" Carol grabbed his arm. "Was it Virginia?"

"She's fine. She's okay. A little shook up. Well, a lot shook up." He paused.

"And?"

"Officer Blaine's in the hospital. He's hurt bad. He's hurt real bad." Chief Bert choked.

"It was him again, wasn't it? Boudreaux. He won't stop. We have to get—"

"Did you hear what I said?" Irritation hung on his words. "Officer Blaine is in the hospital. I know what we need to do. I'm just asking for your help to do it my way. I think you know more than you're telling me."

Carol's heart dropped. "I'm so sorry. Is he going to be okay?" She asked, diverting his accusation.

"He's pretty bad. It's a waiting game at this point. He got a pretty nasty concussion. Someone tried to abduct Virginia when he was on a stakeout."

"What? That's ridiculous." Carol scrunched her nose. "Any idiot would know that's not going to work."

"Yes, unless that idiot meant to hurt Blaine too."

"What about Virginia? Where is she?" Carol's voice escalated.

"She got the day off school to sit down at the hospital. Melanie's with her now. I'll take you there if you'd like. But we have to talk."

"No, I'll drive myself. I just need to get Tina to open up for me this morning."

Chief Bert left, and the shop phone rang. "All right, Mel, I'm coming," Carol yelled as she ran for the phone.

But it wasn't Melanie.

The call went to voicemail before she could get there. Carol listened. "Carol? Please, it's me, Eleanor Perrin. Please. Please call me."

The voice was frantic, and Carol called her back without hesitation. "Hello, Mrs. Perrin?"

"Oh, thank God. Please, I don't know what to do. They won't give her back. My daughter. They're refusing to let me see her. I just want to take her away from here. Please meet me? I have no one else to call." Her voice sounded genuine, but it had before. Carol almost waited for it to change.

She hesitated. Eleanor was hysterical, but that was not unusual. Every encounter with her had been frenetic or paranoid. But the woman needed help. It was her daughter. *Oh, Lord, wisdom, please?* Instantly the thought arose that she didn't have the right to call on God after taking matters into her own hands. A hint of wisdom nudged her that it was false thinking, but she ignored it and barged ahead with a plan.

"Yes, I can meet you. Can you come to Second Chance.?"

"I don't have a car. I've never...." Her voice broke.

"I can pick you up. Where are you?"

"I'm at my daughter's Social Worker's office in Jackson."

Carol went silent. That was three hours away. But it sounded legit. She wasn't sure she could get Tina to run the shop for the rest of the day. "Mrs. Perrin, could I speak with the Social Worker?" Carol took a chance that Eleanor was really there. She heard some shuffling, and a strange voice spoke.

"Hello, who is this please?"

"Hi, this is Carol Scape. I'm a...a friend of Eleanor Perrin's. Is there any chance you could call a ride for her? And send her to my address in Bay Town. I could send you the money by phone."

"Are you sure, Mrs. Scape? Hang on." Carol heard the woman giving instructions. "Okay, Eleanor is out of the room right now. A clerk is attending to her. Are you sure you want to get involved? We've not had any progress with this woman, and her daughter has been temporarily placed."

"Yes, Yes, I'm sure."

"And you want to secure her a ride and not the bus?"

"I don't think Mrs. Perrin is the bus type. A ride would be better."

"That will be awfully expensive."

"I know. It's fine. By the way, how's her daughter? Is she safe? Is she cooperating?"

Carol thought of Acadia and immediately of the other young girl. Wanting to help both, she had to concentrate on one at a time.

"Yes, she's safe. Not very cooperative, but manageable. But that's not your concern."

Carol bit her lip. She took the reprimand as from God himself. "Yes, I know. But I'd like to help with Mrs. Perrin. I just can't leave to pick her up right now, so if you could help me out here." There was silence. "I mean, aren't you about reuniting families?" A loud huff blew out across the line. Carol regrouped her thoughts. "Listen, I work with The Refuge down here."

"The Refuge?" The worker went on to ask questions, confirming the house parents' identity, the address, and details that confirmed that Carol knew the organization well. After she seemed satisfied, she agreed to help. "I can send her down. What are your intentions?"

"Well, I'm not sure. I guess I'm going to have to let the Lord lead me on that one."

Another silence. Carol winced. But when the woman spoke, her tone took on a much friendlier vibe. "Well, you can't go wrong with that. But let me warn you. Eleanor Perrin is very unstable. We've had her evaluated and suggested treatment with a therapist, and she's refused. I'm not sure what you can do, but I'm sure it's worth a try. Thank you for investing."

"Well, thank you for all that you do too, ma'am. Is it possible to get updates on Acadia Perrin? I mean, so I can let Mrs. Perrin know?"

"I'm afraid not. She'll have to call herself."

"I understand. Thanks." Carol gave the address, and the woman assured her she'd send her down.

"There is one more thing." The woman paused. "I think Mrs. Perrin is in an abusive relationship. It's required that she tell us who she is living with or involved with, and she insists she lives alone."

"I think she does," Carol added.

"Well, then I think she's recently been attacked."

Carol sucked in a breath, knowing too well by whom, but she remained silent.

"She wore large sunglasses throughout our meeting today. A fairly sure sign for us. We see it often. And she was in obvious pain as she sat and stood. You wouldn't know anything about that, would you?"

"I'll see what I can find out. Thank you for helping to get her down here."

Hanging up, Carol took a deep breath. Now, what was she going to do? She couldn't take the woman in, could she? Walking to the front entrance, she leaned against the door jamb and stared. Cars drove slowly by. Such a peaceful and serene scene, and yet evil lurked around almost every corner. *Where is he? What will be his next move?*

Carol stood up straight. A cold fear gripped her. *What if he comes here, and she's here?* Running back to the counter, she called the chief. "Chief? I need to tell you something."

"I was just there. What's up?"

Carol drew a deep breath, gaining courage. "I've met the mother of the runaway daughter."

Silence.

"You know? The Acadia Perrin girl. The one was taken last year? Then she ran away again, but just last week, they found her?" Carol's head spun just relating the story.

Chief Bert cleared his throat. "Why would you meet with her?" His voice had a hard edge.

"Well, I just wanted to help her. She called my shop and talked all crazy like.... Oh, shoot. It's a long story, and she's coming here this afternoon in about three hours. Anyway, you offered to patrol my house once. I'd like to take you up on that."

"Why would she call you?" Carol heard his voice talking to someone other than her before he continued. "Listen, we need to talk. You need to tell me everything, but I'm being dispatched right now, so wrap this up quick. So why do you want a patrol now?" The Chief wasn't naïve, and Carol knew he was an expert in law enforcement and reading people. She hoped he would let her slide.

"Because she's coming to my house, and she's very unstable. Her daughter was removed from her home the same night the authorities brought Acadia home."

"Why?"

"Acadia reported that her mother was abusive. Anyway, the mother is distraught and needs help. But I think maybe she's manic, bipolar or something, and I'm not sure what she might do." Carol paused.

"You've got to be kidding me." The Chief huffed.

"I wish I were. Can you just do a drive-by a few times and check on us tonight? Maybe check on the alley behind my apartment?"

"Yes, I can. But I got a feeling you still aren't being completely honest with me. If this has got anything to do with Boudreaux..." Carol heard a door slam and a siren strike up. "I need to go now. But I'll be by this evening." His tone was commanding as he clicked off.

She took a deep breath and organized her thoughts. She

promised to meet John for breakfast, but she had to go see Virginia at the hospital, then be back here for Eleanor. Carol's hand dropped to her side as she clutched the phone. *Lord, give me strength.*

As John and Carol sat in the corner at The Mockingbird Café, she felt flutters again. They spoke of the horrific event at The Refuge the night before, and Carol felt a little sheepish that while they shared a passionate moment, lives were in peril across town. They had sat and talked in John's car until all hours of the morning. Both longing for more, but both showing restraint. Carol laughed at the thought. Restraint.

That was a foreign word in her vocabulary, but John seemed to navigate it well. She loved that about him. She loved everything she knew about him, but that wasn't much. She shivered, thinking it didn't take much for her to be attracted to any man, but this was something else. Something different. A pang hit her heart, and she thought of home. She'd once had a familiar feeling back then, and she ran.

John's sandy-gray hair fell across his forehead, and his gray eyes sparkled. What a gentleman, she thought. *Why me?*

He gazed back at her, and she didn't bother to turn away. She loved the way he looked at her, and they remained uncomfortably silent until a voice spoke.

"Hello? Good morning?" Desmond grinned. "So you two playing the staring game?"

Carol hit his arm playfully, and John sat up straight and blinked. His face took on a red tint, and he quickly stood to extend a hand.

"Good morning, Pastor. I thought you'd be over at the hospital this morning?"

"On my way over now. Just getting a latte for Melanie. She sat there with Virginia last night." Desmond wore a puzzled expression. "Melanie tried to call you several times last night. Is everything okay?"

This time Carol flushed. "Everything is just fine." She smiled at John but nodded towards Desmond. "Oh. My phone was dead. I was just about to return her call when Chief Bert dropped by this morning." She glanced at her watch and pouted her lips. "Sorry, Mayor. I have to run. I need to get to the hospital and back before opening time."

John stood and simply nodded. His shoulders heaved a little, but smiling, he reached out a hand to help her up.

"Hey, Carol, can I give you a ride? I'm heading there now," said Desmond.

"No, thanks. I need to make a phone call. I'll be there in a jiffy."

Desmond picked up Melanie's latte and left. John walked Carol outside, and they stood for a moment with the sun warming them. Carol smiled. The good Lord is indeed shining down on me, she thought. "I have to run. I'll see you when I see you then?" Carol shrugged.

"How about I meet you for a late lunch?"

The elation continued, and Carol felt as if she would float, but just as quickly, it was as if something dragged her down. Eleanor Perrin. She hated secrets. "Can we eat really late? I'm meeting someone at the shop in a couple hours."

"Perfect. How about I pick you up? Text me when you're free." His hand caught hers, and he laced his fingers between hers. "Will your meeting be over then?"

She squeezed his firm fingers but let go, wishing she'd never agreed to meet Eleanor. "Yes. It will. I'll text you." Another deep breath, and she turned. *Keep walking, keep walking.* "Bye." As Carol hurried down the sidewalk, she couldn't help but feel sneaky. *But why?* He didn't need to know every detail of her life. Not yet anyway. Maybe not ever.

As she reached Second Chance, she called Tina. Thankful

for her friend that would cover for her almost any time she asked. She checked that off her list.

The morning visit to the hospital was short and sweet. Melanie had stayed the night with Virginia, and they were just getting ready to leave. Virginia had put up a fuss about leaving, but Carol convinced her she needed to go home to freshen up, and Melanie offered to bring her back later. She gave in.

Desmond planned to stay by Officer Blaine's side for the rest of the morning. His prognosis was stable but still serious, and Carol's concern for him overshadowed her hate for Boudreaux. He was one busy bad guy, she thought. Beating Eleanor, and almost killing Blaine, or at least responsible for it, boiled her blood. One person at a time. Right now, her focus was on Eleanor.

CHAPTER 21

A compact car drove up to the front of the shop and parked. The door opened, and Eleanor Perrin, moving very slowly, unfolded herself from the backseat. As she stepped out, her black heels planted on the sidewalk, and her tall, slender form followed. She carried a large black satchel and wore a simple red and white geometric print sheath with a red sweater. Carol could smell the subtle yet expensive perfume from the shop door.

"Hi, Eleanor. I'm glad you could make it."

Carol swung the door wide open and stepped aside. "Let's go sit down."

Eleanor wore oversized sunglasses, which she didn't remove, and after following Carol inside, she shut and locked the door. At the sound of the click, Carol spun around and tilted her head.

"Why'd you do that?"

Removing her large sunglasses, redness betrayed Eleanor's trauma and fear, as well as a darkened blue bruising surrounding one swollen eye. Her shoulders slumped a little as she leaned her back against the door. Her ankle wobbled, and she grabbed her side, wincing in pain. Carol looked her over and gasped at the purple marks on Eleanor's wrists as her sweater sleeve rose.

"What happened?" She sucked in a breath. "Boudreaux? Did he do this to you?"

"Please, may I sit?"

"Of course, I'm so sorry. Come." Leading her to the settee, she offered her hand, and to her surprise, Eleanor took it as she eased herself down. Holding her side with her free hand. She lowered her purse to the ground as she tried to get comfortable.

"Why do you keep calling him Boudreaux?"

"That's his real name, Eleanor. Whatever he's told you, it's a lie. They're all lies. The man is evil."

Eleanor gasped a shallow breath and tilted her head. "You know, I vaguely remember you telling me that once, and it seemed so long ago." She breathed but winced. "But our history doesn't go so far back, does it?" Eleanor stiffened and scooted to the edge of her seat.

Carol slumped. Weariness enveloped her, but she knew she needed strength for the long day ahead. Wherever that might take her. "Eleanor, please. The past is the past. Either you let me help, or I'll send you back to Jackson right now."

Eleanor glared as if she might walk out. Slowly, twisting in pain, she reached back and gripped the back of the settee. As if it took all her strength, she pulled herself back. Tears welled. Not bothering to cover her face, she let them flow freely.

"Cash…Boudreaux, or whoever he is, he promised to help me get my daughter back. He said if I'd help him with his daughter first."

"What?" Carol frowned but suddenly raised her brows. *Did Boudreaux mean Virginia?* "That's not his daughter," she said. "The girl is somehow related, but not that way. Eleanor, the man abducts girls and traffics them. I don't know how or exactly where. But he was convicted of it a year ago." *How could she not know that?*

"But he was acquitted. He told me." Eleanor didn't sound convinced herself but simply stated the facts.

"You knew? And you believed him?" Carol stared at the woman's eye. "Eleanor, what did he do to you?" Carol pointed. "He roughed you up good, didn't he?"

Eleanor glanced around the room. "The fire. I heard him talking to someone on the phone about the fire." She gripped her hands tightly together. "I wanted no part of that and told him I was through. I tried to leave, and he did this to me," her voice broke as she covered her face, sobbing.

"How did you get away?"

"The Social Worker called when he threatened me. He made me play the message back. She reminded me of my appointment this morning saying, that if I didn't keep it, my chances of getting my daughter back were slim, diminishing. So, he said he'd drop me off and warned me that if I said anything, he'd kill me."

"I wouldn't put it past him," Carol said unapologetically. Her mind reeled. She knew she should bring in the authorities. "Eleanor, does he know where you're at now?"

"I don't think so. He was supposed to pick me up at a bar in Jackson. I stayed in the office until the car you sent arrived.

"Do you think you were followed?"

Eleanor chuckled, the first lightness she'd shown in the last hour. "How should I know? I didn't know we were playing detective." She glared at Carol. "Who are you anyway, and why do you care?"

The woman was starting to turn, and Carol didn't know what direction, but she didn't have a good feeling. "I just want to help. I was confused when I was young. Just like these girls. Just like your daughter. They need all the help they can get. We all do. Especially me, and I finally came to the end of myself, and my life is turning around. But it's taken me thirty years. I don't want others to live like me. It's a hard life." Carol paused. "You know it's Jesus that changes all that."

Eleanor tipped her head, and her jaw clenched. "Don't you start talking religion to me."

"It's not religion. It's faith." *Oh, Lord give me words.* "There will be a time when you need Him. So, when you're ready, and you come to that point, I'm here to tell you how God worked in my life." *Don't push it, Carol.*

Eleanor's lips pressed tightly together.

Carol switched gears. "Hey, do you know anything about another girl that Boudreaux might be keeping somewhere?"

Eleanor shook her head slightly. "Another girl? And you think it's him?

Carol was sure she knew nothing.

Eleanor's back hunched a little, and she exhaled. "Maybe we can have that talk another time. But for now, what do you want me to do? I can't promise anything, but if it gets my daughter back, I'll try."

"You need to do more than try. Everyone's trying to help, so the best thing you can do is follow what the authorities tell you to do. The social worker, the police. You need to go to them and tell them about Boudreaux." A pang of hypocritical guilt hit her heart.

"What do I tell them?" said Eleanor in a fearful whisper.

"Tell them he assaulted you. Tell them what you heard about the fire at The Refuge."

Eleanor shook her head. "No. No, I can't do that. Look at me. No man has ever treated me like this."

"Are you sure about that?" Carol was always blunt, but even she surprised herself at the question.

Eleanor slowly slumped, and her face sagged. Carol wondered if the inside pain was as deep as the outside.

"I think you're right. That man is evil," said Eleanor quietly.

"You don't know the half of it." Taking a deep breath,

Carol finally stood, and just as she did, pounding resounded from the front door. The women froze, and it didn't stop. That couldn't be good. Carol peeked around the large Boston Fern. She heard footsteps, so whoever it was, had already taken off.

"Let's go. I'll take you up to my apartment." Carol hustled Eleanor up the stairs. The woman moaned, obviously in pain, but Carol let her in, and instructed her to wait. Then she texted Chief Bert.

<Come to the shop now. I think he's here.>

She clicked off and tiptoed to the front door. Peeking the curtain, she saw Chief Bert. Relief flooded her as she threw open the door. "Wow, that was fast."

Chief Bert stood sweating and breathing heavily. "You, okay?" He pushed past her. "He's out there."

"I know! He was pounding on the door."

He threw up his hands. "That was me."

"Well, why didn't you say so?" Carol's voice rose.

"I was out patrolling and saw Boudreaux walking to your shop. Before I could get out of my car, he saw me and ran down the alley. I pounded on your door to alert you, then ran after him. I couldn't find him, so I came back here. Is Eleanor Perrin here?"

She nodded and pointed up the stairs.

"She's up there? Staying here?" Chief Bert pushed his hat back and rubbed the bridge of his nose. "How about you give me the Reader's Digest version and quick."

"I reached out and tried to help Eleanor. We met in Gulfport, and Boudreaux must have followed me." Carol rubbed her forehead. "I think she went home with him from the bar."

"Bar? What bar?"

"It's not what you think." Carol shook her head. "Never mind. She's been with him and heard him talk about the fire and tried to get out. He beat her up bad."

Chief Bert's lips pressed so tightly together they turned white. "Great, and you're just now telling me this? I've got to call in the Hancock County Sheriffs for extra support. When I get back, we have a lot to talk about."

He left, and his reprimand stung, but she was thankful that she could at least do something to help. She ran to check on Eleanor, who lay sound asleep on the sofa bed. Carol crept back down the stairs, approaching the register counter. She took a step and planted her foot a little too close to the base of the counter. She screamed. Pulling her foot away, she looked down as blood gushed from a gash on the side of her foot. The nail she'd forgotten to fix poked out the cornice of the baseboard. *Shoot.* When she'd yanked her foot back, she tore a good size chunk of flesh, and blood splattered all over her clothes. She quickly grabbed her long skirt and dabbed at the wound. It wouldn't stop. Ripping off her scarf, she tied it around her foot and limped to the back room.

By the time she hobbled around and found her first aid supplies, she dripped blood everywhere. Instead of calling Tina to come open the shop for her, she limped to the front door, turning the "Be Back Soon" sign visible to the outside. *Now what?* Carol wasn't used to taking care of so many people. She needed to check on Virginia, but she needed to get to the hospital herself. Yet, she couldn't leave Eleanor. *Heck, I should take Eleanor to the hospital with me. She needs it more than me.* But her bandages soaked through, and she had to take care of it.

Hopping on one foot and grimacing at each step, she reached the stairs. "Eleanor?" she called. "Eleanor?" No answer. Carol hoped the woman was down for a long nap as she gathered her things and dragged herself to her car, forgetting about Boudreaux.

Her foot throbbed, and the pain was almost unbearable as she drove herself to the hospital.

Just as she arrived at the Bay Town Hospital, she realized she had forgotten to ask the Chief where Blaine was admitted. She asked the clerk and was informed that he was transported to the trauma hospital in Gulfport.

That's a half-hour drive away, she thought. Her foot throbbed, and her face felt clammy. She wondered if she could make it that far. Then she could get her foot looked at and see Blaine at the same time.

"Is there anything else I can help you with?" said the receptionist.

Carol shook her head and limped away.

"Hey," the admitting clerk called after her. "Are you okay?"

Carol waved just as the double doors whooshed open. Not entirely stable on two feet, she toppled as something hit her foot. She screamed out in pain as she dropped to the ground. An older gentleman hunched over a wheelchair didn't stop and rushed straight to the admitting counter. "Help, my wife is having chest pains."

Carol closed her eyes, trying not to scream again. Her excruciating pain almost drowned out the man's words. Instantly, another nurse knelt beside her.

"Are you all right? Did you hit your head?"

"No. That man clipped me with the wheelchair. But he needs help. You better take care of him."

He glanced down her leg. "You're bleeding. What happened?"

Swallowing hard, Carol chewed on her lip, trying to bite down the pain. She shook her head and reached for her foot. "My foot. I hurt it this morning."

As the nurse reached forward, he gave a gentle tug at the slip-on sandal. Her foot had swollen, and the shoe wouldn't budge. He wiggled it, and Carol screamed.

"Ma'am, can you tell me what happened?"

Her pulse quickened, and sweat broke on her forehead, but she didn't answer.

He placed a firm hand on hers. "Ma'am, can you stand? I want to take you back."

"Just pull my sandal off." She pressed her lips tightly.

Once again, he gave a little tug, and the sandal came off. Carol collapsed backward, and a stifled moan escaped her throat. He yelled out orders, and a nurse brought supplies. He unwrapped her soaked bandage, and more blood flowed. He slapped on a gauze pad and immediately applied pressure. A wheelchair and more nurses joined him.

They finally got Carol back in one of the ER bays, and she huffed and puffed but felt so much better with the sandal off that she foolishly tried to talk them into releasing her. She was instructed as to the danger of infection and blood loss. She also needed stitches and would have to stay off her feet for twenty-four hours.

"Can't do that. I have to go to Gulfport."

"What's this about, Gulfport?" A young physician introduced himself and offered his hand. "Hello, ma'am. I'm the attending physician. Can I take a look at that?"

"Have at it," said Carol.

When he was done examining it, he removed his gloves and faced her. "We're going to have to wash and clean that wound and stitch you up. I may need to remove some flesh as well. That's quite a tear."

"Yeah, well, it hurt like heck when I stepped on that nail, so I practically ripped my foot off."

"When was your last tetanus shot?"

"I have no idea," said Carol, and she glanced at the clock on the wall and remembered Eleanor. "Oh my goodness, I have to go. Where's my purse? Where's my phone?"

The doctor placed a hand on her arm. "Ma'am, most everything can wait. We have to take care of this now."

They had a friendly banter, and Carol finally gave in. She winced as they gave her a tetanus shot and administered the anesthetic. She scrunched her face as he sutured her foot, blaming herself for her haste and trying not to blame God for the inconvenience.

CHAPTER 22

Feeling much like a loser, Carol sat in the Bay Town Hospital ER waiting area. Her bandaged foot ballooned like a cartoon. It rested on the footrests of the wheelchair, where she sat helplessly. She wanted to cry but wouldn't.

"Ma'am, can we call someone? Or maybe an Uber to get you home."

"My car is out there, you know. It's a beautiful neon orange, 1972 El Camino classic." As if that would make a difference, she thought.

"Yeah, you're on pain medication. That won't work." The nurse smirked.

Carol felt a little groggy and nodded. "Listen, can you call John Taylor?"

"Who?"

"Are you kidding me? You don't know the mayor of Bay Town?"

The nurse hunched. Her ponytail swayed, and strands of sun-bleached blond hair made her tan pop. The curves of her ears were dotted with holes up and down the cartilage, but only one actual earring rested in each lobe. "I'm not from around here."

"Let me guess. California?"

"Yes, how'd you know?"

"Oh, it was the skinny body and Nike shoes." She winked. "Okay, can you hand me my purse?" She giggled as she searched for her phone and scrolled for his number.

"Hi, John. It's Carol. Listen…what? Oh, okay…I just needed to ask…Okay. Fine. Bye."

Carol bit her lip and hung up. That's strange. *Can't talk. He can kiss me in the Town Hall parking lot in front of the whole community, but he can't speak to me today?*

"Ma'am? Did you get a ride?"

"What? Oh, no." She felt in a daze. He shut her down. John Taylor shut her down. "I'll try someone else."

Her eyes burned. Her foot throbbed, and the little bit of her heart that she gave away felt like an open wound bigger than the one on her foot. She tried calling Melanie, Desmond, and finally, Chief Bert.

Carol peered up at the bright sky. Seagulls flitted everywhere, and the cloudless blue bathed her in serenity. She sat in the wheelchair with her foot propped on a red metal chair. Bubba came out with his percolator and a tin cup. Staring at her leg, he shook his head.

Smiling, she welcomed the hot coffee and nodded at Chief Bert. "Thanks for picking me up at the hospital and for bringing me down here."

Chief Bert raised a hand, shading the sun. "I should have taken you straight home, but I don't know how you could make it up those stairs."

"I'll manage," said Carol. Though she didn't know how.

"We got a couple extra men out searching for Boudreaux. Miz Carol, you should have…don't matter now."

"I know. I should have reported everything. But it happened so fast."

"Yup, but I got a busy day, and I can't be your private chauffeur. How are you going to get home from here?"

"I'm fine. Just need to clear my head, and it's so beautiful down here."

The Chief glanced at the little building with paint peeling off the "Bubba's Crab Shack" sign. Though clean, everything was worn and sparse. He shook his head and glanced at Bubba. The unruly beard, red bandana rolled tightly around his white forehead, and his vast white apron spattered with grease and hot sauce was quite the sight.

"Yup, hard to beat the view." The Chief chuckled.

"Don't worry about me. I'll call Melanie or something. I'm just glad to hear Blaine is resting okay." She paused. "Eleanor. She's still at my house, isn't she?" She eased herself up.

"I hope so. I was patrolling for Boudreaux when you called, but I'll swing by and check on her. You sure you're all right?"

Carol slumped. "Yes. As long as these pain meds don't wear off. Oh…" She opened her bag and pulled out a spare key to her house. "Here. It opens all of my doors."

"Oh, that's really safe." Chief Bert shook his head and pocketed the key.

"So, Virginia?"

"She's fine. I'm surprised that little girl could sit so quietly in the ICU. Except for when Officer Blaine woke up. She screamed so loud they almost had to give her a sedative." Chief Bert stopped and gave Carol a sideways glance. "Hey, how come I'm the last to know about that little romance thing between her and Officer Blaine?"

Carol laughed, "Well, I was hoping they'd take it slow, but they've got chemistry." She watched as a lone, wispy cloud floated by. "Maybe sometimes you have to grab it before it's gone." She watched as the thin cloud dissipated.

The Chief scratched his head. "I have no idea what you're talking about. Anyway, I'm picking her up later, and I'll take her back to The Refuge."

"What's next?"

"Investigation, again." Removing his hat, he wiped his brow. "I spoke with the mayor this morning."

Carol's stomach flipped. "When? Where?" Her lips pursed as she breathed deeply through her nose.

"He was at the hospital. Dropped by to see Blaine. He was there when I had to leave to come get you."

Carol's lips fluttered as she breathed out. "You didn't tell him where I was, did you?"

"No. Why would I? He didn't ask." The Chief replaced his hat. "You sure you're okay here? I best be going."

"Yes, I'm good. Thank you, Chief."

He waved and urged her to take care as he drove off.

Bubba returned, asking if she was hungry.

"No thanks," she said but had second thoughts when he returned to the kitchen and she heard the crackling sound of hot grease. Then she thought of John, and the thought of food became tasteless.

The water lapped against the rocks, and she wanted it to lull her to sleep. But a mind at unrest was unfit for sleep. Why was John so cold on the phone? The one time she thought to ask something of him, he bailed. *Just like a man.* She turned her face toward the sun. It felt good and warm...much like John's warm embrace.

Forcing her mind to put the thoughts to rest, she prayed. For Virginia and Blaine, for the girl in the drug store, and other girls like her. An uneasy rumbling soon churned in her stomach, and it wasn't hunger. She prayed for The Refuge, and when the image of the fire and the thought of men trying to abduct Virginia clouded her mind she got so mad she could spit! *What are you doing, God?* Carol crossed her arms and stared across the water. Beyond the docks, beyond the small harbor, she thought of her mom and her dad. *What did they think when she ran amok? Did they wonder what God was doing then?* Raising her head, a crossroad seemed to rise before her.

She was tired of worrying about everyone. And she didn't like the longing she felt for John. It was different than before when she lived one day at a time. No responsibility, no commitment. Always out for a good time. Looking for men. Accepting the fleeting passion and not taking anything more. Yet always hoping, but forever hitting a wall of disappointment.

Thirty years ago, she'd given up a chance for a meaningful life. For what? Fun, freedom, and fruitlessness. *Put them behind you.* The inaudible voice caused a quiet peace to surround her.

"Hey, girl? You here again?" A jogging Melanie stood before her.

Carol breathed deep. "Therapy." She waved at the sky. "Seeking wise counsel."

"You're a wise woman."

"What can I get ya', Mel?" Bubba's broad grin beamed from behind the pass-through window as he waved.

"Nothing. I'm good, Bubba. Thanks." Melanie waved back. "So any news?" She visibly shivered, running her hands up and down her arms. "I've been in New Orleans all afternoon, checking out a hotel for a wedding venue."

"What hotel?"

Melanie crossed her arms, her fingers clenching her skin tightly. "The Bourbon Hotel. The bride is adamant about having her wedding there."

Carol recalled the incident she knew Melanie was probably thinking about. Her ex-husband had been found dead at The Bourbon Hotel last year after the human trafficking bust down in the Lower Ninth District of New Orleans. It was after he and Desmond had succeeded in rescuing Virginia. While Bay Town celebrated the rescue, Melanie's husband remained in New Orleans. The next morning he was found dead in his suite at the Bourbon Hotel.

"You sure you're up for that? I mean, there are a lot of other ritzy hotels there."

"I'll be okay. Lord willing. Most venues are not as iconic, but I did suggest the Mont Leon. We'll see." Melanie breathed deep and blew out slowly. "So, Officer Blaine?"

"I heard he's doing better, but I didn't quite make it there today." Carol glanced towards her foot hiding under the table.

Peeking down, Melanie bent over and gasped. "Your foot! What happened?"

"It's a long story. I'll tell you later. Hey, can you give me a ride home? I'm in no hurry."

"Sure. I'll run home, clean up and head back with my car. Should I give you a ring before I leave?" Melanie glanced back and pointed at the Catch Shack. "I mean, in case you need more counseling."

Laughing, Carol said, "Nope, I think I'm all counseled out here. Except for some food therapy." She leaned back and craned her neck towards the shack. "Hey, Bubba, how about some French fries?"

She heard the oil spatter, and he called out, "Sure thing. Up in a minute."

"Okay, well, I'll be back in a half-hour or so." Melanie first checked her watch, then took a few steps. She stopped. "Hey, Carol. Have you heard from the mayor today?" She grinned. "You had him so flustered last night.

Carol's heart crushed, reminding her of how he had held her so close to his chest. She breathed out. "Yeah, well, he has me pretty twitterpated too. I called him this morning, and I think he's miffed at me for something."

Melanie placed her hands on her hips and gave Carol a sideways glance. "That's not like him. I'm sure it was something else."

"Maybe." She tipped her head. "But maybe not. Maybe I'm just not right for him."

"Carol? I thought we had this conversation. And you've been praying about it, about him, right?"

"That's what scares me. I might want him for the wrong reasons."

Melanie pulled a leg to stretch. A breeze blew, and her hair flew about her face. "I don't think so. You may have some wrong reasons lingering, but that doesn't make this whole scenario wrong."

"You don't understand. I tried to make a good thing work a long time ago." The pain of lost love pressed a heavy burden on her heart. She was afraid Melanie could see it all. "I was engaged to a good man. Well, my goodness, back then, he was a boy, just in college. He loved me, and I loved him. But I don't know. This stupid free spirit in me couldn't be tamed. I hate what I've done since then."

Melanie pulled out a metal chair. The girls winced when it screeched across the small patch of concrete.

"We all have things in our past that we hate. The important thing is now. And now, Carol, you're a different person. Sure, there are consequences, but learn and let God have them. Your new life doesn't include suffering and grieving over your past."

"You sure about that?"

"Positive," said Melanie firmly.

"But I hurt so many people."

"Me too. My parents and my sister. I ran away and got married and pregnant at nineteen. Now, that's another story, but God redeemed my life. So I know about trusting Him. Just believe in His grace."

Carol liked that word. It went a long way with her. "Grace." Her eye sparkled. "Thanks for the reminder. That's the magic word. And right now, I'll take it."

"Good. I'll be back in a few." Scooting out, she hugged

her friend but stopped once more before returning to a jog. "So, your leg?"

Carol rolled her eyes. "My foot. I ripped it on a nail in the shop."

"Oh, my goodness! Did you get stitches?"

"Yes, and I about passed out. Anyway, I'm supposed to be off it for a day or two. I've got to call Tina to see if she can come help out."

"I'll ask her. She was working in her yard next door when I left. She's so bored. Rudy has some commercial painting project, and she wants nothing to do with it. No creativity, she says. See ya." Melanie jogged off.

Carol's phone buzzed, and she checked the text message from Chief Bert.

<Took Eleanor to a hotel. She insisted. We'll keep patrolling. I'll drop your key off tomorrow. >

Carol dropped her head back. The lapping of the water and the warmth of the sun heated her body. As she nodded off, she hid behind large sunglasses. She finally drifted off into a deep sleep for what seemed like hours.

"Carol?...Carol?"

So startled, Carol jumped, and her foot hit the underside of the tabletop. "Ouch!" She pulled off her sunglasses and glared in the direction of the voice. A tall shadow blocked the sun, She swallowed hard and tried to speak, but her foot hurt so badly, tears welled,

John Taylor sat down and laid a hand on her leg. "Are you okay?" His words weren't as soft as his touch. "I didn't mean to startle you." John pulled out a handkerchief and handed it to her. She wiped the tears wet on her lashes. His actions were kind but not tender.

She immediately felt the tension from his first words and his touch. His intensity shook her, and in almost a whisper, she asked, "What's the matter, John?"

"Well, for starters, we were supposed to have lunch today."

Carol cupped a hand to her forehead. "Oh, my. I'm so sorry. I completely forgot. No wonder you cut me off when I called."

"Not hardly." He placed his hand in his pocket and pulled out his cell. The lines on his forehead appeared deeper than she remembered, and she'd never before experienced this hardness from him before. It was as if he'd slapped her face.

"Listen, John, I didn't mean to put you off today…." She stopped short as he moved his cell in front of her face. She gasped. The same photos that showed up on her phone the night of the Crawfish Festival glared back at her. The images displayed made it appear that she was partying at the bar in Gulf Port when in fact, she hadn't ever wanted to be there.

"I'm so tired of making a mess of things. I'm sorry, John. I should have told you."

He placed his phone away and straightened again. "Well, I guess now you don't have to. I understand." He turned to walk away but stopped. Turning aside, he shook his head. "You know, maybe I'm the one who made the mess." His eyes narrowed. "You were pretty clear from the start. You really didn't want me around."

Tears fell, but they weren't sad tears. She swiped them away. "Do you believe those pictures? You think I was stringing you along, all the while trying to pick up lowlifes in bars?"

John said nothing.

Carol wiped her face and managed a chuckle. "Oh, I get it. You believe whatever you've heard about me before. I mean, you're the mayor. You can find out anything you want about someone." Carol tried to stand but dropped back down, even letting out a little shriek.

"You okay, out there, Miz Carol?" Bubba yelled from his window. He nodded at the mayor.

John nodded back but fixed his attention on Carol. "Go ahead, then. I'm listening."

Swallowing hard, Carol struggled to catch a breath as she contemplated giving him the silent treatment, but the sadness in his eyes changed her mind. Suddenly, her own inner and outer pain diminished, and she felt only his.

"John, it's not what you think. Those are blackmail pictures or something. I was trying to handle a situation." Her voice cracked. "I haven't been to a bar in I don't know how long."

"I don't care if you've been in a bar. I got these photographs in the mail. I took pictures of them on my phone to show you. So just tell me what this is and why or how I got them."

Carol nodded. "It's such a long story. Someone is trying to get to me because…heck, I don't know why. A crazy lady keeps calling me, and I think I'm in the way between Boudreaux and his next victim."

"Wow. The little I knew about you was dramatic, but this is over the top."

Carol picked up the basket of French fries and threw them at him. She immediately covered her mouth, horrified at what she'd just done.

As John deflected the golden spray, a roar of laughter came from the Catch Shack. Bubba's large stomach jiggled.

"Oh, my goodness, I'm so sorry," shouted Carol.

"Guess there must be some truth to it. That's quite an arm you got there." John sat and leaned in. "Just answer me this. Do I have a chance with you? Are we something you want?"

"Yes," Carol blurted without the hesitation she felt in her heart. Between the pain, the medication, and all the terror going on in her life, she had no restraints left. Feeling trapped, she pulled her scarf, covered her face, and gulped air, trying to hold back.

John sat next to her and placed his arm securely around her shoulder. "Shhh."

The sound soothed her.

"Listen, when I got those photos, I was angry. Sure I was, but I care for you, and I wanted to give you the benefit of the doubt. That's why I came." He looked at her foot. "I'm sure glad I did. Otherwise, I'd be feeling pretty rotten right now."

"John, there's so much to tell. I haven't even told the Chief everything. I don't even know where to start." Carol could already feel the burden lifting.

His smooth hair fell across his forehead as he nodded. "Hey, we'll navigate this."

His words were meant to reassure, but her heart still weighed heavy. "But there's a lot more. Like really a lot more." Carol stopped. "Wait a minute, how did you know I was here?"

"Guess it was a leading? Those photos were driving me crazy, so when you called, I just couldn't talk to you."

"Well, they weren't that bad." Carol raised her brows and chuckled. He moved to pull out his phone, and she stopped him. "Oh, all right."

"Anyway, I finished up some work at the office and went for a drive. I don't often come down here, but the gulf is always soothing. I ran into Melanie. She was running home."

"Ah, my conniving friend."

Pulling back, John sat straight and stared at Carol. He took a deep breath. "Is that a bad thing?"

He was too perfect. How could he always be so forgiving? Just like her mom and even her dad of late. Oh, God, why did relationships have to be so sticky? "Nope. It's a good thing." Carol touched his hand. "I'm glad you're here." Glancing at her fries scattered across the boardwalk, she chuckled, "Well, the seagulls are feasting tonight. Can you take me home, Mayor? I mean, John?"

"Always happy to be of service, ma'am."

Carol raised a finger, quickly texting Melanie.

John stood and leaned toward her. He bent and gently

pressed his lips against her cheek. Reaching up, she touched his face, pulled his forehead against hers, and closed her eyes. This time, the sweetness of the moment replaced the passion of desire.

CHAPTER 23

John Taylor drove Carol home, euphoria enveloping her. She slid a finger across her lips, feeling like a teenager after her first kiss. She struggled to remove her shawl as heat rose within, and he reached over and helped. His tender action prompted uncomfortableness. The attentions of a southern gentleman were new to her, and she hardly knew this one, but she longed to know more.

"So, how'd you become Mayor?" Carol winced. Hoping to avoid the whole ex-wife topic, she feared opening an old wound.

Her fears went unfounded as he casually opened up and told her about his career and his family history in Bay Town, never mentioning the ex. His life was not that eventful, but she welcomed it and loved just hearing his voice. He sounded happy.

He pulled into the alley behind her shop and parked, then walked around and opened her door, offering his hand. She stepped out and gritted her teeth, struggling to balance on one foot. Gazing upwards, she sighed at the long flight of stairs. *It might as well be Mount Whitney,* she thought.

John stood by her side and moved in closer. His arms

reached out like a delivery man carrying a package. His face beamed. "You ready?"

"Ready for what?"

"A ride up those stairs."

"Yeah, right. You're no spring chicken, and I'm not Giselle."

"Who?" John furrowed his brow.

"The supermodel? Tom Brady's wife? The quarterback?"

He nodded and smiled broadly. Seeming to brace himself, he swooped her into his arms and walked towards the stairs. Carol winced again and had no struggle left in her. The foot throbbed, but her heart soared.

He stared up ahead, like an athlete with his eyes fixed on the finish line, and up he climbed. Carol marveled at his strength, and after he settled her inside, she invited him to get a drink from her refrigerator, and they spent the next hour talking. The conversation somehow turned to Boudreaux and Eleanor. His calm professionalism took it all in. When the conversation lulled, he looked at her with longing. Typically, this is where she'd invite a man to stay, and oh, how she wanted to do just that. She glanced around the room and spotted her Bible.

"Well, John. I'm mighty tired, and my foot is killing me, so we better call it a night."

He stood but his shoulders dropped just a little. He nodded. "All right then, but can I get you your pain relievers before I go? Something to help?"

"If I was still a drinking woman, a shot of whiskey would do the trick!" She chuckled and waved him off. "Nah. I got some ibuprofen and something the doctor prescribed in my bag here." She patted the floppy cloth, paisley print oversized hobo purse.

He leaned in to kiss her goodnight. His lips brushed her cheek ever so sweetly. *That's the best pain reliever of all,* she thought. He quietly left, and Carol fought off the regret of not inviting him to stay. It took all the strength she had to resist the longing she saw in his eyes as well as the desire in her own body.

Immediately after he left, loneliness set in, and the first thing she longed for was family. Something she hadn't felt in a very long time. She glanced at the clock. It wasn't late. Following a gnawing sensation, she called her mother. The hair on her arm raised as she heard her mother answer. But the little girl within her succumbed to the lilt of her mother's voice, and she fought back the tears.

Their long conversation held nothing but love, and renewal flowed through her veins. Although her mother expressed concern over her injury, she seemed almost thrilled that she could share in Carol's trials. How much had her mother agonized over not knowing all these years? They spoke for what seemed like hours, and sometime during the night, Carol had fallen asleep right where John had left her on the sofa.

A ray of daylight peeked through a slit between her drapes. She blinked. Stretching, she didn't realize how stiff she was. She hadn't moved since her phone call with her mother, and her cell phone lay on the floor. She stood, and once again, the pressure of putting weight on her foot was too much, and she dropped back down. She picked up the bottle of pain meds on the end table.

A knock at the door startled her, and the bottle dropped to the floor. Now how in the world would she make it to the door? Suddenly it opened.

Tina's bouncy head of curls peeked in. "Hey, sweetie, hope you don't mind. I took a chance that the shop's front door key might work up here too."

"What time is it?" said Carol.

Swinging the door open, Tina ushered in a guest, much like Vanna White on the TV show. "Ta-da! Look who I found wandering outside your shop."

"Hello, Caroline."

A beautiful mature woman peeked in. Her loosely tousled gray hair glinted with a hint of auburn highlights. She wore a sage-green cotton twill coat, and a purse hung on her arm. A colorful silk scarf hung from her aging, but slender neck and taupe shoes with stacked heels matched her simple sheath.

Carol gulped and reached out a hand. "Hello, Mother."

Aurora Scape handed everything over to Tina and walked in. She knelt, enveloping her daughter in her arms. They hugged silently until they heard Tina bawling like a baby by the still-open door. Carol waved her over. "Come on, Tina."

Always in her high heels, Tina's shoes clicked as she joined the reunion. "Group hug." She yelled.

When the excitement died down, Carol's mother stood. A little shaky from kneeling, she eased onto the sofa. Touching the pillows, she glanced around. "It's so quaint, Caroline. I love it. You always did have a unique sense of style. I wished I'd appreciated it before...before you left."

"Mother, let's not go there. At least not yet. Now, Tina, how did all this come about?"

"Hey, I just found Mrs. Scape lingering around like a tourist outside. She was peering in your window just as I walked up to open."

"I'm sorry, Caroline. I should have called. After our conversation last night, your father agreed to send me out. Why he even booked me on the red-eye. Can you imagine? Him letting me fly late at night all alone."

Tina clapped her hands together and pursed her lips. "How sweet is that?"

Rolling her eyes, Carol glanced at Tina. "I have been flying solo for...never mind. Mother, it's good to see you."

Aurora reached out and patted her daughter's hand. "Let's enjoy the day, and then we'll talk. How about some breakfast, my treat?" She glanced at Tina. "You too, dear."

Carol's long hair was a tangled mess, and her flowing

clothes bunched up all around her. The little makeup she had on smeared under her eyes. She drew the chenille throw close to her neck and scooted down. "Mother, how about we eat in?"

Tina jumped up. "Yes. I can pick something up at the Mockingbird café. Mrs. Scape, would you like some yummy cherry-almond scones? And they make the most amazing lattes in town. All kinds of specialties."

"Thank you, dear, but I think Caroline needs some fresh air. I'll help her get washed up."

Carol pulled up straight. "I should say not, Mother. I can manage." Carol stood and hopped on one foot, resisting the urge to put weight on the other. As she moved forward, her bad foot clipped the leg of the end table, and she drew in a breath. "Well, maybe you can help me to the bathroom."

Tina and Aurora took Carol's arms, placing them on their shoulders. By the time she made it to the restroom, she had untangled herself from her mother and Tina and shooed them out.

"I'm fine. I'll just sponge off and be right out. Mother, my armoire is against the wall. Could you please fetch me a change of clothes?" Carol peeked out.

Aurora's moist eyes gazed back just as Carol closed the door. "I'd love to, Caroline."

Carol heard footsteps across the apartment and the creak of her antique wooden closet door. A few moments later, there was a light knock, and her mother's head peeked in, her eyes closed.

"Just hang it on the hook behind the door." Carol sat on the closed commode, a towel around her, washcloth in hand. She heard another knock. Much bolder but further away. "Who is that?" She yelled.

"I'll find out, dear. You finish up in there." Her mother closed the door.

Curious, Carol turned off the faucet and heard a familiar voice.

"Well, hello, ladies. I brought some breakfast for the patient." It was John Taylor's voice. Carol slumped back against the tank and listened.

"Hello, Mrs. Paulson," he said.

"I told you, Mayor, it's Tina. Mrs. sounds so...so old." She scrunched her face. "By the way, this is Mrs. Scape." Tina winced, "Oh, my, I mean, this is Aurora Scape, Caroline's mother."

Carol rushed to finish up and grabbed the drab gray dress hanging on the hook. Of all the clothes, her mother picked the funeral dress. She threw it on, brushed her hair, and stumbled to the door. Flinging it open, she leaned on the door jamb.

Tina frowned. "Oh my goodness, we're not doing that look again, are we?"

Carol glared at Tina, then looked at John and smiled. "Why, John? What on earth are you doing here?"

His brightened face quickly faded at her harsh voice. "Well, I thought you might be hungry and didn't think you could make it down those stairs." The smell of bacon wafted from the package he held, but no one seemed to notice.

Tina asked, "The stairs? My goodness, how in the world did you make it up those stairs in the first place?" Her brows knit close together.

Carol blinked long and hard. She pointed at John. "He carried me."

"Ahhh," Tina oozed admiration.

Aurora clapped her hands, and they both grinned at John.

"Such a gentleman," said Aurora.

"Why, I do declare. I'm just speechless." Tina sang.

"Mayor, please, please sit down." Aurora glided across the room, taking him by the arm.

She took the containers from him and handed them to

188 | KATHLEEN J. ROBISON

Tina. Aurora motioned to the sofa, took a seat in the chair adjacent, and turned to face him. "Mayor, it's such a pleasure to meet you. I can't thank you enough for all your help with my daughter. She's told me so much about you."

Carol swallowed hard. "About everyone in Bay Town." Her voice felt unnaturally high-pitched as she tried to take a step in the direction of the pending interrogation huddle. John stood to help, but she waved him off and gave Tina a look that made her come running.

With Tina's help, Carol maneuvered to the sitting area. A struggle ensued as she tried to sit in a chair across from her mother. Tina won and forced her next to John. He silently mouthed, thank you.

He patted Carol's arm. "Good morning."

Carol took a deep breath and couldn't help but smile. He was dressed for business in his classic tan suit, white shirt, and subdued tie.

"Good morning," she said loudly but added in a whisper, "Thank you for everything." She glanced at the food containers on the table. Taking a whiff with her nose in the air, she mumbled. "Mmm, mmm. Smells good." Glancing at her mom, she added, "Guess we don't need to go out this morning?"

John wore a puzzled but concerned expression. "And how were you going to manage that?"

"I may be injured, but I'm not incapacitated."

"Still, dear, we'll just stay put. We have a lot of catching up to do." Aurora gave a loving nod to her daughter.

Carol's body went rigid. The last thing she wanted was to sit here alone with her mother. "We have lots of time for that. Let me show you Bay Town. I can scoot down the stairs on my rear if you can drive."

Aurora's face reddened, and John broke out in a hearty laugh. "Now, if I weren't so concerned about your injury, I'd like to see that. But the doctor said, take it easy today."

"John Taylor, I've taken care of myself for...well, for a long time."

"Yes, we know Caroline." Aurora waved a hand in the air. "But I thought you were working on surrendering some things in your life. Maybe letting others help and submitting to sound advice would be a start."

"Mother!" Shouted Carol. Feeling convicted immediately, she regretted her reprimand. It didn't help that her foot was throbbing, and the pain added to her irritation.

Aurora lowered her eyes, John clasped his hand, and Tina, still standing, moved toward the door leading to the shop. "I best be opening up down there. See you all." She yanked a thumb in that direction.

"It was a pleasure meeting you, Mrs. Scape." Tina wiggled her fingers. "Bye, y'all." And off she whisked.

"I'm sorry, mother," she whispered while wringing her hands.

Aurora nodded and stood. "How about some breakfast?" She retrieved the containers that John Taylor brought and placed them on the coffee table. She smiled as she opened the boxes. "Mmm, breakfast croissants."

"My goodness. Those look heavenly." Carol licked her lips. "Thank you, John."

"Let me get some plates and napkins," said Aurora.

"Oh, no the boxes are fine."

Aurora's pinched lips betrayed her dismay, but she sat anyway. "Would you like one, Mayor?" she asked.

"No, thanks. You ladies go ahead. I have a breakfast appointment soon."

Aurora bowed her head and clasped her hands.

Carol's brows scrunched. "Mother, you can bless the food out loud. I pray now too, you know."

A chuckle erupted from John, but he quickly stifled it. Aurora nodded and proceeded to ask the Lord's blessing on the food. When finished, she asked, "Mayor, tell me about your little town here." Aurora took a dainty bite of her croissant.

Carol sat amused as John gave a rousing speech about their little town, with Aurora hanging on every word.

Finally, John finished, then stood. "Mrs. Scape, it was a pleasure meeting you."

"The pleasure is all mine, I assure you."

"Will you be in town long?" He asked.

Aurora's unparted lips formed a straight line, and she threw a sideways glance at Carol.

"As long as my daughter needs me." Aurora smiled.

"Sure, Mother, but since you're here, I might as well show you the town." Carol shifted in her seat, groaning as she tried to move her foot.

John smiled, then his brows rose. "Mrs. Scape, I have an idea. why don't you help your daughter with some shoes?" He looked at Carol. "That is if you want to wear shoes today." He winked. "I'll help you."

She shook her head so that emphatically, her hair tumbled around her shoulders. "You are not carrying me down those stairs. We're both liable to plunge to our deaths!"

He threw his head back and laughed. "That's a little dramatic, but I can *assist* you then. Aurora, can you drive a manual transmission?"

"I'm afraid not," said Aurora.

Carol sat in the middle, glancing back and forth between them. She felt like a child while they discussed her care. Tapping both hands on her knees, she sat rigidly and breathed deep as mixed thoughts floated in her brain. Pride. With just that realization, she blew out a hefty breath and plopped back. A silly grin spread across her lips, and she was ready to listen to the resolution they would propose to this predicament. It felt kind of good.

"Aurora, you can drive your daughter around in my car.

And Carol, would you mind if I drove your El Camino today?"

Carol smiled back, amused that the mayor of Bay Town would be driving around in a classic hot orange truck. "Not at all, Mayor. Not at all."

He nodded back as if he agreed to her approval. "I can put the wheelchair in my trunk, and I'm sure wherever you go today, someone will be there to help unload it as needed."

Carol tensed a bit at the mention of the apparatus but slowly let it go.

Aurora bent down and picked up a pair of earthy-looking sandals. She frowned, but her lips took an upturn as she swiveled around to the Mayor. "That would be wonderful, Mayor. Thank you so much. I can manage the wheelchair just fine, though." Turning to Carol, she asked, "Are these all you have, dear?" Her face scrunched.

"Of course not. But those will do. And please, mother, call him John. Not mayor." She glanced at him. "I mean, if that's what you'd like."

"I'd love it, ma'am."

"Then, John, it is." Aurora walked to the sofa. "Carol, let's get those monstrosities on and go see your town."

CHAPTER 24

The secluded grassy green belt across from the gulf provided the serenity needed for Carol's visit with her mother. The sun reflecting off the choppy water almost blinded the women as they sat on the wooden park bench under an old fruit arbor. Established thorny vines rose high from the ground encircling the four pillars.

"Why, Caroline, is that a wild blackberry plant?" She reached out to touch the delicate pink and white blooms.

"I think it's called a bramble bush. But yeah, they're a lot like blackberries. Be careful, Mother. Those thorns are brutal."

While Aurora had driven all over town, Carol had played navigator and given her the grand tour. Although she wanted to go to Bubba's Crab Shack, she didn't know if her mother was ready for that much down-home southern charm. Instead, they picked up lunch at a gourmet deli and chose to eat in the grassy belt.

Carol unwrapped her sandwich and glanced at her mother, delicately balancing a boxed salad on her lap. "You sure you don't want a bite of my pastrami?" As Carol picked it up and took a bite, mustard dripped. The wrapper caught some of it, but the rest dotted the front of her dress. She quickly grabbed a napkin and dabbed.

"Oh, Caroline, your dress. Now that won't come out."

"Oh, well. Guess I'll have to toss it." She shrugged.

Aurora took a dainty bite of her salad and chewed. Lifting a napkin, she patted her lips and set down her fork. Taking a long drink of bottled water, she set it down and stared straight ahead. They ate in silence for a while, and finally, Aurora spoke first.

"Caroline? You have a beautiful life here."

A shiver went up Carol's spine. She felt thankful that her mother didn't know the life she'd lived before. A weight of despair seemed to envelop her whole body. She didn't like the feeling. *How much would Mother want to know?*

"You seem so happy. And I'm happy for you." Aurora faced her daughter. "Do you ever think you might come home?"

Carol's stomach dropped. *Come home? Home?* She stared at the churning water. Too much. Too much time and too much life had passed.

A rusty old fishing boat noisily chugged up the jetty. Gray smoke blew out the back, staining the sky with wisps of darkness, and the rolling white water disturbed the calm inlet. Gliding past in the opposite direction sailed a beautiful new boat with white canvas flapping effortlessly in the breeze. The two boat captains waved at one another. One weathered and worn, the other pristine and proud. Yet, a pleasant peacefulness was shared in their wave of camaraderie.

Carol watched as the boats diminished from sight. "Mother, the things I've done…."

Aurora waved her hand, much like the two captains did. "Shhh. I don't want to hear about that. It makes no difference to me. Unless, of course, you need to speak of it. But, Caroline, we can start from here. God says we are new creations in Christ. We can start over, can't we?"

Carol felt much like the worn and weathered boat captain but reached over and hugged her pristine mother. "Sure, we can. I love you, mother. And I'm so sorry...."

"I said, shhh. And I mean it. Now that I've met some of your friends and have gotten a glimpse of your life here. Would you like to know what's going on back home in Santa Fe?"

Carol shrugged and nodded, knowing she didn't have a choice in the matter. She picked up her sandwich, devouring it as her mother spoke.

"Well, your father is anxious to see you too. He would have come, but he had a board meeting with one of the charities we support. He's about ready to retire, but this project has him so fired up, you'd think he was a young man starting a new venture."

Carol only half-listened. The thought of her father coming to see her made her shiver. She'd hurt him so badly. She couldn't help but flinch.

"Anyway, that's the newest thing on our horizon. I'm so glad you've connected with your sister. I don't know who's enjoying the restored relationship more, her or her sons. My grandsons are crazy about you. They call you the cool auntie."

Carol smiled. "I'd like to meet them in person. They seem like a lot of fun. As for my sister, well, she unloaded on me, but it's all good now. I mean, she never pushed me away, and for that, I'm thankful. I love being back in a relationship with you, but it's so hard not to think about how much I've—"

"Caroline, you stop it. God loves you, and I love you, but you have to love yourself."

"I have. I did. That's why I took off, mother."

"That's selfishness," said Carol's mother. "I mean, you have to receive God's love. That's different than this self-love that's so popular right now."

"I guess you're right. I was only thinking of myself and

I'm just beginning to grasp that God loves me. I just don't understand how he can."

Aurora took her daughter's hand. "Look at me, Caroline. None of us deserve God's love. But He gives it freely. It's only through Him that you can love freely as well."

Carol sniffled and grabbed a napkin, blowing her nose. "How could I have left? You haven't changed, mother. All that wisdom spouting. Why didn't I listen?"

"It goes both ways, Caroline. I'm sorry too. You didn't fit our world. And I was too blind to see your gifts."

Laughing and coughing, Carol slapped her chest. "Gifts? Mother, I fly by the seat of my pants. What gifts?"

Her mother's eyes grew glassy, and she pursed her lips tightly as if trying to hold in years of pent-up emotion. She spoke softly, "Your shop, Caroline. You, dear. You're beautiful, and I'm the one who missed out. Not because of you, but because of my standards. My worldly standards."

Carol shook her head. "Now you hush, mother."

"No. We tried to push you into a box, and you had nowhere to go." She gave a sideways glance toward her daughter. "Not that Alexander wasn't good for you."

Carol drew a sharp breath. She hadn't heard that name spoken aloud in a long time. Her gut wrenched. Alex, the boy she'd left behind. And he was going somewhere. Just not where she wanted to go, and even she didn't know where that was back then.

Waving a hand in the air, she flicked her wrist. "I wasn't good for Alex, mother. He's probably got a beautiful trophy wife and a pile of kids by now." She forced laughter.

"He's single, never been married. Like you." Aurora spoke sweetly.

"Not like me, mother." Her eyes grew hard. "I've never been married, but I've not often been single."

Her mother covered her ears as if anticipating more

reveals. "That's in the past. He's a good man Caroline, and he loved you. I dare say he still does."

"Mother."

"Well, he does often come for Sunday dinner."

"Are you kidding me?" Carol attempted to stand but gave up the effort and instead faced her mother.

Aurora didn't appear fazed. "I'm not expecting you to come home and marry him. I just thought you might like to know. He's on the Board of Directors for the charity I spoke of earlier."

Like to know? She hadn't much thought about him and never once imagined what he looked like now. He was tall but not overly handsome and not much of a dresser, so he didn't draw much attention from the girls back then. Besides, Carol had intercepted any attention that might have been showered on him by her loud, brash, and overbearing self.

"Well, I don't want to know about Alex. This is my home and has been for a long time. Mother, I think maybe God might have a purpose for me here."

"Oh, that's right. How could I forget? The mayor."

Carol fell back against the park bench and opened her mouth to speak but chose not to. Instead, she patted her mother's hand and gripped it tightly for a moment before releasing it and letting it rest there. She felt her mother lean against her shoulder, and they sat in silence for quite some time. The lapping of the ocean just beyond Beach Road was the only sound heard. Even the highway was devoid of cars. And as they gazed upward together, a pair of graceful herons glided through the blue skies, Their wings almost touching. Carol moved her hand, barely brushing her mother's.

Aurora stayed the week, and Carol made sure it was filled with lots of activities, so they had little time to dwell on the past anymore. Her mother fit right in, right into Carol's new life. She attended Women's Bible Study and happened to be in town for the Monthly Church Potluck, meeting many of Carol's friends and acquaintances. Some tried to pump Aurora for information about her intriguing daughter, but instead, Aurora boasted of Carol's talents and a knack for style. Melanie hosted a dinner with some of their closest friends.

Yet, their reunion was overshadowed when Carol got word that Eleanor had checked out of the hotel without notice. No wonder Eleanor had not returned her calls. Chief Bert had informed Carol that Eleanor had refused police protection. She wanted so much to find Eleanor, but helpless and injured herself, she instead focused her attention on her mother. They'd had a lovely time, and Carol couldn't think of spoiling it with the rottenness that seemed to follow her.

On Aurora's last day, Carol insisted on taking her mother over to The Refuge. She remained quite secretive, anticipating her mother's surprise and admiration for Carol's involvement at the home for abused and trafficked girls.

Pulling up to the curb, Carol opened her door. "Here we are, mom." She hobbled out and grabbed her intricately carved and colorfully painted walking stick that served as her cane. "Come on."

Aurora stepped out and smiled at the beautiful old Victorian. "We don't have many of these in New Mexico."

Carol felt a flush of pride at her mother's approval. Even though it wasn't her home, she felt a little ownership in the repairs they'd been making since the fire. One part of her life she hadn't yet shared with her mother.

As Aurora perused the property, Carol walked up and hooked their arms. Her mother stared at the hanging wooden sign, swaying from two posts. With a puzzled expression, she looked at Carol.

"Yup. The Refuge. I'm volunteering here, mother. It's a home for—"

"For abused and trafficked young girls." A breeze blew, and Aurora's short wavy hair blew around her face. Carol's long locks likewise wrapped around their arms.

"What? Have you heard of it?" Carol drew back. A little disappointed that maybe her surprise was ruined.

"Caroline, remember the charity I told you about that your father and I support?" Her eyes remained locked on the sign.

Carol's good leg buckled a bit, and Carol leaned on her cane. "You mean the one that Alex is on the Board of Directors?" *Why did she think of him again?*

"Yes, dear. Well, it's the Refuge House." She pointed to the sign. "We take in abused girls from all situations, but mostly human trafficking." She sighed. "It's a terrible thing, isn't it?"

"Mother. It's a wonderful thing."

Aurora's mouth gaped. "How on earth could you say such a thing?"

"No. I mean, yes. I mean, both. Terrible that it happens, but wonderful that we're both working on it. Like, together." Carol almost whirled, catching herself. "Mother? How did you get involved?"

Aurora took her daughter's arm. "Well, now, maybe we may have to delve into the past yet." She patted Carol's hand. "Let's just say Alex was more than a little concerned at your disappearance."

"Carol! Carol!" Virginia stood on the front porch, waving vigorously. "Hi, y'all. Are you Miz Carol's mother?" Virginia pushed back her crop of blonde curls and hugged Aurora.

"Mother, this is Virginia. She's an exceptional young lady in my life."

Once again, Aurora's mouth gaped. "Caroline? You have a daughter?"

Virginia and Carol laughed. "Heavens, no." Carol hugged Virginia. "But I'll claim her."

"Why, ma'am, I'm her shop assistant. We work together. And Miz Carol here, she headed up the committee to restore our home here."

Aurora beamed, and tears brimmed as she gazed at her daughter. Carol stared at her mother, and her chest puffed. She didn't know who was prouder, her mother or herself. And yet, it was also a humble feeling. Something she hadn't remembered ever experiencing before.

CHAPTER 25

The dark, rich earth felt good beneath Carol's bare foot. However, her injured one, still lightly bandaged and encased in a sandal, hindered the full enjoyment of the ground oozing between her toes. The smell of spring earth and fresh new greens lingered. Balancing, she leaned on a hoe in the garden. Volunteers from all Bay Town Community church and others from all over town had come to replant the front yard flower beds of The Refuge, and a few folks were out back, planting the back entrance to the kitchen.

With the updated electrical work done, the women decorated to their hearts' content. Carol hadn't taken part, but Tina had been ecstatic about it and threw a painting party courtesy of her husband. The bathroom and kitchen were ready, and the community had donated appliances. It was all coming along. Looking around, Carol smiled and nodded in approval, but a pang hit her heart, and she wished her mother could have seen it. At least her mother had experienced Carol's joy in The Refuge before returning to New Mexico.

A large, warm hand reached around Carol's waist, and soft lips brushed across her cheek, causing her to turn. She flushed as her face was just inches from John's. Playfully, she pushed him back. "Why, Mayor, what will folks think?"

"Makes no difference what they think. It's what you think that matters." His eyes were deep and intense.

Carol blew out a breath.

He dropped his hand and turned away his gaze. John had brought morning coffee and dinner every day during the last week. He attended to her every need and was her private chauffeur, and while she didn't feel smothered, unrest stirred within her. She'd never let a man's heart get so close and never kept a man so far away either. Her mind wandered back. Well, maybe once, but that was long ago. Carol shook her head as if clearing the thought and forced herself to look at John. Really look at him.

John seemed to respect her distance but didn't hesitate to take every chance at gaining her affection. The latter raised an internal struggle that battled out within her gut and heart. It didn't help that her mom had liked him so much. The pressure again of living with decency, honor, and all that stuff clouded her mind. Could she settle down?

Carol's gaze fell on Melanie and Desmond, working side by side. They'd helped her navigate this new life, this renewed faith of hers.

She glanced up at John. For an older man, no one could hold a candle to him. Not even a younger man, for that matter. His blue t-shirt stretched over his well-formed biceps, and the casual blue jeans he wore fit perfectly. No middle-aged paunch there.

"Why don't you go sit down? You should get off your feet," he said with concern in his voice.

She waved him off. "I'm tired of sitting down. I got this shovel here, and I'm ready to use it."

Taking the long handle from her, he threw it aside. She glared back at him, but he bent and picked her up.

"What? Oh my goodness, John Taylor. Mayor put me down." Carol kicked but winced at the movement of her still injured foot. She whispered, "Everyone's staring at you, and you're making a fool out of yourself."

"I already did that in front of the Town Council. I think I can handle a little church scrutiny."

Walking over to the sitting area under the gnarled old oak, he plopped her down in a white wicker rocker. "Keep Officer Blaine company. Besides, no one believed you were going to work in that long skirt of yours. Lemonade?" He pointed to a little drink station set up by the porch.

"Sure. I'm working up a sweat here." She rolled her eyes as she watched him saunter away.

She gazed at those working in front of her. Pink and white peonies lined the walkway border, compliments of Max, the florist from The Pink Rosette. His wholesale license had come in handy when purchasing the night-blooming jasmine and rose and azalea bushes. The bright blue hydrangeas went in below the front porch railings. The hope of full bloom by Easter break was envisioned by the hearts of the community.

Blaine sat on a whisker settee. He leaned against the armrest, hiding behind dark shades and an Atlanta Braves baseball cap. The brim sat low on his brow, touching his dark glasses.

"Hey, there, Blaine?" said Carol.

His gaze rested on Virginia as she dug in the dirt. Occasionally Virginia would toss a dirt clod at him, and he gazed at her adoringly.

"Hey, Miz Carol. How's that foot, ma'am?" He asked.

"It's all right. It seems to want to fester more than heal right now. But I'll be fine. I hope your head is doing a whole lot better."

Officer Blaine nodded. "I'm getting there. The headaches are still pretty bad. I wish I could get back in my squad car, but with the dizzy spells, the doc won't release me." He pushed up the sunglasses on his nose and pulled down the baseball hat even tighter. The bright sunlight seemed to bother him.

"Well, I should hope not. You just take it easy. Chief Bert's got that replacement officer for now." Carol laughed. "And is he driving the Chief crazy or what?"

"That's what I'm afraid of. Chief's getting crankier every day from what I hear."

"Well, the world goes on without us. I need help at the shop myself. Tina comes in for a few hours a week. Helps me unpack and stuff."

"I thought Virginia did that?"

"Oh, she does, but sometimes I do a little retail therapy, and a big order comes in." Carol chuckled, and Officer Blaine stared back blankly. "Retail Therapy? You know shopping like crazy 'cause you feel sorry for yourself?"

"Nope. Never done that, ma'am."

Carol scrunched her face. Men. "Never gone crazy shopaholic or never felt sorry for yourself?"

"Neither, ma'am."

Carol reached over and gave him a shove, almost toppling him. Scooting up straight, he sighed. "Well, maybe a little." He glanced at her. "Not the shopping, but I sure wish I could get back to work. And I'm not sure what's going to happen with Virginia right now. I can't be there to protect her much."

Carol rubbed her arms as if a breeze blew by. It didn't. "I know, Blaine. Me too. God took us both out of commission. Maybe we were getting in his way?"

Blaine chuckled. "I never thought of it that way. It's a good thing we got a lot of other people that can step in." He glanced around. "At least, I hope so. That Boudreaux, he's inflicting some damage."

Carol could feel his angst, even though she couldn't see behind his mirrored sunglasses. She bit her lip and couldn't say a word at the mention of the monster's name. He'd gone silent the past week or so, and so had Eleanor.

"You know, today is Virginia's birthday." Officer Blaine watched Virginia work. "She hasn't even mentioned it. I mean, she asked me yesterday if we could get a cake, but other than that, all she cares about is me." He smiled, and Carol followed his gaze.

Virginia bent over a patch of ground. Her blue denim cut-off shorts were slightly too cut-off but fortunately revealed nothing more than her shapely young legs. Her blonde curls fell forward and swayed as she stabbed at the hard ground. Sitting up she arched her back, and with a trowel in hand, waved at Officer Blaine. Dirt flew from the tool and flung smack into Melanie's face, who was working next to Virginia. Melanie tilted her head and smeared the clot off her cheek.

"Oh, I'm so sorry." Virginia apologized but, at the same time, couldn't control her giggling.

Melanie squinted and picked up a small handful of dirt, flinging it at Virginia.

"Truce," Virginia screamed.

The women laughed and wiped the dirt off their clothes but turned as singing erupted, and a chorus of Happy Birthday rang out. The housemother approached from the porch carrying a beautiful white cake covered in coconut flakes. The candle-lit masterpiece rested on a sparkling cut-glass pedestal. As she walked down the Victorian House steps, she set it on the picnic table. Virginia ran over as the small crowd gathered. Carol felt a sinking feeling because she hadn't planned the intended birthday party. Seeing Virginia's excitement over the cake washed away Carol's guilt, at least for the time being.

"Mmm. Is it coconut crème?" yelled Virginia.

The housemother nodded, and Virginia squeezed her so tight, that a cough escaped as everyone clapped and laughed.

"It's my favorite. Well, come on, y'all. Give me that knife so we can eat this thing."

As Virginia held the knife in the air, an older model, plain white van rumbled up the street and parked in front of the house. Everyone turned. They waited. Finally, a uniformed man exited the driver's side, clipboard in hand. Carol thought it a little odd. His uniform was somewhat generic, and what delivery company used clipboards anymore? Everyone nowadays uses electronic sign-off. Blowing out an exasperated sigh, she wondered if she was paranoid, but when she glanced over at John, he wore a puzzled expression.

In appearance, the thin young man held no threat. But the entire scenario seemed ominous. He walked up to the small group and with a high squeaky voice, called out, "I have a delivery for…." He searched his clipboard as if he'd forgotten the name. Straightening up, he started again. "I have a delivery for a Ginny Boudreaux?"

The crowd froze, and all eyes fixed on Virginia, then back at the man.

A smile burst across Virginia's face, and she blurted out, "Why, he must mean me." Jumping from the picnic bench, she yelled, "I'm Virginia. My uncle is Boudreaux."

A collective hush emitted from the crowd. Virginia pushed out her lower lip, and she huffed. "I mean, who's it from?"

"I don't like this," said Officer Blaine. "Not one bit." He straightened and called out, "Hey, Virginia, get away from him, ya' hear."

It seemed as if only Carol heard Officer Blaine, as everyone's rapt attention fixed on the delivery man. He cleared his throat, "May I have your attention, please," he said it as if reciting a line from a script and continued. "The benefactor of this delivery insistently desires to remain graciously anonymous." He held his head high as if nailing the final act in a play.

A loud, lone clapping sounded, then Carol lowered her hands. "Are you kidding me? Who do you think you're trying to fool here?" She stood.

John walked over and laid a gentle hand on her shoulder

as he asked the delivery man, "Thank you, sir. Mind showing us what you got in the van there?"

The man backed away, and John walked forward with Pastor Desmond and the housefather of The Refuge following close behind. Reaching the van, the three men stood formidably behind the shivering delivery man. As he opened the back doors, he pulled out colorfully wrapped boxes and packages and handed them back to the three men. Virginia clapped as balloons accompanied the packages brought to the table. The delivery man leaned back into the van.

Officer Blaine yelled, "Watch him!" This time loud and forcefully enough for John to act.

John dropped the packages and ran. He pulled on the man's arm, spinning him around, but a small, white fluffy ball of fur jumped into John's arms. Its pink tongue lapped at John's face.

The delivery man picked up his clipboard once more. He walked over to Virginia. "Ma'am, please sign here."

Carol pushed herself up and limped over to Virginia. She took the pen out of Virginia's hand. Grabbing the clipboard as well, she shoved it into the man's chest. "Oh no, you don't."

The scene played out awkwardly. Expressions fluctuated between surprise, disgust, and joy at the puppy wiggling in Mayor Taylor's arms. The delivery man fidgeted, and he swiveled his head from Carol to the crowd and back.

"Thank you, sir, but I think we might need to decline these gifts." The housefather glanced at Virginia's pouting face. "We need to know who the gift giver is."

All eyes rested on the strange little man in uniform. Suddenly, he dropped the clipboard and ran. Before anyone thought to chase him, he jumped in the van, and the engine roared. The back doors swung wildly open, and a little cage fell out into the street as he sped off.

Laughter broke the silence as well as the barking puppy.

Virginia took the adorable animal. He licked her face as she scratched behind his ears. "I think I'll name him...." She glanced at Officer Blaine. "I'll name him Officer. Ain't that a cute name?" she cooed as she snuggled him tightly.

CHAPTER 26

"How in the world did I land up with you?" Carol waved a hand, and the tiny puppy, Officer, ran around her apartment. She'd had the puppy for a week now and still wasn't used to having a pet. He stopped in front of her, not looking the least bit guilty, wagging his silky, white tail, and panting his tongue. A tipped head and adorable eyes stared at her. Carol started to limp but caught herself and walked a little straighter. She picked up the chewed black ballet slipper and stared him down.

"Bad dog." She waved the slipper at him, and he ran off to his hiding place. Safely under the bistro table, he peeked out, arrogantly barking at her.

Flinging the slipper in his direction, she missed on purpose, and he ran in circles, mocking her as he barked. She took a step, and he boldly hopped on a chair and onto the table. Cocking his head at her, he wagged his tail but quickly turned and poked a paw into a potted African violet planted in a mosaic pot. Tauntingly, he lifted his paw and with one last pant at his new owner, proceeded to dig, flinging dirt everywhere.

Carol screamed, and he jumped, knocking over the plant. Bits of broken blue and green mosaic tiles and were dirt scattered everywhere. The purple violet root ball sat on its side intact.

The door to the shop flung open. "Goodness, are you okay up here?" Tina peeked in.

"Are you always sneaking in behind closed doors? And to answer your question, of course, I'm okay. I always scream randomly. Don't you know that by now?"

Bells jingled downstairs. "Coming! I'm coming all right." Tina yelled as she disappeared, her voice trailing and her heels clicking down the steps.

Carol shook her head, staring at the mess. She searched for the guilty culprit and found him, eyes closed on her favorite crocheted, striped afghan. "What in the world am I doing with you?"

Recalling how Virginia had put up quite a fuss about refusing the gifts, especially the puppy, Carol smiled. The whole incident had been enlightening, even life-changing for Virginia. Carol had noticed a stirring in Virginia when Blaine asked her why she wanted anything from that man. It was as if some reasoning and reckoning were taking place in her soul as well. Carol could only hope that Virginia would understand that being lavished with gifts could never replace the joy of God's eternal gift in Jesus. She was still trying to grasp that one on her own.

When Virginia asked if she could sell the gifts and donate the money to the Refuge, Carol's heart swelled, but the house-mother implicitly rejected the idea. Blood money, she said, so the unwelcome presents were disbursed elsewhere. Only the puppy remained. Like an innocent baby, how could he be rejected? But the Refuge had a No Pets rule, and Carol reluc-tantly landed up with little Officer. Not being an animal person, she had no idea what to do, and the new houseguest was giving her a run for her money.

"Officer," she yelled, and he merely opened one eye. "If

you don't settle down, I'm going to throw you out the window. And we're on the second floor!"

He opened the other eye and stared up at her under his furry brow. If it weren't for his winding down in the evenings and how cuddly he was, Carol was tempted to follow through on her threats. But as if he could understand, he tucked his head under his two paws, and Carol's heart melted. She was discovering a softness inside of her that she didn't know was there. "Oh, come here, you. I didn't mean it."

Sitting next to the puppy, she picked him up and stroked his back. He perked up and licked her face, raising his head for an under chin scratch. Carol complied and nuzzled her new companion.

With all the things wrestling in Carol's mind of late, Officer was a welcome distraction and comfort. Especially in the evenings. Boudreaux once again went silent, so anxieties regarding him took a back seat. But since her mother's visit, Carol had a longing to go home.

She let the thought of a homecoming dissipate as she busied herself with Bible study, followed by the accounting for Second Chance. The numbers were tedious, but Carol's sharp mind handled them well enough. She stretched as she closed her ledger. Dusk was descending, and Tina had locked up and left for the day. Carol sat upstairs, with too much to think about, all alone.

Knock. Knock. The sound came from the front door leading outside.

Why was Tina knocking from that entrance, she thought? "Come in!" She fidgeted, tying a blue bandana around Officer's neck.

"Hey, sweetheart." John walked in.

Carol cringed at the greeting but smiled at seeing his handsome face. He always came at the right time, but she sensed his feelings were growing, where hers were...well, what were they doing? He walked over and leaned down to kiss her cheek. She consented. They hadn't had any more passionate kisses. She had placed an invisible barrier, and John must have sensed it. With the threat of Boudreaux work at The Refuge, the reconciliation with her family, and the shop, she really had no time for a relationship. At least a relationship that she was sure she could keep clean and pure. Temptation still loomed. Resting her chin on a propped arm, she stared off.

"What's up, Caroline?"

"Only my mother calls me that."

"Sweet Caroline. I like that name. You never told me that Carol was a nickname."

"I never told anyone." Although, secretly, she liked her given name. It was nice and proper, but she never felt like she could live up to it. She tipped her head, "Maybe it's about time I took a grown-up name."

Sitting on the sofa adjacent to her, John caught Officer as he bounded over and licked the light rough scrub on John's face. He scratched, patted, and finally lifted the puppy and placed him on the ground. "You keeping him?"

Carol shrugged.

"How about some dinner?"

Carol nodded but looked up with a furrowed brow. The pit in her stomach hurt. *Why God, why bring him now? Couldn't he have entered my life before? Before I messed it up so badly?* Another face popped into her head, Alex. Carol sat up straight. Her brows knit together, and she drew a breath.

"It's just dinner, Caroline. I promise," he said.

A sigh followed, so audible she imagined his frustration.

"When you're ready for more, you can let me know." He stood and offered a hand as a ray of hope broke across his face. Somehow it always filled her with secure patience. It held a strength that she admired, although his eyes expressed a sadness that made Carol hurt.

"I'm sorry, John."

"Let's go out and have a good time. It's been a crazy week. I just want to be with you."

~

The aroma of a rich marinara sauce, with hints of garlic and onions, greeted John and Carol as they entered the Manière Sister's restaurant. The restaurant jutted out across the gulf and was a Bay Town favorite for locals and tourists alike. White linen cloths covered every table, and old-fashioned raffia-covered wine bottles topped with a tall candle graced the centers, the dripping tapers diffusing soft ambiance. Melodious strings filled the room as an older violinist played, and a younger man accompanied on the keyboard in the corner on a small platform. The slow, haunting melodies floated out from the soulful, expressive performance. Unfortunately, it had to compete with the chatter, crying babies, and squeals of families who had come for the All-you-can-eat-Pasta Night.

John pulled a chair out for Carol, and she relaxed in her seat, appreciating the family vibes. It lessened the chance of her getting caught up in the moment. Yet, the sweet whining strings of the violin messed with her heart as she gazed back at John through the candlelight. "You know what, John? I think I'm having the All-you-can-eat-Pasta." She slapped the menu closed.

"Why not?" He waved at one of the Manière sisters.

She glided over in her 50s style dress, wearing black orthopedic shoes. The permed hair and bright red lipstick flooded Carol with nostalgia.

"Good evening, Mayor...ma'am." The Manière sister nodded at Carol. "Love the outfit." She pointed at Carol's lacy top and floral silk kimono. "You got style, girl."

"That she does. Listen, I guess we're here for the same as everyone else."

"You got it. What pasta can I start you off with?" She

offered a palm toward a long salad bar situated in the fresco-painted archway. "You can help yourself over there, too."

Both John and Carol ordered linguini and helped themselves to the salad bar. Toasted perfectly with a buttery crust, fresh garlic bread sat in a little basket waiting for their return. Carol picked up her Coke and drank it halfway down. She stared at John as he sipped his glass of red wine. Funny how people thought wine gave them an air of elegance. John didn't need the wine for that. It came from within.

Placing his glass down, he reached out and took Carol's hand. She froze and swallowed hard. Oh no. What's he doing? A panic arose, and she felt her body heat up. *This is bad.* She removed her hand and grabbed her cola with both hands. The cold felt good.

"Relax, Caroline. I wanted you to know that I'm leaving town for a week or so."

Suddenly, Carol wished he still held her hand. "What? Why?"

The joy that broke across John's face lit up the room. "Oh, so absence does make the heart grow fonder? And I haven't even left yet."

Carol felt a warm flush. She didn't care and grabbed his hand. "Why so long? What will we...what will Bay Town do without the mayor? I mean, especially now with that creepy Boudreaux."

He squeezed—his large, safe hand covering hers. "We have a town council that can handle anything. I'll only be a couple of hours away. My mother is aging, and I need to check in on her."

"I didn't know you had a mother...I'm sorry. I mean...."

John laughed. "I know what you mean. We haven't had much time alone together, but we've spent enough that I know who you are, Carol. And I love everything about..." His voice trailed, and his grip loosened.

Carol reached for her water glass and gulped.

"Anyway, yes. My mother is ninety-four years old and lives with my older brother and his wife. Mama's in good health. She's just getting along in her years. I call her almost every day and try to get out there once a week. But with all that's going on, it's been a month."

Carol warmed at the sweet moniker. This man of authority had a *mama*, and it made him all the more endearing. "And you'll be gone a week?" She heard herself squeak.

"Miss me already?"

He seemed to be enjoying this. A knot formed in her stomach. Carol didn't want him that far away, and her heart and her mind swirled. "Yes, John. I do. And I will. I guess I've depended on you more than I thought. I've always handled everything on my own. Except for the last year, I think God's been taking things out of my control."

"That's a good thing. He's the only thing that got me through my divorce."

Her brows furrowed. *But didn't he say that's when he took a break from God?* This was the most positive thing he'd said about faith. She stared back, knowing her eyes questioned.

"I'm still working on that. So, I'll be gone for a week or more. It depends on how Mama is getting along." He squeezed her hand. "I'd ask you to join me, but I'm not sure I can take any more rejection." He didn't give her time to answer. "I'll be back before you know it, Caroline."

Carol hadn't really noticed, but most families had left, and couples, young and old, had repopulated the place. Suddenly she was aware of the quietness. The evocative melody of the movie theme song from The Godfather began to trill, and John stood, offering a hand.

"You think you can manage with your foot?"

A feeling of joy flooded her. She really loved dancing, and with John, the music, and the moment, she didn't hesitate to stand. "Whether I can or can't, I'll sure try." She smiled back at him.

Twirling her once, twice, and three times, they reached the center of the tiny dance floor. She stumbled most of the way but didn't care. He pulled her in close and wrapped his arm around her waist, and with his other hand, he clutched hers tightly against his chest. The flesh of his palm felt smooth and firm. Their bodies pressed close together as her head rested under his chin. As the violinist plucked out the melody, her heart beat wildly with the moment surrounding them. As he glided her around the floor, his touch, his steps, lifted her to another world.

The song drew to a close, and John eased back, but the heat between them grew. Their eyes searched one another, and as she lifted her chin, his face drew close. His lips swept her forehead, moved to her cheeks, then rested softly on her lips. He let them linger there, and before she could catch her breath, his mouth pressed deeper onto hers.

She would have clung there forever if not for the applause that interrupted the moment. While still in one another's arms, Carol realized that they were the only ones left on the floor.

In typical Carol fashion, she yelled, "Whoo, wee! Mayor, you are quite the dancer." Breaking his hold, she lifted his hand high in the air and took a bow herself. All the while, she was dying inside. *And where do we go from here?*

CHAPTER 27

Carol was thankful the drive back to her apartment was short. It didn't afford them much time to talk or express what had just happened on the dance floor. His kiss tonight was every bit as magical as the night he first kissed her after the town meeting, and she had told herself that wouldn't happen again.

Shining stars in the clear night sky continued the magical aura, and as they stood on the top steps of her apartment, John's strong arms gripped her about her waist.

Carol placed her hands on his chest and pushed back. "John..."

He dropped his hands. "Don't say you're sorry. I don't like it, but I think I understand. Maybe time apart will do us good. You have some things you need to figure out." The hard edge in his voice toned down and all but disappeared as he continued, "You are a special lady."

"No, I'm not."

"Shhh. I don't know what voice you're listening to, but you deserve all the respect this town is trying to give you. And all the love...well, let's leave it at respect. Caroline, you are an amazing honorable woman." Lifting her chin, he ran a thumb across her lips.

The heat rose inside. Could she turn away if he bent to kiss her again?

Slowly and tenderly, his thumb swept across her cheek instead. She closed her eyes, and his soft kiss barely graced her forehead. He left her standing on the landing as he retreated down the stairs.

He stopped at the bottom. "I'll call you when I get back." Pushing back his hair, he grinned that bright smile full of strength, but when he waved, she already felt an emptiness creeping in. She watched as he got in his car and drove away.

Turning towards the door, Carol pushed it open. Something wasn't right. It was too quiet. She peered at the knob and then the keyhole. No key. She hadn't inserted her key. She never left the door unlocked. Especially nowadays. Stepping in, the room was brightly illuminated, but she hadn't left the lights on, and the silence, she couldn't place the still quietness. She turned to yell for John, knowing he was long gone. She shut the door behind her and fished through her purse for her phone. She stopped. There was no friendly bark.

"Officer?"

The apartment was just a small studio, and her eyes swept the room. There was nowhere for him to hide. Just the same, she called out, "Come on, boy, quit playing with me."

Carol shuffled to the bistro table and stooped to look under it. She sucked in a breath, closing her eyes tightly. The movement put too much pressure on her foot. Her wound hadn't completely healed yet, and her foot ached as she lumbered around the apartment. It had gotten infected and slowed her recovery. She walked to the laundry area where his food and water were, but he wasn't there. A hitch caught in her throat. Fear gripped her heart. Boudreaux. She grabbed her cell phone.

"Chief, I think someone broke into my apartment. The dog is missing, and...Okay, thanks."

With all the events happening of late, the Chief took issue

with everything. He was on his way. Carol stood, arms crossed, chewing on her bottom lip. She tapped her forearm. She couldn't give in to fear, and before she gave herself over to anger, her heart stirred. She had to trust. *God, please. He's just a helpless puppy.*

A knock at the door and a shout from the chief sent Carol across the room. Opening the door, she fought back the tears. "The dog is missing. I don't know what to do? It's going to kill Virginia."

Removing his hat, he patted her arm. "Mind if I come in?"

"Of course." She opened the door wide.

Looking around, he asked questions. "Did you touch anything? Is anything besides the dog missing? Any visible evidence of a break-in? He kept walking and circling the little room.

She followed.

Walking into the bathroom, he pointed to a small window high above the toilet tank. "Where's the screen?"

Carol's eyes widened. "Are you kidding me? There's no way that little thing could jump up there, much less push out the screen." She faced the Chief but could only envision Boudreaux.

"What's out there?" He asked.

"It's the side alley. The garbage bins are out there. They're full, so the smell is pretty bad right now. That's why I keep the window closed." She bit her lips and shivered at the night air coming through. "Trash pickup is in the morning."

"Shhh." The Chief held out a hand. "You hear that?"

A muted whimper floated into the window.

The chief and Carol both rushed for the bathroom door. Getting stuck, Chief Bert glanced down at Carol's shoulders wedged between his and the door frame. "We ain't both going to fit, and I don't intend on being a gentleman right now."

He glared at Carol, and she backed away. He ran for her

door, and his body pounded down the steps. Carol followed much more slowly and caught up with him in the alley. He had already hoisted himself on the top of one bin and was wearing glove she lid on one container was closed, but the other was propped open.

"I'm sure I heard something." As he squatted atop the bin, his fingers wiped up a thick liquid on the rim, and the moonlight revealed the dark red color. He followed the trail and peered into the full garbage bin. The sound again.

"That's him! Officer, we're here! He's in there. Come on, Chief, we have to dig him out."

"Ma'am, if I get in there and he's still alive, my foot alone could finish him off. I'm afraid we gotta do this the messy way." He hoisted himself atop the closed side of the bin and laid out his 6'2 frame, scooting his upper body over the open container. He began throwing garbage out, one piece at a time. "Phew. This is bad."

"What do you expect?" Carol ducked as the pieces flew over her head. *Please, God.*

A louder whimper came from the bin, and the Chief called, "Hey, there, buddy. Hold on, we gotcha." He straddled his body strategically over the container. Bending down, he removed a few more pieces of garbage and lifted the battered, injured pup. Handing him over to Carol, Chief Bert nodded. "I think this was a job for the firemen." Hoisting himself out of the bin, he scrunched his nose as he shook his whole body.

Tears fell as Carol buried her face in his fur. Officer continued to whimper and even squealed as she maneuvered to hold him gently. "I have to get him to the vet. Do you know where one is? Do we even have a vet in Bay Town?"

Chief Bert pulled back. "Of course, we got a vet, lady. Where you been living?"

"Not in doggy land, that's for sure." Carol stroked Officer. "You poor thing."

The chief pulled out his phone and dialed. After a short

conversation, he wiped the phone on a somewhat clean spot on his shirt and replaced it. "My wife says there's an animal clinic over behind the Mockingbird Café. She called, and the vet said he'll meet you there in a few minutes." He gently patted Officer's head. The dog made a noise that might be interpreted as a happy yelp.

Tears dropped onto the dirty, matted fur, and Carol's concern turned to anger. "He is just plain wicked. Who would throw a dog out a window?" Carol winced, recalling how she'd threatened the same many times. But she certainly didn't mean it.

"I wouldn't put it past him, but we need to take prints. I'll call forensics. It'll take a while for them to get here. You want to leave a key with me?"

"Sure. But I touched the doorknob," said Carol.

"Anybody else touch anything tonight?"

Carol flushed red and blew out a breath. "Yeah, the mayor, maybe. I don't remember," she said quietly.

"Who?" The Chief seemed to be stifling a snicker, but he waved her off. "Got it. If it was Boudreaux here, he more than likely wore gloves. It's a good thing that bin was open. Too bad they both weren't. He probably hit the closed one and bounced into the open."

"Poor little thing." The veterinarian scratched his head. "What happened?"

"I think someone broke into my house and threw him out my bathroom window into the alley."

"You don't say? Who would do such a thing?"

He gave her a sideways glance as he gently cradled Officer. Not waiting for an answer, he took the dog to the back office, and Carol waited. Thirty minutes later, he returned.

"He's a lucky little guy. He's got a nasty gash on his back

leg, but there doesn't appear to be anything broken. I'm sure he's pretty bruised up, though. I can give him an x-ray to check for a concussion, but if you want to stay up with him and keep checking on him, I think we can wait till tomorrow. I don't want to traumatize him anymore. On the other hand, if he's hemorrhaging…."

Carol stared at him. "He's not." She took the puppy in her arms. "He can sleep with me, and if he takes a turn, I'll call. Either way, I'll bring him back in the morning."

"Good." He pointed next door. "We have a groomer over there, and she's pretty booked up, but I can get you in. That little thing needs a good washing. I cleaned his cut up pretty good, but I'd like to recheck him after a bath and cut."

"Good idea. Thanks. I'll do that." She stood and carried him carefully to the door. "Thank you."

As she opened the door, she ran into a tall, imposing figure. It was dark out, and she caught her breath.

"Sorry, ma'am. I just wanted to return your key." Chief Bert held up her house key dangling from a big fuzzy purple ball.

"Why is everyone always scaring me half to death around here? Are you done already?"

"Yes, they dusted for prints. We'll find out tomorrow. I'll let you know. How's the little fella?"

"He's a lucky little guy. I'm amazed that fall didn't kill him."

The Chief followed Carol back to her house and checked things out once more in her apartment. As he was leaving, he stopped on the front porch. Looking down, he scratched his head. "Miss Carol? The mayor, he's not a smoker, is he?"

Carol nodded, nuzzling the puppy in her arms, half ignoring the rhetorical question. Everyone knew the mayor didn't smoke, and he'd tried to pass ordinances to outlaw the nasty habit around downtown. So far, he hadn't succeeded.

The Chief pulled out a pair of gloves and a baggie. He bent and picked up two cigarette butts.

"Whoever it was, he's a bold character. Smoking two cigarettes under your porch light."

Carol seethed. "I'm sure it's been him around here smoking for the last month. I've seen more butts around here than I care to count." Carol laughed nervously at the chief's raised brows.

"All right then. I need to knock on some doors. Find out if anyone else saw anything around here this evening."

"Won't do no good. I'm the only one who lives up here."

He stared back at her with a hard glare. "Well, Miss Carol, maybe it's about time you moved in with Miss Melanie for a while. I'm going out to the alley, going to take a look around. Lock up tight, now."

She did as he said, and instead of feeling sorrow or fear, her anger rose. *Like heck, I'll move in with Melanie.* Carol had already given up her home once, and now she was sure that it was Boudreaux's actions that had forced the move. After Grady was killed, she couldn't bear to live in her home, where she had last shared her bed. That house had been home to her for the last ten years, and she'd downsized from the two-bedroom bungalow near the woods to this claustrophobic little studio loft. But it was home, and Boudreaux wasn't pushing her out this time. She reached for her phone.

"Tina? I need your help in the morning. Can you be here early? Say eight o'clock...great. Thanks so much." She kissed Officer and stroked his head as his eyes closed. *Boudreaux's not getting away with this,* she thought. She glanced down at the puppy sleeping in her arms. *That I can promise you.*

CHAPTER 28

Everything was set. Tina arrived early, agreeing to handle the shop for the day, and Carol dropped the puppy off at the vet, who would keep him until she picked him up at the arranged time. If she didn't, Tina would pick up Officer and take him home until Carol returned. She got in her car and drove.

Thankful that Tina could pitch in, Carol couldn't worry about tomorrow. She had called the Refuge and made arrangements for Blaine to pick up Virginia after school and take her to the shop. He'd finally gotten the okay to drive but wasn't released for work yet. He'd also return her home at the end of the workday. She told no one of her plans, but for a brief moment, she thought of John. Then her cell rang. She pulled to the side of the road and answered.

"Hey, Chief Bert?"

"Where are you?" Chief Bert's voice was no-nonsense.

Did he know what she was up to? How could he? "I'm...out. What's up?" Her body tensed.

"We found Eleanor Perrin. She——"

Carol fumbled with her cellphone righting it to her ear. "What? Where? How is she?" Her questions shot out like gunfire.

224 | KATHLEEN J. ROBISON

"Let me finish." He took a deep breath. "Her body was found floating in the gulf." Chief Bert's voice dropped, and he went silent.

Carol slumped in her car, gazing in the direction of the water. She wanted to cry but couldn't. A hardness took over her heart. "Are you sure?"

"I'm sure, but they're waiting for a positive ID. Her purse was on her person."

"No more. I don't want to know anything about the body. It was Boudreaux. That I know for sure."

"No. No, we don't know anything for sure."

"I have to go. I'm late for an appointment. Goodbye, Chief." She clicked off.

Carol wanted to believe that this was confirmation that what she was about to do was the right thing. Still, an inclination told her otherwise. She ignored it. Carol drove over the Bay Bridge. Hoping to get to Pascagoula early, she avoided the beautiful beach drive and took the main inland highway instead. She imagined the blue skies lighting up with the orange sunrise and reflecting off the gulf waters. Just the same, the dazzling rays of the rising sun bounced off her windshield, blinding her. Blindness, all right, that's what the day held. Still, she moved forward, purposely ignoring the urge to pray and seek God in her scheme. She hoped she knew the answer, but she wouldn't wait.

An hour later, Carol arrived in the familiar strip center where she'd seen Boudreaux with the teen girl. Driving around, she doubted she'd find him again, but she had to try. She parked her El Camino and stepped out. Shading the sun, she fumbled through her bag for her sunglasses. Spring was warming up, and it felt more like a hot, humid summer day. Carol removed her light denim jacket and threw it in the truck. The thin, colorful scarf tied around her neck hung down, as did her hair, already heating her back. It would be a hot one. The smell of bacon coming from a café lingered in the air, and her stomach growled. Ignoring it, she walked into the drug store.

"Hey, there. Remember me?" Carol wasted no time approaching the same clerk she spoke with the last time she was there. She was thankful that this was his shift.

"Oh, yeah. I remember you."

"Yup, most people do." She tipped her head. "It's my charm, right?" It was her brash aura coupled with her wild dress that always made an impression. Good or bad, she didn't much care. A pang hit her heart. Well, maybe a little these days. What was that thing, *a gentle and quiet spirit*? She shook it off. Time for that later. "Hey, have you seen our friend…" She winced at the word. "I mean that slick, creepy guy?"

He nodded. "But not with no new girls."

"Well, listen, I need some help."

He shook his head. "I don't want to get involved. I got a wife and kids. I don't need no trouble."

"Oh, settle down. I just need a phone call." She pulled out a business card and slid it across the counter. "Here's my phone number. I'm parking out behind the building. Call me when he comes in."

He glanced at the psychedelic business card with her phone number. "What for?"

"I just want to follow him. Find out where he lives. Report the address to the police. I promise you. I won't bug you again. That is unless you change your mind about helping me out."

"Nope." He pushed the card back.

Carol's first instinct was to lash out. Instead, she took a deep breath and put on her sweetest face. "Listen, mister. You got a daughter?"

He raised his hand to stop her, then picked up the card. "Okay, okay. But just a phone call." The clerk glared back at her. "If he even shows."

"Fair enough. Thanks." She reached over and squeezed his hand, but he quickly pulled it away.

Driving her car around the back, she parked in the empty alley. Her bright orange truck stuck out. Carol wished she'd thought of renting or borrowing another vehicle. Something less conspicuous. On the other hand, she didn't know whether Boudreaux would even know what she drove. *Of course, he would.* Unfortunately, he wasn't stupid and knew what he was doing every step of the way.

Settling back in her seat, she tried to get comfortable. She picked up a book she'd left in the car and started to read the psychological thriller by Nancy Brashear. *Great, just what I need right now.* Still, she chuckled. *I might get some tips.* She read, but anxious butterflies fluttered in her stomach, and the time dragged as she waited for a phone call. Laying the book aside, she started the car's engine and turned up the volume. Talk radio. She listened to her favorite preacher speaking on trust and God's grace. A few minutes later, she flicked it off and sat quietly. She glanced at her watch and huffed. It was still early.

Buzzz. Buzzz. She felt the phone in her skirt pocket.

"Hello?"

"He's here." Click.

Carol's hands shook as she returned the phone to its safe place. A prayer for help nagged at her, but she ignored it. *I can't wait,* she thought. *He's already gotten away with murder.* Thoughts of Grady and Eleanor fueled her revenge, but fear for the teen girl and Virginia spurred her to reckless abandon. She drove slowly around the building, being careful to hide on the side of the long strip mall. She crawled forward until she got a view of the parking lot. It was there. The blue Lincoln. She waited.

It was him, and the girl was with him. Carol's stomach lurched. Her intention was to follow him. Get his address and report it, so the authorities would keep an eye on him. But seeing the girl again changed everything. How could she just leave her?

He walked out with his hand on the girl's shoulder. From the back, they appeared normal, almost like father and daughter. Carol shuddered as she watched him open the door for her and forcefully seat her in the front. He looked around before slipping into the driver's seat.

Carol stayed a reasonable distance behind him. Blocks away, he pulled into an old trailer park. It wasn't as bad as some she'd seen but run-down enough that she guessed no one cared about anyone's business. Good cover. She had to act quickly. *One chance, that's all I got.* The entrance led to rows of lefts and rights. She watched until he turned, then she followed. A few toddlers played in the street, and young mothers sat in lawn chairs watching them, waving at cars to slow down.

Finally, he pulled into a double-wide trailer carport. Carol sped up until she reached the toddlers, then stomped on the brakes, then drove again slowly. The mothers stood and yelled expletives as they grabbed their children.

Carol waved and smiled, calling out, "Sorry." Still, she sped to Boudreaux's space, reaching it just after he parked. The girl, who had exited the car, was by the trunk when Carol screeched up.

She threw the car in park and left the engine running. She opened her door and stood. "Will Boudreaux?" she yelled.

Her hatred for the man clouded a much-needed healthy fear. His head swiveled, and his narrowed eyes connected with her. Before he could speak, she yelled at the terrified girl, "Girl, get in my car now. This is your only chance."

As if an invisible force moved her, she flew to the passenger side of Carol's car and jumped in. Boudreaux was already by Carol's side and grabbed her arm. Carol tried appealing to the young mothers, who stood gaping. "Hey, ladies?" she yelled. "This guy is a predator! He kidnapped this girl. Call the police, now!"

Boudreaux let go of her arm and seethed. "Ladies, you go on and tend to your young 'uns. This lady is crazy." His laugh sounded friendly and convincing. But it was enough time that Carol broke his hold, jumped in her truck, and slammed and locked her door.

"Can you drive stick?" *God, please let her.* The plea came so naturally, and she was willing to sacrifice herself if need be.

The girl nodded but jumped when a loud rap threatened to break the driver's window. Carol turned, and her eyes widened at Boudreaux's gun pointing at her. She hadn't really expected to get out of this situation this easily, but still, her pulse raced. His face seethed, but his body blocked his actions from the view of the neighbors. He barely nodded, and Carol raised her hands and pointed to the lock and handle.

"Turn off the engine," Boudreaux said.

She barely heard his voice through the window, but he slowly reached forward.

"Drive to the drug store. The clerk will help. I promise." Carol spoke quietly.

The girl's frightened face froze.

"God help us." With one swift movement, Carol unlocked the door.

Boudreaux took only a small step back, with his hand on the outside handle. He pulled, and with all the weight she could muster, Carol slammed her shoulder against the door. The old heavy door swung wide and knocked Boudreaux down. Still sitting in the driver's seat, Carol reached to pull the door closed, but it swung too wide. She put a foot on the ground and leaned to pull it shut. The sandal exposed her bandaged foot. The heel of Boudreaux's boot kicked the wound, and Carol screamed and fell out of the car. With nothing to break her fall, she lay dazed, lying under the door. Adrenaline flowed, and she grabbed the bottom of the door with both hands, and with all the force she could muster, she slammed it shut.

"Go!" She screamed as she rolled to the side.

Before either herself or Boudreaux could stand, the girl ground through the gears, peeled backward, and jolted down the street. Carol glared back at Boudreaux and glanced at the mothers. "You see that? Now, call the police!"

Boudreaux stood over Carol, his gun blazing in plain sight. The mothers screamed, grabbed their babies, and ran inside. He hissed at Carol, "Get up now."

She blinked, wincing at the piercing pain. Blood dotted her bandaged foot, and her elbow and shoulders scraped from the pitted blacktop. Her skirt pocket ripped, and her cell phone lay beside her, exposed on the ground.

"You stupid woman. Where'd she go?" He yelled.

Carol kept a peripheral eye on her cell. If he saw it, she didn't have a chance. But in his rage, he didn't seem to notice. Fiery eyes bored into her, and he took a step. She tried to roll her body to conceal her lifeline, but he bent over her, yanking her arm.

"Git up!"

As he pulled, she let her body go limp right on top of her phone. Losing his grip, he kicked at the rocks, and in that instance, Carol slipped the phone back into her skirt pocket. Without hesitation, he grabbed her hair and dragged her to his car.

He held the gun to Carol's head while he twisted a clumped bushel of her hair. "I said, where'd she go?"

She tried to stand but couldn't. Blood trickled from the side of her face where her head hit the ground.

Carol swallowed. *This is it*, she thought. "Wouldn't you like to know?" She spoke sweetly.

Boudreaux smiled just as sweetly back. He let go of her hair and smoothed it down, lowering his gun. He cupped her chin. "Yes, I would, darling." He stood straight, lifted his boot, and ground it onto her injured foot, much like he extinguished a lit cigarette.

The pain was like a sharp knife slicing through her open wound. Carol felt light-headed, and black dots formed in her eyes, threatening to connect. Her body slumped against his car.

Boudreaux flung open the back door and shoved Carol in. "We're going for a drive, sweetheart. And you're going to be my navigator." He slammed the door on her hip. She stifled another scream.

Carol keeled over in the backseat. Her bandage lay open, and she shuddered at the flesh of her wound lying open. The searing pain all but diminished the sting of her other newly inflicted injuries. She lay across the backseat, not attempting to buckle up. She tried to think but instead prayed. *Lord, get her to safety. Please.* Carol found the strength to pull herself up.

Boudreaux's movements were quick but calculating, and Carol memorized every move. He backed out of the carport. He paused. Then drove past the trailers where the mothers and their children had sought refuge. One by one, Boudreaux went by their homes. Behind thinly worn curtains and battered blinds, the frightened women peeked out. To each one, he raised his gun after a friendly nod. All quickly drew back away from their windows. Carol glanced back and saw one mother peek out again, a cell phone to her ear.

CHAPTER 29

"I wouldn't try anything back there if I were you."

Boudreaux stared at her in the rearview mirror, and Carol didn't know how he could shoot her while driving, but she didn't doubt he'd try. An evil mind was capable of anything.

"Now, you want to try again and tell me where she went?"

Carol shook her head. "I have no idea. Where'd you get her from?" She shot back.

"You stupid woman. She's a runaway. The bus stations are full of them. Everyone knows that."

Anyone that knows about human trafficking, Carol felt ashamed that she wasn't more aware. She'd assumed it was mostly done through kidnapping. She thought back to the days when she ran wild and never imagined that she could have become a trafficking victim. Yet, somehow, she'd been protected.

It helped that she had money. Her parents had never cut her off. Her bank account was always full. She thought of the teen girl and the others. Was it God that had protected her? She forced the thoughts out. This wasn't about her anymore.

Boudreaux drove the streets of Pascagoula, and she knew he was searching for her bright orange El Camino. He seemed to be going up and down the same roads repeatedly. Soon, things took on familiarity. He pulled into a Quick Stop on the corner near the drug store.

"You best stay put." He said as he exited the car. "Don't think you can get far with that poor little foot of yours." His grin made her sick to her stomach as he patted his hip. "Besides, my little ole' gun, it can reach as far as you can crawl." Rapping his knuckles on the roof, he slammed his door.

Carol watched as he approached the building. He yelled something inside, threw his hands up in exasperation, and returned to the car. Raising a hand to shade his eyes, he froze. Carol heard the sirens. He glanced down the street, and at the end of the long strip center that housed the drug store, two Pascagoula police squad cars sat parked. Boudreaux jumped in just as he saw two more screech in front of the drug store.

He yanked open the car door. "You stupid woman. See what you've done?" His face flushed, and the veins in his temples bulged. As he climbed into the car, perspiration dripped down his neck. He pulled out slowly and waited at the light, all the while checking his rearview mirror.

"You're done," said Carol. "They got your car, your license plate." Hope gave strength to her voice. The sirens came in all directions, and when the light turned, he drove one block in a direction they'd not yet traveled.

"No, lady, you're done." He pointed, and Carol's heart sank. Her car sat on the side of the highway just past the intersection. Empty. He moved swiftly. Parking behind the car, he jumped out and peeked in. He checked the door. It wasn't locked, and she could see him gloating. He walked back and opened her door, "Well, this is my lucky day. Get out."

Carol's gut wrenched, and she prayed that the girl had gotten to the drug store. Maybe she'd stalled out, but she could have run from here. *Oh, please, God,* she begged again. Boudreaux dragged her battered body to the El Camino and threw her in the passenger side. Jumping in to drive, he glared at her and cursed. "You drive a stick?" He slammed the steering wheel. "Scoot over here, now!"

He couldn't drive a manual transmission? She wanted to laugh, but everything in her screamed with pain, and trying to drag her leg over to the driver's seat prevented her. He walked around to the passenger side. Yanking open the door, he cursed again. She couldn't move.

"I can't drive. I need two feet," Carol said.

"You're going to need more than that when I get through with you. Now get over there."

Boudreaux pulled out his gun.

Do I give up now? The girl is safe, and he can't get away. Virginia will be safe. Carol smiled inside. *At least I can end on a good note.*

"Are you deaf?" Boudreaux pulled his gun. "You think I can't get out of this? How do you think I only spent one year in jail? I killed your boyfriend, lady. And I got all those girls. I'll get more."

Carol felt her body strengthen with each hateful word. She yanked her leg and shifted her body across the bench to the driver's seat. The keys were in the ignition, and she stepped on the brake with her good foot and took a deep breath as she stepped on the clutch with her bad one. Her face scrunched as she maneuvered the car on the road. Her pressure and release on the clutch caused the vehicle to jerk and stutter. Boudreaux screamed at her, and with every vile word, she sat straighter. She clutched, accelerated, and clutched and accelerated more. She had control now. They could both die. She didn't care. She drove toward the Interstate.

"Don't even think about it." He hissed.

Most likely, there were roadblocks by this time. Boudreaux directed her onto a highway and ordered her to increase her speed. She accelerated past the limit.

Tensing at his screams and threats, she recklessly passed other vehicles, weaving in and out while cutting drivers off. Hopefully, someone might report her. Many cars entered the highway, and traffic slowed. So did she. The bright orange truck crawled along with the flow. An hour went by, and he gave her no directions, so she continued to drive north. *Why weren't there any police?* Every time she stepped on the clutch, she felt blood ooze. Feeling lightheaded caused moments when she thought she might faint from the pain. She focused on staring at the road ahead, and suddenly, the car lurched a bit.

"What are you doing, woman?" Boudreaux glared.

Carol glanced at her gas gauge. *Thank you, Jesus.* "I have to pull off. I'm out of gas."

"The heck you are. Keep going."

Better for me, she thought, letting the El Camino crawl along until it started to chug and choke.

Boudreaux sat up and slammed a fist on the dash. "Pull off now and get to a station."

Could she make it? Exhausted, she coasted into the nearest station. It was a huge truck stop with lots of activity. She let out a sigh.

"What are you smiling at? This just makes lots of good cover. Ain't nobody going to notice us." The tone of his voice displayed otherwise.

Carol's mind raced. If he used his credit cards, they'd get him. If he used cash, he'd have to go inside the building and leave her in the car. There was no way she could walk now, but she could scream for help.

He looked at her and grabbed her head. With his white handkerchief, he wiped the blood off her temple. "That's better. We wouldn't want anyone asking questions, would we?" He stepped out and pointed a finger at her. "And just in case you think of doing anything…" he smiled sickeningly at her and patted the bulge in his coat pocket. "I'm pretty good with this."

Carol slumped. His gun. She didn't doubt that he'd kill anybody that got in his way. Boudreaux walked to the pump in front of him, and she watched as he approached a hunched over, gray-haired gentleman pumping gas. A woman with a head of curly white hair barely peeked above the passenger seat.

Carol rolled down her window and leaned out but couldn't hear a thing. Boudreaux pulled out his wallet and handed the man a couple of bills, then took over pumping gas. The man grinned and walked towards the building. Boudreaux was clever. She had to give him that. He looked around and grinned.

A young woman stood on the other side of the pump. He leered at her while replacing the nozzle and cap. She hunched her shoulders and tilted her head sweetly, smiling.

He banged on the roof of the car, and called, "All done, ma'am."

The curly white head nodded and waved. Boudreaux took a few steps over and joined the young woman. Carol watched them exchange words, and the young woman smiled. Her low-cut sundress blew in the breeze, and she giggled as Boudreaux took the nozzle and pumped her gas. Carol felt sick.

"Carol?"

Her body jerked in her seat, and she rolled down her window. "John? What are you doing here?" Her hair was drenched in sweat, and her face flushed, but she felt a new wave of perspiration washing over her. She glanced at the car in front of her. The old man was back, but Boudreaux was not in sight. *He can't be far*, she thought.

"You should go, John."

"What? How'd you know where to find me?"

"I didn't. John just…" Carol reached out and touched his hand. "Just go."

"Carol, you don't look so well. Are you all right?"

"Hey, mister. Are you bothering my woman?" Boudreaux walked up from the rear of the El Camino. He laid a hand on John's shoulder, pushing him back. Leaning in, he grabbed Carol's chin and kissed her hard on the lips. Everything in her wanted to slap him, but she worried about John's safety. Just the same, she pulled away.

John stood staring, puzzlement all over his face. "Carol, who is this guy?"

Before she could answer, Boudreaux spoke. "Why, we're old sweethearts. Got hooked up on that Facebook, you know." He winked and stroked Carol's shoulder. She pulled back.

"Please, John, just go." He wasn't budging. She sat up straight, wincing and forcing a smile. "I'm sorry, John. I should have told you. Will—"

"Honey, it's Beau. I told you to call me Beau." He glared.

She faked an adoring smile. "Beau here. He just came back into town and swept me off my feet." Carol practically choked on the words.

John's eyes narrowed. "I just left yesterday. When did this happen?"

Her heart broke. Her only alternative was more lies. When this was all over, and it would be over one way or another, she hoped he would understand. Understand that she wasn't fit for him. This mess proved it.

Boudreaux pointed a finger in John's chest. "You, sir, are a sore loser. You best be going."

Fists clenched on both men. She glanced between the two. "Honey?" She said, and they both turned. She died inside. "Beau, can we go? We got a long drive. I'm sorry, John." She shrugged. "I tried to let you go."

His hard eyes seemed to search hers, and finally, he nodded. He drew up straight and unclenched his fists. "You sure about this, Carol?"

She didn't answer.

John shook his head. "My mistake, I thought...."

Looking back at him, Carol feared that she had betrayed her heart.

"You thought wrong, mister," said Boudreaux.

"Maybe. Maybe not." John tipped his head.

Carol reached out but took Boudreaux's hand. "Yes, John. It's him. Not you. Now leave us alone."

"Be gone, mister." Boudreaux laughed.

John walked away, and something inside her felt much like the final nail in a coffin, but she thought this was the right thing. She would take care of this mess of her life once and for all. Her rearview mirror reflected John walking to his car behind them. From the side window, she could see Boudreaux topping off the gas as he watched John's retreating figure.

Boudreaux finished and slid in. Carol took a deep breath and groaned in pain as she started the car. She pulled out too quickly, almost hitting the car in front of her. It caused Boudreaux to crash his head as his body flew into the console. He immediately reached over and slapped her. Stunned, she swerved, and another car honked. A few onlookers shook their heads. She didn't care anymore.

Boudreaux berated her with questions about John and why he was there. She refused to answer, staring stoically ahead. Her hands gripped at ten and two on the steering wheel. With each refusal of hers to answer his questions, he slapped her again. Her cheek swelled, but she kept driving. He turned the radio to a news station and waited. An alert was now out for her vehicle. Carol knew he would soon be plastered all over the news. She sighed, hopeful of the outcome for everyone but her.

It wasn't long before they were on an empty two-lane road heading nowhere. Carol saw a few signs that indicated state marshlands and bogs up ahead, and he directed her to a dirt path, barely wide enough for her truck. A wall of trees and thick growth rose on both sides. The damp earth gave way to wet dirt, soon turning to mud. Still, she sludged along, the ground getting thicker and deeper until she couldn't drive anymore. The car stalled.

Boudreaux pulled his gun. "Looks like you got me. Right?" He pulled her hair, but she refused to scream. "Well, you don't. I grew up here, here in this rotten stinking place. I know my way around Mississippi better than any police. I'll get out. I always do." He opened his door and sunk a little as he stepped into the mud. He walked around to her door and yanked it open. "Now get out."

"Are you serious? I can't even—"

This time, he used a fist and hit her jaw. Her head flew sideways. Stunned, she rested against the seat. Finally, she prayed. *Oh, Lord, help* and wondered if this was the end. Dark spots flickered before her, then blackness started to converge. Boudreaux yanked and pulled until she fell on the soft, muddy ground. He took her arm and dragged her a few yards into thick, damp bushes, and dropped her. Of all things to pray, she gave thanks for the cool mud that soothed her open wound. But just as quickly, her eyes focused, and bile rose. Her body went rigid as crawling insects slithered across her shoulder.

"Well, sis. You are done interfering with my plans. I can leave you here to die," She heard his gun click, "Or I can finish you off quick. Either way, your journey is over."

Carol raised and saw his gun pointing at her head. "Well, at least mine will end in glory."

"Have fun in glory then, stupid woman." He fired the gun.

CHAPTER 30

Leaving her lying in the mud, Boudreaux sloshed back to the road. He slid into her El Camino and started the engine. Shifting gears and rocking the car back and forth, the car almost lurched out of the mud hole, but not before the roar of another engine screamed up behind him. As he turned, a large Mercedes sedan barreled toward him. Boudreaux jumped out and pointed his gun at the car. The Mercedes flew into the back of the El Camino, and it burst into flames. The explosion flung Boudreaux through the air. His body slammed into a tree and dropped to the ground like a rag doll.

Flames engulfed the El Camino, and red spires blazed high into the air. The crackling and sparking sounds joined the hissing Mercedes. Exploded airbags filled its interior, but the driver's door opened, and a man fought down the airbags before falling out of the seat. Blood trickled down his brow, and he swiped it away.

"Carol? Caroline?" John yelled, his voice booming through the woods.

As he stepped forward, his feet sank, and he fell once more. Covered in black ooze, he pushed himself to stand and struggled forward toward the woods, attempting to shield himself from the ball of fire raging behind him. A glint of the sun's rays shined through the trees and reflected off something shiny coming from a mound. He staggered forward, and bangled bracelets flashed in the mud. Crawling, he dropped to the ground next to Carol's limp body. He began to shake, and his body heaved.

He leaned in and whispered, "Dear God, please."

CHAPTER 31

Her eyes flew open, and she tried to scream. Her voice gripped in silence as her mouth gaped. She tried to give notice with the horror on her face. Look behind. It's him. An almost unrecognizable body rose. Bloodied and battered, a blackened form beneath fragments of burnt cloth struggled to stand, but the gun in hand pointed forward with strength. With all her might, she expelled a blood-curdling scream. Like a dark fog, blackness surrounded and suffocated her.

Carol felt a gentle touch. Her eyelids fluttered, but bright lights overhead blinded her. Blinking, she tried to turn her head, but every muscle in her neck hurt. Any part of her body that she attempted to move ached and throbbed. Closing her eyes again, she heard voices. *Who are they?* It pained her mind to concentrate enough to make them out, and anxiety rose within her. A monitor beeped.

"Her blood pressure is rising." A female voice called out.

Carol felt the gentle hands of pressure once again. Her body settled, but her mind was alive. "The gun!" She screamed, trying to lift her body.

"Caroline. Shhh. Shhh. There's no gun. He's gone." A deep, soothing voice spoke, but she could barely hear it. It was like cotton was stuffed into her ears.

But the pressure of a gentle hand calmed her. John Taylor smiled at her, and he bent to kiss her forehead as he smoothed her hair.

"Caroline, stay still. You're safe. No one can hurt you now."

Her eyebrows scrunched, and now, the pain she felt was of the heart and not the body. If only she could remember. She hated the cloudiness in her brain as she glanced around. The clicking machines glared back at her, and she frowned. She struggled to understand every word around her.

"Can you wean her off the drugs?" The deep voice spoke again.

"We have been each day, but when she gets restless, we need to increase to keep her calm. But I'll check with the doctor," said the nurse.

A knocking sound came from somewhere. It was so faint, that Carol could barely hear it. The hand comforting her slid off her body, and she heard rustling footsteps. Quiet voices spoke, and she wished they'd talk louder. With all her strength, she said. "Speak louder." Though hushed and hoarse, the command silenced the voices. She heard shuffling approaching her bedside.

"Ms. Scape?" A loud voice asked.

A weak laugh crackled, and Carol slowly forced her heavy eyelids. She stared straight into the face of a handsome young man. "Honey, call me Carol. Mrs. Scape is my mother." Her eyelids closed again.

"Well, I think Caroline is coming back." The deep, strong voice came again.

Carol dragged in a breath but couldn't control the tears. They rolled down the sides of her face. Her body shuddered as she worked to hold back the pent-up deluge. She turned her head aside, away from him.

"Can you tell me what hurts? What's going on?" The young doctor spoke.

She shook her head and heard John speak. "Doctor, can we have a moment?"

Once again, she heard footsteps. This time retreating away from her bed. She weakly lifted her hand in a wave. As much as she tried, she couldn't stop the tears. "Go, John. Go, now," she whispered.

He placed a hand on her cheek and gently turned her head to face him. She had no physical strength to resist his touch.

"You told me that once before, and you didn't mean it then. I don't believe it now."

He bent forward, and his face hovered over hers. He pressed his soft, warm lips onto hers. Her tears flowed, and although she welcomed the salty kisses, her cheeks burned, and she moved her head aside.

"Carol?"

Her eyes met his, and she expected to see pain. Instead, she saw nothing but kindness.

"We'll talk another time," he said. "Right now, we need to get you off these drugs and get you back to your ornery self." John reached for a tissue, wiping her tears. "Get some rest, girl. Melanie will be here soon to sit with you." He kissed her forehead and brushed aside her hair. "I'll be back."

John left, and the doctor reentered.

"Carol. Can you tell us what happened? It would help us with your diagnosis and treatment."

Carol shook her head, not wanting to recall anything that happened.

The doctor continued. "It appears you have difficulty hearing, and we found some gun powder residue near your temples when they brought you in. But there's no gunshot wound."

Finding the strength to chuckle, she said, "He didn't shoot me?"

"Did he try?" The doctor asked.

She blinked and remembered how Boudreaux had pointed the gun. His words about finishing her off rolled around her head, and she mumbled out loud.

"Excuse me?" The doctor said.

"How's my foot, doctor?" Carol asked abruptly.

"Well, that's part of your problem. You picked up some nasty swamp bug, and infection set in. But we got the right combination of antibiotics, and that's under control. When you're feeling better, you need to see an ENT and get your hearing checked. I'm sorry, I don't have a more concrete diagnosis. If someone shot at you, they must have aimed right at your head." He winced. "I'm not sure how he missed, but you're a pretty lucky woman."

"It wasn't luck, Doc. The good Lord saved me."

What felt like days passed, and darkness hovered outside her window. Inside, the lights were dim. With great effort, she turned her head. Melanie and Desmond slouched on the window seat. Both asleep, his arms cradling her.

"Hey, if you two would just get married, you could go to sleep together in your own house."

Both stirred at her voice. Melanie jumped up. "John said you woke this morning."

"This morning? Are you sure? That felt like ages ago," said Carol.

"Sometimes, sleep is God's way of getting us through difficult times," said Desmond.

Instead of being comforted, Carol fidgeted. Each movement caused pain, and snippets of memories flashed before her eyes like still photographs—ugly, graphic black and white pictures. Taking a deep breath, she sighed and tried to poke around. Her arms wouldn't move.

"Carol. You're safe." Desmond stood by her side.

"Was I shot?" Carol asked, having a vague memory of the doctor's conversation.

"What? No. You keep moaning about a gun, but there's no bullet wound," said Desmond.

"He was just leaving me to a painful death."

"But you're safe, now. And Boudreaux is dead. We'll tell you all about it later." Melanie's voice perked up. "Hey, your mom is staying at my place. She's been here sleeping every night with you."

"Mother? When did she get here?"

"Carol, you've been in the hospital for over a week." Melanie's voice wavered a little.

Patting her hand, Desmond said, "You're a tough woman, Carol. It was touch and go. You've got some nasty injuries."

A weak chuckle escaped. "That's my life, touch and go."

"No, Carol. God's got you. You've been steady for the last year. He's not letting you go." Desmond's words comforted her.

She nodded. "I know. I had a nice respite from my past. But I've got a lot to think about now."

"Why you're the town hero," Melanie chuckled, then squeezed Carol's hand. "We're here, Carol, and we'll help you get through this."

Melanie's soft voice lent some comfort, but Carol shuddered. The short time with Boudreaux flooded her. His harassment, his beatings, and his harsh kiss. She couldn't erase it. Reminiscent of a past life with insignificant men she thought she loved and those she didn't.

"Carol. It's over. Whatever has happened, God will use it for good. Just believe and trust in that. We'll weather this together," said Desmond.

"And Carol," Melanie smiled. "Virginia is safe. The girl, her name is Ashley, she's safe too. It's because of you."

A ray of hope beamed from Carol's face as she recalled the girls. Beauty from ashes. Hope quickly diminished to despair at the thought of ashes and flames. She shut her eyes tight. The flashbacks wouldn't stop.

"Hey, Carol? Do you mind if I read a little to you?"

She nodded. Desmond reached for a black leather bible. He opened the book and let it fall smack in the middle. Turning a few pages, he began to read the Psalms. Carol felt her anxiety release and tension float away. As if the words of scripture bathed her soul, she felt the cleanliness of God's mercy, and grace wash over her.

~

"Right, sweetie. I'll have your room ready. Everyone is so excited about your return."

Carol held her phone and picked up her fancy cane. She limped to the bistro table and sat. Her body tensed while she gazed out her window into the stark, empty alley.

"Me too, Mother." Though excitement wasn't what she felt now.

"Caroline, are you sure you're all right to travel? I can come out and fly back with you."

"Thank you, Mother, but I already have my ticket. I'll be there before you know it, but I have to tie up some loose ends."

"All right. I just can't wait." Carol listened as she heard a light panting as if her mother was ascending stairs. Through the phone, she heard a door close and knew what was coming —a whisper.

"You know your father can't wait either. He's fit to be tied that we had to leave before you were discharged from the hospital."

"Well, I would have been fit to be tied if you'd stayed. That hospital room was getting to be a grand central station." Carol heard a rustling under her feet and felt a tugging at her skirt. With her cane, she lifted the paisley tablecloth. "Officer, you let go of my skirt. Go on, now git. Mother, I need to run. I love you. Tell Father I love him too."

Her mother clicked off in protest. Everything was in place. Virginia would graduate from high school next week, and Carol would leave the day after the party. The thought of returning home to New Mexico gave her new hope. She anticipated a reconciliation of sorts but wondered if it might also be like a restart. She picked up the fluffy puppy. He hadn't grown much, but then he wouldn't. The Lhasa Apso licked her face. She shivered a little. Would she always think of Boudreaux when she held this treasure? Another reason to leave.

"You'll have a good home, boy. I promise." She held him high. "And don't I keep my promises? Virginia is going to love you to pieces."

She set him down and checked her calendar. A Town Hall meeting tonight. She wasn't going. Having sworn Tina to silence, which was near impossible for her, she would go in her place. Tina had agreed to run Second Chance in her absence. Carol had given her free rein, and she jumped at the chance to take over. Virginia would help full time after graduation.

Carol smiled. She'd hoped to give the shop to Virginia and Blaine for a wedding gift. Lots had happened when she was in the hospital. Blaine had proposed, and the timing was perfect. As Virginia aged out of The Refuge, they would marry and live in Blaine's little cottage.

Ashley was now in The Refuge, and though having a difficult time, she agreed to terms. She was a runaway, and her parents were contacted and were in full cooperation with her rehabbing at the house. She'd been reluctant to help the police, but with love and gentle coaxing, she understood the urgency to stop human trafficking.

Checking her watch, Carol grabbed her purse and her Bible. Her eyes moved slowly around her apartment. Her stomach growled, reflecting the emptiness she felt. One year. She'd only lived in the studio apartment for one year, and it was supposed to be a new life. She locked her front door. She longed for the days when she wasn't concerned about that anymore. Carol stepped out on the landing as darkness settled in. Her first instinct was to cower and huddle back into the little studio, which no longer brought her comfort. Instead, she straightened, shoving her Bible in her hobo bag before hoisting it over her shoulder. Grabbing the rail, she stepped down. Wearing an orthopedic boot on one foot, the other sported a fancy cowboy boot with a modified heel.

When she reached the bottom step, she drew a breath. The shadow of a tall, dark figure approached. "Good evening, Caroline."

That voice. That soothing, loving voice. "Mayor, you about scared me to death again."

She waved her colorfully carved cane at him. The light from her porch silhouetted her frame.

He stared back. His eyes seemed to cover every inch of her face.

She fingered her hair nervously. The tight bun atop her head was such a contrast to her usually long flowing locks, but it matched her mood. She moved her fingers across her lined forehead.

"So, it's back to Mayor, is it?" It sounded like a half joke.

She shrugged. "Oh, John. No need to be so serious." She glanced at her watch. "Don't you have a town hall meeting to tend to?"

He stepped forward and reached for her bag. She pulled back.

"You've been avoiding me since you left the hospital. I've given you time, Caroline."

"Please don't call me that."

Staring back at her, his eyes reflected the hurt that matched the wound in his heart. Darkness lingered there, and she was the cause. She knew it. She'd tried to let him go. Heck, she pushed him away, and he kept coming back. Like a lost puppy. No. Not a lost puppy. He saved her life, and she was forever indebted to him, but he was another reminder of the mess she always made of things.

"All right. Carol." He took a deep breath and stood straight. Placing one hand in his pocket, in a gentlemanly form, he offered his arm. "May I help you to your car?"

Her lips pouted, and she shook her head. "I do believe I don't have one anymore." She winked. "Thanks to you."

He chuckled. "No rental?" He glanced around, but there was no car in sight.

"I thought I'd try the bus."

"I can give you a lift to the town meeting?" The conversation changed to cold and formal. "That is if you're going?"

"Actually, I'm not." She didn't offer any more information.

He nodded, and they ambled out of the alley. His car was parked on Main Street, and the City Hall was a few blocks at the far end. She let go of his arm as they stood under the lamplight. The clear sky twinkled with a myriad of stars, and a slight ocean breeze blew loose tendrils across her cheeks. John brushed back one behind her ear. Reaching up, she took his hand and pressed it to her lips. "I sure wished I'd met you a long time ago, John Taylor."

"I'm here now, Carol. Maybe you should accept God's timing." His warm hand squeezed hers.

"Yeah, I always seem to have a hard time with that. God's timing, I mean." She raised an index finger. "But that's my goal for the rest of the year."

She avoided his comment about him being there. The truth hurt. He was always there for her. Like no one else. *I'm not ready yet, John. Your goodness shines too bright a light on my garbage.* She wiped his hand on her skirt as if trying to clean it, then let go. She pointed to the bus stop across the street.

"I'm going to catch a bus."

He stood staring back. Suddenly, almost stumbling, she reached up and brushed her lips across his cheek. She felt his hand brush up her side, but slowly it dropped. She eased back down off her tiptoes and pressed her head under his neck, hearing his heart beat...or break. She didn't know which. Placing a hand on his chest, she pushed away. His smileless face stared back at her, and she couldn't avoid the sadness in his eyes. He lifted his chin and pointed to the bus.

"I don't know where you're going, Caroline, but I hope you find yourself. You can't run forever."

"I'm not running. For Pete's sake, John, I'm just heading to the church." For now, anyway. "I got a counseling appointment with Pastor Desmond."

"Just get on the bus then. I won't leave until I see you safe." He threw a nod in that direction.

Carol's heart dropped. Her stomach filled with butterflies. *Will he forever be my knight in shining armor? If not mine, someone's, Lord?* Taking one last look at the tall, broad figure in the pristine tan suit, she took a deep breath and hobbled across the street. The bus opened its doors, and Carol watched John walk away. "Does this here bus go by Bay Town Church?"

"Yes, ma'am. About ten minutes away."

CHAPTER 32

Tapping her fingers on the counter, she waited. She waited for the coffee to brew—her last cup in the little studio apartment. For the time being, everything was covered and would be left as is. She bent to pick up Officer's water and food dish. He had already made himself at home at Blaine's cottage, and Carol missed his barking and chewing.

All her suitcases were packed, and she'd shipped some clothes and a few other things. Tomorrow, she'd be staying at her parent's home in Santa Fe. She gazed at her teal sofa, Tiffany lamps, and antique wood pieces. No need for furniture. She wouldn't miss them. They were all a reminder of things she wanted to forget.

Her counseling with Pastor Desmond was effective. He'd helped her clear her mind and settle her heart. She wasn't running away. She was heading for a new start, and open to whatever God had for her. And right now, she believed it was for restoration with her family. She lowered her head as dark thoughts broke through.

Carol closed her eyes. *I'm restored. I'm forgiven.* She stood up straight, pulled the coffee pot from the maker, and poured a cup. Carrying it to the little bistro table, she set it down and sat. Her eyes rested on the opened Bible, and she read the marked passages. She knew God's grace had saved her. God's grace on earth and in heaven, but she had to continue to remind herself, and that was hard in Bay Town. Squinting at the print, Carol tried to make out the words going in and out of focus. *Now, if God would only restore my eyesight.* She'd been fighting glasses for quite some time. *Maybe that's part of the new me. I am a new creation. Thank you, Jesus.*

As the crowd watched Virginia walk across the stage, everyone whooped and hollered. Her black mortarboard hat sat atop loose platinum curls, which set her apart from the crowd. As she took her diploma and shook the Principal's hand, she faced the crowd. Raising her diploma overhead with both hands, she stomped up and down, kicking her red platform heels in the air, and cheered. The crowd went wild, and Carol and Melanie shed tears of joy.

After the ceremony, Virginia's friends met at the church community room for her celebration. She had no blood family, but this group was even closer. With Melanie's event planning expertise, the party was a huge success.

True to church tradition, it was a potluck, and everyone brought their specialties. The covered table boasted salads of every variety, elaborately sculptured fruits, macaroni and cheese, baked beans, and even a roasted pig, compliments of Chief Bert and his wife. The dessert table across the room held delectable homemade pies, coconut cream cake, and Lyla's famous Praline Pecan candy.

Carol stood, plate in hand, enjoying a little of everything. For the first time in a long time, her appetite returned. She smiled, watching Virginia so happy and excited. A new life for her too. Things were changing for good without the threat of Boudreaux hanging around. Carol shivered at the memory. Thankful he was gone but left with the horror of his demise.

"Lemonade?" Melanie offered a glass.

Carol took the sweet drink and sipped. "Mmm, mmm. You did a great job, Melanie."

"Well, thank you. But it's nothing compared to what you've done." She smiled. "Are you sure you have to go?"

"Now, don't start that again. Virginia's got a new start, and it's here. Mine's not."

"And you're positive about this?" Melanie glanced at John, standing across the room. He seemed engrossed in a conversation with someone Carol didn't know. A polished, put-together, professional woman. Not from Bay Town.

"Oh, I don't know. I think he's doing okay." Carol raised a chin, staring across the room. "He'll be fine. He's moving right along." Carol winked with a pang hitting her heart. She forced a chuckle. It had been three months, and other than a passing *hey*, they'd not spoken since the night at the bus stop.

Melanie shook her head. "Uh, no. That's my sister. She's tougher than you. Come on, I'll introduce her."

As they walked across the hall, Carol felt light-headed. She didn't know if she was ready for this. "Wasn't she the one that helped with the whole trafficking ring last year?" Carol asked.

"Yes. She challenged everyone to work harder and fight more for the girls. She gave John a run for his money too."

"Hey, Charlene?" Melanie touched her sister's elbow.

"Hey, sis. What's this? I hear about the mayor being some kind of James Bond hero or something."

John laughed. It was good to see his merriment, but then his gaze settled on Carol. As his voice died down and he stared, it felt like no one else was in the room.

Charlene glanced back and forth. "Oh, so you must have been the damsel in distress."

Carol frowned and tipped her head. Long and wavy, her hair flowed around her shoulders. The shiny brass butterfly clip swept back one side. Her peasant top and paisley skirt could be mistaken for a damsel. But not her determination and grit. "Excuse me? I'm no damsel."

"Whoa, ladies. You two are too much alike. Carol, this is my sister Charlene. Charlene, this is my good friend, Carol. Believe it or not, you two are the fighting inspiration in my life." Melanie set a hand on each of their shoulders.

Carol smiled, and they shook hands. She noticed that Charlene's plain, simple pantsuit was quite a contrast to her own colorful outfit. Charlene seemed to match John Taylor's handsome conservative blue slacks and polo shirt reasonably well. Again, a pang hit Carol's heart.

Charlene spoke, interrupting her thoughts. "Thanks, sis. I'm a fighter, all right. Sometimes, I just need to remember what for." Raising a finger, she struck a pose. "A fighter for justice and peace. Sometimes I just forget the peace in my own life."

"Sometimes?" John raised a brow. "So, fighter for justice and peace, where were you when this last Bay Town madness came down?"

Charlene pounded his arm playfully with a closed fist, then she gave him a friendly shove. He laughed back at her.

Carol gulped, her heart hurting.

"Well, Mister Mayor. For your information, I was doing surveillance," said Charlene.

John Taylor furrowed his brow. "Where, may I ask?"

"In Thailand. And that's another story. If you want to get involved, you should come with me sometime."

Carol watched and listened to their banter, dying inside.

"Maybe, I will. When's your next trip?" Asked John.

Before Charlene could answer, Carol whispered to Melanie and stepped back. She waved weakly, staring at John. He appeared not to notice as she walked away. Approaching the exit, she gazed after the tall, handsome Mayor John Taylor, savoring everything about him. As if he felt her gaze, he turned and stared back. She embraced the rise and fall of his chest and the sad smile lifting at a corner of his lips. Finally, he nodded.

Stepping out of the terminal in Santa Fe, the hot, dry air assaulted her like a hairdryer on high temp. Thirty years. *God, I hope this is the right thing.* She peeled off her light wrap and held up her hair, hoping for a breeze to cool her neck.

"Taxi?" A driver yelled.

She shook her head and waved him off. Her parents were supposed to be here. And they were never late. Her suitcases stood around her, and she plopped herself atop one of them. Even those were colorful and eclectic. She fanned herself. Although Mississippi had humidity, living by the gulf provided a constant cooling breeze. Perspiration dripped down her back, and she wiped her brow, staring at the line of cars coming and going.

Where are they? Looking around, she noticed the bronze metal sculptures of native Americans and Cowboys dotting the sidewalks. She was impressed as she continued to notice the colorful terminal. Painted landscapes covered the walls of the airport inside and out. Not a body of water in sight, but the picturesque desert scenes lifted her spirits. There was no reminder of the horror she'd lived in her last days in Bay Town. This was definitely a new start and a new hope.

She crossed her leg, resting her bad foot on one of the smaller suitcases. Everyone seemed to wear cowboy boots and hats of some sort. More than a few women wore colorful tiered skirts, much like the old Mexican style...much like her. She chuckled.

Almost before the thought finished, she saw a slim, dark-haired, and very handsome man in the crowd. What stood out was his navy suit, blue plaid shirt, and yellow tie. It was a bowtie, and no boots. Conservative. She tipped her head. Was there a familiarity about him? He seemed to be making a beeline straight to her and waved.

"Hello, Caroline. It's been a long time." He flashed beautiful white teeth. "You're still as beautiful as the day you left." His deep, sultry voice sounded like the feel of lush black velvet.

Drawing a deep breath, Carol tipped her head. She opened her mouth to speak and promptly shut it.

He laughed a low, hearty chuckle, and extended a palm. "Alex? Remember me? Your ex-fiancé?" His full head of dark hair laced with gray strands complemented the mature light lines across his forehead. His dimples recessed beneath a dark stubble on his cheek and chin. Gorgeous.

She clasped her hands together and sighed. *God takes away, and he sure gives back*. She winced inside. Well, maybe he didn't take away. *Maybe I just ran away.*

"You okay?" he asked.

She stood quickly and put her hands on her hips. "Why, what happened to that gangly, goofy kid I used to know?" *And love*, she thought.

He laughed. "That was a long time ago."

Carol breathed deep. "Yup, and it's sure good to see you." He opened his arms wide, and she flung hers around his waist. Slowly, his strong arms enveloped her, and he drew her close. After a moment, he pulled back and gazed into her eyes as if searching for something. Before he could ask a thing, she blurted out.

"I'm glad you came, Alex."

"Phew! Because I wasn't sure how this was going to go down. I asked your parents if I could pick you up." He dropped his chin. "Well, I didn't exactly ask. I insisted."

Carol's chest tightened. "Alex...I'm sorry I ran away from you...Well, I ran away from everyone but mostly, I ran away from Him." She pointed up. "I'm home, Alex. Home to figure things out, and I'm not running again. I'd be throwing God's grace in His face if I did." Her eyes sparkled.

Alex smiled, and the longing in his eyes reached her soul. And Carol knew she had the power over the next moment, but she laughed.

No. God has the power over this moment and every next moment of my life forever after.

The End

AUTHOR'S NOTE

The theme of grace runs throughout this story. I hope as you read it, you experienced the pain of those who find it hard to receive God's grace. Perhaps you do yourself, and just as Carol Scape was learning to understand God's love for her, I pray that you will too. And for those of you who have the pleasure and joy of knowing how much he loves and forgives you, I pray you will take every opportunity to share His love. That you will reach out to those, who hurt from past mistakes. Those more broken than ourselves. Just as Melanie did to Carol, and Carol tried to with Eleanor. We are God's messengers and instruments of His grace. How can we not share with others what He has done for us?

ABOUT THE AUTHOR

Kathleen J. Robison is an Okinawan-American. Born in Okinawa, raised in California, Florida, Mississippi, and Singapore. Her travels are the inspirational settings for her stories. She and her Pastor husband have eight adult children. Seven are married, blessing them with fourteen grandchildren and counting. The diversity of their 31 family members provide the inspiration for more lively characters than can be imagined. Her husband grew up in the streets of Los Angeles raised by a single working mom, and that life provides fodder for many of the conflicts of her characters.

Tackling difficult life's trials with God's strength are the central theme of Kathleen's stories. She hopes to inspire her readers to trust God and with His strength, weather through and rise above trials and tragedies. If you like suspenseful stories with a thread of romance, you will enjoy Kathleen's Bay Town Series!

facebook.com/kathleenjrobisonauthor

instagram.com/kathleenjrobison

bookbub.com/profile/3794692396

ALSO BY KATHLEEN J. ROBISON

Bay Town Series

Shattered Guilt (Book One)

Revived Hope (Novella)

Restored Grace (Book Two)

ART'S JOURNEY

RESTORED GRACE BONUS STORY

KATHLEEN J. ROBISON

CHAPTER 1

S ometimes, a journey of love is going no place at all.

Art Anderson was in love, terribly, hopelessly in love. The object of his passion was Victoria, his childhood best friend. She'd long since moved away, but he hung on every summer vacation and holiday for her return to Bay Town when she'd visit her grandmother, Sally Trotman. Because he lived across the street from Miz Trotman, he spent most of his time with Victoria at her grandmother's house whenever she blew into town. And then, one day, she didn't.

"Mornin', Miz Trotman." Art ran to take her elbow and helped her up the church steps.

She pulled away. "I'm not that old. I been creaking up these old steps since before you were born." She stopped and patted Art's arm. "But thank you, son."

He grinned that boyish smile that lit up the world— anyone's world except Victoria's.

"So, have you heard from Victoria?" He hated asking.

"She still calls me every week. But no, she's not coming this holiday."

"Oh, I wasn't asking. I just…"

Miz Trotman patted his arm. "I know. I miss her too. But

don't give up." She winked. "She's just on some strange journey right now."

He tried to chuckle but instead exclaimed, "You know, I have a job interview in California? I mean, it's a phone interview."

Sally's eyes widened. "Really? You're not getting some crazy notion to move out there, are you? We need you here, Art."

His heart dropped. Little ole' Bay Town wouldn't let him go. That's why he'd turned down every IT job he'd previously been offered.

Sally reached the top step and took Pastor Brooks' extended hand. "Good morning, Pastor Brooks."

The pastor greeted her kindly, as he did everyone. Art waited till Miz Trotman finished drilling him about the Sunday sermon, and he looked back at the filling parking lot. He watched a car pull in, blowing smoke as it parked. Before he turned around, he took a double-take. A big black truck stopped right behind her. She was so busy getting her kids out she didn't notice. Art took a step down, but the truck pulled out quickly, the tires spitting gravel.

"Hey, there, Art." Pastor Brooks extended his hand.

"Oh, hey, Pastor Brooks." Art took another glance over his shoulder.

"Are you okay this morning?"

"No, he's waiting for my granddaughter to come back," Sally interjected, though she was already at the church doors. She was one of the oldest members of the church, but there wasn't anything wrong with her hearing.

Art forgot about the truck. He tried to smile again but shrugged instead. "Life is good." He lied—sort of. "I mean, good here. Yeah." He pointed to the white clapboard building, double doors opened wide, plotting his escape.

"How about lunch today?" Pastor Brooks asked.

Art glanced, then pointed at the line of people waiting to greet the pastor.

"I'll meet you at Bubba's after church," said Pastor Brooks.

Art nodded and slipped into the church, and soon the building was packed.

Pastor Brook's sermons brought a new dimension to teaching. His exposition mingled with application motivated Art to love and serve God more sacrificially. He was thankful for the message that took his mind off of Victoria, too.

After church, Art crept out quietly, and with his head down, he headed for his car. The squealing of tiresstopped him, and he looked up. A pregnant woman struggled with her three kids. It was her car that blew smoke upon arrival earlier. One child squirmed in her arms, and Bobby, the eldest, ran around her legs. She held the middle child in a hand-cuff grip, and he almost yanked her off her feet. Art ran over to help, and she thanked him while arching her back and patting her protruding baby bump.

"Hey, Cindy. Where's Collin?"

Cindy's husband worked at the local grocery store, grave-yard shift.

Her brows furrowed. "He didn't come home this morning. I mean, that's not all that unusual. Sometimes he works over-time and misses church. But he didn't call."

Little Bobby ran around Art's legs, weaving in and through them, giggling all the while. Finally, Art caught him, threw him in the air, and rested the toddler on his hip.

"I can drive over to the market and check."

"That's okay. Most likely, he's home and sleeping by now. Thanks, Art." She reached for Bobby's hand.

Art quickly scooped him up. "Come on. I'll help you buckle this rascal in."

Making sure the kids were secure in their car seats, Art waved and turned to leave. The whining car engine caused him to turn. Cindy's head rested on the steering wheel, and her wrist cranked the ignition key repeatedly. The banged-up car was acting up again.

"Stop!" Art ran back. "You'll flood the engine. This old girl needs a rest. I'll take you home."

"This old girl? Are you talking about the car or me?" Cindy teased, but her eyes watered. "Are you sure you don't mind? Collin can bring me back later to get it."

"Sure, no problem. Let's move the seats into my car."

"Your car? Yeah!" Bobby yelled, and his little brother screamed too.

Art took care of switching the kid's car seats and buckled them all in. He then ran back to Pastor Brooks.

"Hey, Pastor. I'll be a little late for lunch. I'm taking Cindy home."

"Her car, again?"

"Yup."

"Sure, no problem. You're a good man, Art. I'll order lunch. The usual?"

Art nodded.

Instead of turning towards the gulf waters, Art turned in the opposite direction and headed for the train tracks on the other side of town. It was a short drive, but the terrain drastically changed as they drove across the tracks and down a dirt road. Bramble bushes lined each side of the road, but the discarded old furniture and trash marred the landscape.

Arriving at Cindy's RV, Art parked. Trying to hide his sadness over their living conditions, he quickly jumped out.

Cindy gasped.

"Is it the baby?" Art rushed to the passenger door.

Cindy pointed. The RV door was wide open, and Collin stood just inside. His lip was bleeding, and one eye was swollen shut.

Art rushed to help.

Collin waved him off. "I'm fine. Get the kids," he said.

As cramped as the RV was, Cindy always managed to keep it clean and tidy, but drawers were turned upside down, dishes lay broken on the floor, and even her hand-sewn curtains hung ripped over the windows. Cindy dropped her body down at the tiny kitchen table and cried.

Art wondered that she asked no questions. It was as if she knew what had happened. He waited, but neither spoke.

Collin covered his face with his palms, breathing heavily.

"Daddy, what happened?" Bobby asked.

Cindy patted his head as the baby she held nuzzled her neck. Wiping her tears, Cindy spoke. "Listen, Buddy. How about some mac-n-cheese?"

Art stood. "I'll make it. Come on, Bobby, you can help."

Cindy stood. "No, Art. Why don't you boys sit outside a spell." She walked to the kitchenette and pulled a dishtowel from the door. Wetting it, she handed it to her husband. "Here, sweetie, wipe your face, and go on, now. Go have some man talk, and I'll feed the kids." She turned her back. "And ya'll pray, okay?" she whispered.

The RV was cold inside, and Art rubbed his hands together. Stepping outside, Art welcomed the sun warming his neck. Collin led him to a rickety picnic table, and they sat.

"I never should have borrowed money from them."

"Who?" Art asked.

"Those guys in town."

"Not the Relief Rescue?" Art cringed.

"Yup. I'm afraid so."

Art looked back at the RV, then at Collin. That moneylending business had opened up shop in an old strip mall and quickly gained a reputation for unethical actions against debtors. Destitute poor people went to them and were loaned money, no questions asked.

"What did they say?"

"I got twenty-four hours. Then they'll come take the RV."

Art blew out a harsh breath. "Why didn't you tell me?"

Collin wiped the blood from his lip and held the rag to his eye. "Cuz I'm sick of getting handouts from the church and everyone."

"I get that. But this isn't worth it."

"It was just to hold me over till I got a raise. But the boss said it wasn't coming until Thanksgiving now." He shook his head. "I don't care about me, but what if they hurt Cindy or the kids. I'll kill 'em, I will."

"You won't do that. I got some savings —"

"No. I ain't taking no more money from church people."

"Okay. Then how about a loan? Just to pay these guys back."

"I got no way of paying it back." Collin's shoulders slumped.

"We'll figure out a way. With the holidays coming, plenty of odd jobs need to be done. Pecan harvesting, chopping fire-wood. Heck, Miz Trotman and the seniors always need help this time of year."

Art had always helped the elderly in Bay Town, never taking money, though they offered. They showered him with home-baked goods, knitted hats, and even afghans when he refused. Heaven knows he didn't need any more of those. The seniors would be happy to help support this little family.

"You think so? I'd be willing to do anything. I asked my boss for another shift, but he's got other guys needing the work." The dejected husband suddenly perked up.

"No worries, but first, we need to report this to Chief Bert."

"No way. Those guys will come after my family. Please, don't tell anyone."

"But you can't let them get away with this."

Collin shook his head vehemently. "No, Art."

"Fine. I'll go pay … how much?"

"I only borrowed five hundred, but they're adding a hundred a day for interest, so it's twelve hundred."

"And you won't let me go to the police?"

"No."

Art huffed, rolling his eyes upward. Staring back, he reached for Collin's hand. "Fine then. Let's pray."

"I been doing that, but more prayer never hurts. That's what Cindy always says." He shrugged. "I know the good Lord's got a plan. I wish I knew what it was."

"I gotcha there. It's easier to take matters into our own hands, isn't it? But that's always a disaster." Art thought of the job in California. The one not too far from where Victoria lived.

"You sound like Pastor Brooks."

"He's a smart man." Art grinned.

Art prayed, assured Collin he'd pay the debt, and left him and Cindy with renewed hope. Art promised to have names, numbers, and jobs lined up. He begged off the mac-n-cheese and left the young family waving from the door. God did that.

Driving away from the trailer park, Art pulled off the side of the dirt road, careful not to get too close to the thorny berry bushes. His classic Ford Mustang was his pride and joy, and Victoria loved it, too. He shook his head. *Ridiculous.* He was worried about his car, and Collin and Cindy were destitute.

Art texted Pastor Brooks, apologizing and asking to meet a little later. Pastor Brooks agreed, explaining that he'd gotten tied up after church himself.

Art drove to Relief Rescue. The small shop was no bigger than half a storefront, and it was sandwiched between empty suites. Although it was clean and nicely furnished, Art didn't wonder why. With the way they ripped off the poor, he was surprised they didn't operate in a newer strip mall, but this was the right neighborhood for their business. The thought angered him.

He walked in, and a man wearing a sleek brown suit, white shirt, and paisley tie stood. Extending a hand, he welcomed Art.

"What can I do for you today?"

"I need to pay off Collin's loan." Art took out his wallet.

"Well, that's mighty nice of you." He picked up his cell and texted.

A younger man came from the back of the office. He slipped a file to the man in the suit.

"All righty then. That will be fifteen hundred dollars."

Art pulled back his card. "Fifteen? Collin said it was twelve hundred."

"Well, today is one week late. That's an extra three hundred for every week he's late." He looked at the desk calendar. "Oh, my mistake. It'll be sixteen hundred. Today is also eight days late, so that's another hundred."

With the transaction finished, Art headed for the door but turned. "Don't ever go near their home again."

The man laughed. "He came to me first, son. We never turn down a customer."

"I'm warning you." Art pointed a finger. His stomach churned, but he didn't attribute it to hunger.

Art greeted Bubba at the Catch Shack at Pier One. It wasn't a wonder that he and Victoria didn't weigh three-hundred pounds. It was their teenage hangout, and Bubba was not the owner then, just the cook. But now, owner and chef, he drew a steady crowd, and the little wooden building served up the best burgers in town. Art looked around before ordering. Pastor Brooks hadn't arrived yet, so he placed their order and sat. He stared at the rocking boats tied up to the docks and thought of Victoria.

"Hey, sorry I'm so late. Did you order?" asked Pastor Brooks

"Yup," said Art.

"Sorry about that. Next time is on me." Pastor Brooks pulled out a red metal chair and sat. "So, why the glum face."

"Excuse me?" Art's eyes widened, but his shoulders drooped. He couldn't possibly know about Victoria. "Do all men of the cloth have a sixth sense?"

Pastor Brooks laughed. "I wish. Everything okay with Cindy?"

Art straightened. "Cindy? Oh, yeah. Well, they got some problems. But God's got them. They're trusting Him." Art cleared his voice, "Sort of," he whispered.

"Anything more we can do? I mean, the church?"

"No." Shaking his head, Art ran a hand through his curly thick hair and blurted. "They'll be okay, now. But... I have this friend. Victoria."

"Oh, girl trouble."

"What? No! She's my friend. My best friend. I've known her since we were kids."

"Then you got it bad, eh?" Pastor Brooks winked. "She's Sally's granddaughter, right? Sally has mentioned her a few times."

"Yeah. She used to live here but moved away to California, to the beach, so we don't see her much."

"I guess not. I'm starting to love Bay Town, but California beaches are hard to compete with."

Art didn't respond, and they sat in silence. Bubba brought out their order. The tray rested on his stomach while he served their burgers. The seagulls screeched overhead, and the water lapping against the rocks should have soothed Art's soul. But the familiar gulf sounds didn't.

"Mind if I pray for the food? Unless you want to."

Art shook his head. "Please." He just didn't feel like praying.

He didn't feel like eating either. *This is ridiculous.* He had no commitment with Victoria, nothing romantic at least. Except for his heart.

A couple walked past, hand in hand, and Art looked away. He breathed deep and sat up straight.

"I have an interview for a job near where she lives."

Pastor Brooks took a paper napkin and wiped his mouth. "Oh. I didn't know you were looking to move."

"Yeah, well, I haven't told anyone, but I updated my profile on the internet, and I've been getting lots of offers from all over."

"A good IT person is hard to find, and you're one of those gifted guys."

"I don't know about that, but I've turned them all down." Art glanced down.

"Except for this one?" Pastor Brooks grabbed three fries.

"I think I'm in love with her." He stared hard. "No, I know I'm in love with her. But she doesn't see me that way."

Pastor Brooks swallowed. "Oh, I see. How so?"

"Like, I said, we've been best friends forever. I've been crazy about her ever since she kissed me in kindergarten."

The pastor coughed. He seemed to be choking and grabbed his water. He raised a finger. "Sorry. I swallowed down the wrong tube. So, come again. Kindergarten?"

"Yeah, we did everything together growing up. Even when she moved, she'd come back every summer and holiday, but when she graduated from college, she got a job out there. Then she came back less and less."

"Do you guys communicate?"

"We used to all the time. She texted me a lot," he shrugged, "but mostly when she needed something."

"So, she depends on you?"

"Well, I live across the street from Sally Trotman, and it's easy to keep an eye on her. Besides, I practically lived at Miz Trotman's house over the summers."

"Does Victoria know how you feel?"

Art's eyes narrowed. "Nah, as far as she figures, we're just best friends. We've never talked about feelings. That would be weird."

"Maybe you need to have that conversation."

"Yeah. No. That's not going to happen."

"Have you prayed about it? Do you think she's the one? Do you have peace when you think of her as being in your life forever?"

"I do."

Pastor Brooks lowered his burger. "Then pray and take the next step. You need to talk to her."

Art shook his head. "I can't do that."

"No, *you* probably can't. But with God's strength, you can."

Art walked into the main house, his white shirt hanging over his shoulder. Pulling out the ironing board from the laundry room, he plugged in the iron. Wearing her robe, his mother walked in.

"Oh, hey, son. What are you doing up so early?" Art's mother placed a kiss on his cheek.

He didn't want to tell her about the Zoom interview for a job in California. With the time difference, he had booked the appointment before work this morning.

"Busy day."

"Do you have time for breakfast? I can make pancakes." She gave him a sly smile.

"Sounds good, but no thanks."

Art finished ironing and headed back to his tiny studio apartment behind the big house. He finished dressing and sat up straight behind his laptop, wondering if this was the right thing to do. Glancing at his watch, he nodded. Fifteen minutes to go. His cell dinged, and he glanced at the notification. Victoria. He grabbed the phone.

<Hey, I need you.>

Art punched her number.

"What's up?"

Victoria sobbed, and Art couldn't understand her.

"Victoria, slow down. I don't know what you're saying?" His heart soared at the sound of her voice but tore at the crying coming through the phone.

"My father had a stroke," she said.

Art gasped. Her father had been in a nursing facility for Alzheimer's for five years. It was one of the reasons Victoria had stayed in California instead of moving back after college. That and her fashion career.

"I'm so sorry, Victoria." Art glanced at his watch five minutes before the interview. "Listen, how about I fly out there. I have an appointment this morning, and I can't leave work today, but I'll call you tonight. Will you be okay?"

The crying slowed, and Victoria cleared her throat. "No, that's okay. But thanks, Art. Just hearing your voice has helped."

She assured him that she would be fine, and her lilting voice thanked him for calming her down. Good ole' Art, she said and told him he didn't need to come. She said that the stroke was mild, and though it left her father weak, not much had changed. He hadn't been able to communicate with her in over a year. This recent episode had startled her was all. So she said.

She hung up seconds before Art's Zoom appointment. The interview went well, and the corporate representative seemed impressed with Art. They told him to expect a call back soon. Art leaned backward. *Now what?* He left his studio apartment and walked back into the main house, letting the screen door slam.

"Mom? How about those pancakes?"

She smiled. "That's my boy."

Walking into the bank, Art quickly picked up the work order list from the office manager. His eyes widened. Though not without reading the details, he hadn't seen a list for computer repairs this long in ages.

"What, did ya'll have a cyber-attack over the weekend?"

The office manager laughed. "No. Just little stuff. You know since the system changed over, everyone needs help."

"Did you schedule the video teaching session?"

"I did, but you know Art, everyone wants you to do it. They can't understand those fancy, visually appealing videos. They want it plain, and no one does it better than you."

Plain. Art blew out a breath. "So, are everyone's computers down, or do they just need help?"

She sipped her coffee. "We just need help. Truth be told, I don't think it's that bad, but we're having a challenging time adjusting to the new system."

"Okay, I'll see what I can do."

Art proceeded to grab the two youngest employees. They were the most computer literate in the office. He went over the list with them, and there didn't seem to be anything they couldn't manage. Dividing up the worklist, he kept the Bank President for himself.

"Mr. Woodley?"

The president waved him in. "I was hoping you'd see me. This darned computer." He stood, moved away from his desk, and motioned Art over. Art sat in front of the screen and tapped a few keys. In less than a minute, he stood.

"All is good."

"That can't be." Mr. Woodley adjusted his glasses.

"I promise it is. If you get stuck, save whatever it is you're working on. Turn off your computer. Count to ten and turn it back on."

The president frowned. "You always say that. One of these days, I'll believe you."

One of these days better be soon, thought Art. "Mr. Woodley, I was wondering if I could take a few days off. I have a friend in California who needs me."

"Needs you? What about us? We can't do without you for one day, much less more."

"I appreciate that, sir, but I'm sure those two clerks," Art pointed out the door, can oversee everything. Of course, I can be available by remote. No worries."

Mr. Woodley frowned. "How soon?"

"I'd like to leave tomorrow."

The president shook his head. "I don't like it. Do you have to go?"

"Sir, I took no sick days last year and no vacation this year."

"I know, I know. But you're invaluable here, Art." His bushy brows furrowed. "Oh, all right. If you're sure those kids can handle it."

"For what's on this list, they can. Call me for anything else."

It was lunchtime, and his travel plans were in order. Art stood straighter, but suddenly he felt hungry. He looked at his watch, then proceeded to take extra care to assure everyone that their computers were fine.

Stepping out, Art put on his sunglasses and peered at the shining sun. He grinned. *California, here I come.* He spun around and bumped straight into Pastor Brooks.

"Whoa!" Pastor Brooks steadied Art by the shoulders. "Someone looks happy. It looks like the Lord answered your prayers. You got peace or what?"

Art winced. Since the call from Victoria, and the job interview, he hadn't prayed at all. Still, he beamed. "Joy of the Lord, pastor. I'm going to California." Art's smile spanned his entire face.

"That was quick."

"Yup. Victoria called and said she needed me, and my interview went well. You never know, I may get the job."

Pastor Brooks stepped back. "It certainly seems as if God's guiding you. Hey, how about that lunch I owe you?"

"Sure, I'm starving."

Over an all-you-can-eat buffet at the Manière' Sisters' restaurant, Art told of his plans to go to California the next day. He chatted away about the job details and seeing Victoria and her dad. They'd been friends before her family moved, but Art hadn't seen the man since his condition deteriorated.

Pastor Brooks nodded, listening quietly. Finally, he spoke. "So, this is a big move for you."

"Yup. Other than college, I've never left Bay Town."

"I can see why. You're needed here. I don't think I hear any one person's name come up more than yours. Not to mention, I was hoping to offer you the Youth Pastor position when the church budget allows."

Art waved his fork. "Ahhh, I don't need a salary for that. I love working with those kids. But I'm sure there's someone else ready to do the job."

"Not likely." Pastor Brooks cleared his throat. "But, if God's moving you away, He'll provide."

They finished their meal, and Pastor Brooks paid the bill.

On the sidewalk, Art's cell rang, and he glanced at the screen. "It's the job offer," he said.

"I'll let you go." Pastor Brooks waved as he walked away.

"Thanks." Art pressed the button, and his feet felt like a hovercraft over the sidewalk. "Hello, Art Alexander, here." He grinned at people passing by, but the smile quickly faded. "Yes...I see...I understand. All right, then. Thanks for the consideration."

That was quick. Figuring the corporation must have found the perfect person, Art clicked off and slipped the phone in his back pants pocket. He breathed deeply, then walked to the pier alongside the restaurant. The old rickety thing had a condemned sign across it, but Art slipped under it and walked a few feet. He stared at the gulf, then glanced up at the clouds, hiding the sun. *I guess I should have prayed first.*

"Lord, what now?"

The clouds parted, and the bright orange ball blinded him. He pulled on his sunglasses once more. *Well, at least Victoria needs me.* His phone dinged, and he pulled it from his pocket. It was a message from Victoria. He grinned.

<Hey, no need to come out. Dad's doing fine.>

Art's stomach churned, and sweat beaded on his forehead. <No worries. I can still come.>

He waited, and no answer came. She often did that. If work or someone got in the way, she'd answer later.

"Hey, son, you're not supposed to be out there."

Art turned to see Officer Bert. They'd never officially met, but everyone knew the friendly police chief.

"Oh, yeah, sorry." Art lifted the yellow caution tape and stepped back on the sidewalk.

"No worries. I just don't feel like diving in the gulf to save someone." The large man's body jiggled as he laughed. "Not that I wouldn't. Have a nice day, son."

Art waved and walked to his car, but before getting in, the

chief showed up again. "Hey, were you out at the trailer park across the tracks yesterday?" His dark eyes narrowed beneath the brim of his hat.

"Yes, at Collin and Cindy's home. Why?"

"I got a report about a disturbance out there. A black truck and that vehicle were reported being seen. Is this Mustang yours"

Art's eyes widened. He opened his mouth but promptly shut it.

"Want to tell me about it?"

"Yes, this is my car, but what did Collin and Cindy say?"

"Nothing. He looked pretty bad." Chief Bert pointed to his eye. "It was all black and blue by the time I got there. If you know something, son, I need to know. You boys get in a fight?"

Art drew back his shoulders. "What? No. They're friends of mine. But I'd check out that black truck if I were you. I've never seen it in town until yesterday. It pulled in behind Cindy's car at the church."

"Church? And you think they're responsible for the assault. I know Pastor Brooks welcomes everyone, but why would roughnecks like that be at church?"

"Maybe you should check out Relief Rescue too." Art shook his head. "But I promised, I can't say anything else."

"Relief Rescue? The loan shark? What's that got to do with …" Chief Bert pushed up his hat. "Oh, I got it. That family is hurting, huh. Ain't the church supposed to help? I mean, I know Pastor Brooks. He wouldn't let that happen."

"He didn't know how bad off they were. None of us did. But never mind about the loan shark. It's taken care of, and Collin and his family will be okay."

Chief Bert wagged a finger at Art. "Oh, I got ya. You're a good kid."

"It's not me. Gods got his ways."

"That's what Pastor Brooks says, but I'm not always so sure. Anyway, you let me know if I'm needed, right? In the meantime, thanks. Town needs good people like you. Have a good day, son."

Art rolled his eyes. If any more people needed him, he'd … well, he wasn't sure what he'd do. He climbed into his restored Mustang and looked down at his shirt.

"Oh, man!"

Spaghetti sauce was splattered down the front. Art headed home for a quick change. He parked out front, glanced across the street, and waved. Sally Trotman was just leaving her house when she leaned against the door jamb. She raised a hand weakly but dropped it as her body slumped to the ground. Art sprinted toward her.

"Miz Trotman? Sally?"

He patted her face and hands, then checked her pulse. It was weak. He pulled out his phone and dialed 911.

The paramedics came and transported Sally to the ER. While waiting, Art texted Victoria.

<Your grandmother's in the ER. She passed out.>

He waited, still no answer. The last message between them was his, asking if he could still come out.

Art was waved into the bay where Sally lay. Her skin was ashen, but her eyes opened. "What happened?" she asked.

"You fainted. How are you feeling?"

"Terrible. Weak. I want to go home."

The curtain sailed across the ceiling rail. "Hello, Mrs. Trotman. It seems your blood pressure dropped. I understand you're on kidney medication."

Art's eyes widened. "You never told me that."

"Are you her son?"

Sally chuckled and reached for Art's hand. "No, but I wish he'd be my grandson-in-law."

The doctor smiled. "Well, we'll stabilize you and then you can go home, but you need to see your renal doctor. He'll need to adjust your medicine, but it might be time to consider dialysis."

Art stared at Sally. "Dialysis? How long has this been going on?"

"Too long, son. I knew it was coming. Now just get me home."

"Soon enough," said the doctor. "Come with me, please." He nodded at Art.

"It'll be a couple of hours. Perhaps tonight before I release her. Will there be someone at home to care for her?"

Art's heart dropped when he suddenly remembered the airline reservation he hadn't canceled. He nodded. "Yes, of course."

"Good. I think she'll sleep the rest of the afternoon. Leave your cell number at the front desk and come back around six tonight."

Art walked numbly to his car. He sat behind the steering wheel, his knuckles turning white as he gripped it. He chewed the inside of his cheek so hard that he tasted blood. Art rechecked his phone and then punched Victoria's number. Not texting but calling. He got the recording and promptly threw his phone in the passenger seat.

He went back to work and put out fires at the bank. Even though the young clerks had everything under control, Mr. Woodley was ecstatic that Art wasn't leaving. They were thankful that Art had confidence in their skills. He finished cleaning up some computers, updated the bank website, and led a small training session. The employees thanked him profusely.

The hospital called and said it would be closer to seven before Sally would be discharged. Art said goodnight, pushed open the bank doors, and stepped out into the dusky night.

Collin approached him.

"Hey, Art. I'm on my way to work and just wanted to

thank you in person. The loan guy came to the RV and said you paid the full amount. They offered another loan –"

"What?" Art brushed past him. "I'm going to the police."

"Art, no. I told him no more. I told him I'd go to the police if they came around again. But he said how much you paid. I'm so sorry."

Art walked back and placed an arm on Collin's shoulder. "Nothing to be sorry about. We all have troubles, sometimes. We just need to trust God, not Rescue Relief." Art laughed.

"You got that right. I dropped off Cindy to get her car last night at the church, and there was an envelope laying on the front seat with some cash and a back seat full of groceries. You shouldn't have done that."

Shaking his head, Art smiled back. "It wasn't me. It had to have been God answering our prayers. I never said a word."

"Are you sure?"

"I promise." Art clutched his chest. "It's God's way of showing you he's got this. You know, even though you have to wait sometimes, like on that promotion. It doesn't mean we have to take matters into our own hands."

Patting his eye, Collin winced. "You got that right. Not to mention what I put Cindy and the kids through. It's taken us two days now to get that RV cleaned up."

"Speaking of clean up, do you have some time tomorrow? Miz Trotman has some yard work. A couple of tree branches fell from the last storm, and she could use some help. She offers a good sum for yard work."

Collin beamed. "Thanks, Art. I'll be over there right after my shift in the morning."

Art nodded. "No problem. And I know a family that needs help with pecan harvesting as well, so I'll give them a call. They're always hiring extra workers."

They shook hands and went their separate ways. Art looked at his phone, and still nothing from Victoria. He arrived at the hospital, and Sally was still sleeping. The nurse assured him she'd be ready to go as soon as she awoke. Art made a few more calls.

"Mom?...listen, I'm spending the night at Miz Trotman's...she'll be fine. I'll call when I get there. You can bring us your super soup for dinner...Thanks, Mom."

Art punched another number, calling the family that needed help pecan harvesting, and passed along Collin's number.

He took a deep breath, and searched, then hit another number. "Chief Bert, please." He waited. "Sir, this is Art. We spoke today at the condemned pier?" Art chuckled. That was the biggest crime he'd ever committed. Trespassing, and now it was his claim to fame with the police chief. "Yes, I wanted to let you know that the Rescue Relief guys went out to Collin's RV again. I just thought you should know...Thank you, sir. I'd rest easier, knowing they were safe."

Every person he called ended with thanks and an expression of how much Art was needed. He'd never paid much attention to those words before. Helping others came naturally. It was who he was—but needed? He didn't want to be needed by anyone except Victoria.

He tapped his cell and couldn't help but go through a mental list of people in his head. People who needed his help. When he couldn't think of whom to call besides Victoria, Art pocketed his phone and rested his elbows on his knees. His hands entwined in front of him. He leaned forward.

Well, Lord, I'm open to your guidance.

His cell rang, not buzzed. It wasn't a text, but it was Victoria.

"Art! What's wrong with Grandmother?"

He smiled. Just the sound of her voice brought joy.

"She kind of passed out. But I'm taking her to the doctor tomorrow."

"Is she okay? Do I need to fly out?"

He wanted to say yes. "No. I'm staying with her tonight,

and my mom will stay with her during the day. We'll find out more tomorrow."

The silence on the other end was too long. "Is she that bad that you need to stay?"

"Yes, and no. I mean, I want to stay. She just spent eight hours in the ER."

"Okay, I'm coming home. I'll find a flight."

Home. Did she say home?

"Maybe it's a good idea. Then you can be at the doctor's appointment with her." His body flooded with warmth at the thought of seeing her again. "Listen, I better go. They're releasing her, and I'll have her call you when we get home."

"I'll schedule a flight out on red-eye tonight. Thanks, Art. I don't know what I'd do without you."

"Hey, how's your dad?"

"He's fine. Everything is back to normal. It was just a TIA, you know, a mini-stroke, and as far as they could tell, nothing's changed."

"Maybe I can fly back with you. I'd like to see him."

"Oh, you don't need to do that, Art."

I want to.

"Besides, I'm so busy with work right now that I couldn't take any more time off. Especially since I'm coming out there. Let's wait for another time," said Victoria.

Art hung up, a little discouraged. She didn't want him out there, but quickly he felt elated. Victoria was coming home.

Sally Trotman was discharged, and Art got her home and settled. While she called Victoria, he headed across the street to pick up his mom's soup.

"Victoria's coming home." Art beamed at his mother while slurping a taste.

Her mother's eyes widened. "She is? Well, that's good. Her grandmother needs her, and I bet you're pretty excited about that. It's about time that girl came home."

"Just a visit, Mom." Though, if Art had his way, maybe he'd get her to stay for good.

"Oh, Art." His mother made a pouty face. "I'm sorry, I know how much you care for her. It seems that California just turned her head." She squeezed his chin. "Not like you. You have a good head on your shoulders. Why, another man might go traipsing off for the girl he loved, but not you. You're needed here, and I love that you're trusting God for Victoria. Why, what would Bay Town do without you?"

Art took the pot of soup and headed for the door. "Bay Town doesn't need me. Bye, mom."

Sally sat propped in her favorite chair, television on, a cup of hot tea on her tray right where Art left it. He entered the kitchen, dished out the soup, and brought it out with some crackers, setting them on Sally's tray.

"Shall I pray?"

"Please do."

Art prayed for their meal, Sally's healing, and Victoria's trip.

"What trip?" Sally took a sip of her tea. "Is she going somewhere?"

"Victoria is flying out tonight."

"No, she's not."

Art gulped. "But I talked to her. She was taking the red-eye."

"Nonsense. I told her you're here, and I didn't need both of you." Her lips formed a straight line, and she stared back at Art.

"But she was going to the doctor with you tomorrow."

"No, Bethie Cook is. I already talked to her. I didn't want you to take off work. I'm fine, Art."

His jaw clenched, and he didn't feel like eating again. Not even his mom's super soup.

"Oh, Art. If she'd insisted, I would have welcomed her. But she fretted about work, and I only want her help if she wants to be here." She stared back, her eyes saddened. "And I don't think she does."

Art stood. He brushed back his curly locks with both hands and rested them with fingers laced behind his head. He nodded.

"You're right. She doesn't want to be here."

Sally lowered her eyes.

"I mean, she misses you, but she knows I can do a better job of taking care of you. Come on, Miz Trotman, she'll just be crying at the doctor's office, and then I'll have to come help both of you." Art chuckled, but his heart twisted at the truth.

Looking up, Sally smiled. "And you wouldn't mind a bit. Art, few people know what the bible says about dying to self, but you do. And one day, son, Victoria will know what a virtue that is. For goodness sakes, maybe she'll learn it from you."

"Victoria knows. She takes care of her dad and doesn't get anything in return." Art breathed deep and blew out a breath.

"That she does." Sally reached out her hand. "You're a good one, Art, and God will work things out. I think you two were meant to be together. Victoria is on some journey right now, and perhaps your journey is here."

Art nodded. He knew Sally was right, and no matter how hard he tried, he couldn't force Victoria to want to be here. At least not for now. His cell dinged, and he checked the message. His eyes widened. It was from the corporation. The other applicant had declined the job offer, and they were extending the IT position in California to Art. Could he fly out tomorrow and meet in person?

"It's not Victoria changing her mind, is it?" asked Sally.

Art breathed keep and shook his head. "Nope. It's me, changing mine."

He texted back. <Thank you, but I must decline at this time. Some situations have arisen, and I'm needed in Bay Town. Thank you.>

"So, are you going on a journey?" Sally winked.

"My journey is right here." He squeezed Sally's hand.

The End

Join Art and Victoria as their story continues in "Let Them Eat Cake," the 2022 Bay Town Christmas Novel. Watch for it on Amazon, just in time for the holidays!

www.ingramcontent.com/pod-product-compliance
Lightning Source LLC
Chambersburg PA
CBHW030425180626
46812CB00005B/2188